The Defender

Diana Ryan

CreateSpace ISBN-13:978-1523924783
CreateSpace ISBN-10:1523924780

To my dearest Maddox and Macy,
who hold my very heart in their hands.

Prologue

A tiny blue service light at the top of the elevator shaft penetrated the complete darkness. My heart beat rapidly as a fat bead of sweat slowly dripped from my hairline. I took a sharp breath.

"This is it," I whispered to myself.

"Just breathe, Nolan." Agent Drew Smith detected my anxiety, and whispered to me from my left. "Ten minutes, buddy, and this is all over."

He was right. I consciously reminded myself to breathe in and out. Heartbeats sounded loud in my ears as I crouched down against the cold elevator ceiling, holding my Glock in the ready position. Several other FBI agents held their offensive positions around me, silently waiting for the signal.

"Outlier, report," my earpiece called.

"The tactical team is in the ready position." I came off confidently, but secretly wanted to vomit on the elevator top. I took a deep breath and the nausea subsided momentarily.

"The task force has almost defused the bomb system within headquarters. Infiltrate on my signal."

"Copy that. Myers is in his office," the voice continued. "You must apprehend him before he suspects the intrusion."

"Affirmative." Seconds passed and the silence of the moment rang out through my ears. Then I heard the signal from Ground Ops.

"Now!" I yelled to my team. Agent Smith cracked open the hatch in the top of the elevator and four agents jumped in. We pried open the elevator door, and Agent Smith rolled in the tear gas canister. Screaming sounds contrasted a calm, but serious voice on the intercom. "System breech. Execute Plan B."

I ran through the open door and shouted, "Get on your knees! Hands in the air!" More tactical teams entered the office from different entry points and fired shots to create confusion. It was Ethan Myers we wanted, not these unsuspecting agents. All the computers had turned blood red, a protection protocol I learned about when I worked here only a few months ago.

I headed toward Myers's office, but stopped dead in my tracks as I passed my old desk. It was a bit too familiar. I ran my fingers over the desktop as memories flooded my brain. Not too long ago I sat right there, hopeful and excited to serve my country faithfully. Familiar faces hid behind their desks around the room, some being dragged away in handcuffs. Pandemonium continued around me, but my eyes moved everything in slow motion. These people had no idea they were not working for the American government. They had been duped, just as I had, most of them probably for more years than the four I was fooled into. I wanted to bring them into a huddle and impart the truth about everything, but the desk agents began to fight back—following their defense protocol and believing they were being attacked by criminals.

Complete chaos ensued—CBB employees sprinted for the exits, furniture was overturned, computers smashed, and sparking wires hung from the ceiling. There were many agents involved in combat, and shots whizzed by my head, but I was still stuck in a trance.

Drew shook me by the shoulders. "Nolan! Myers! We have to get Myers...now!"

He was right. I quickly followed Drew, darting through a maze of desks to where Myers's office was in the back. He kicked down the door and we entered, guns drawn. We circled the perimeter of the office, but Myers wasn't there.

A vent door swung in the ceiling.

"You go up after him," Drew suggested. "I'll have Ground Ops figure out where it leads and meet you there."

"Got it." I jumped up on the desk and hoisted myself into the ceiling. The air duct was just a bit larger than the size of my body, and I wondered how Myers had fit through, being the overweight creep that he was. The metal pathway made a spooky creaking sound in response to my weight as I carefully army-crawled through the duct. Myers couldn't have gotten too far yet—surely his body couldn't snake through as fast as mine could.

What was I going to say when I came face to face with Ethan Myers again? I was filled with nothing but rage for the man. He had forced me to stab my girlfriend six weeks ago, and for four years he deluded me into believing I was working for a legitimate government function when in all reality I was inadvertently assisting him to advance in the world of criminal activity.

What I wanted to do to Myers if I came face to face with him was against FBI code. I'd have a hard time restraining myself.

Just ahead of me I saw a pair of feet crawling as the duct took a bend to the right. They disappeared as I sped forward.

Myers!

I crawled faster through a bend, and as the duct straightened out I spotted the feet again. I activated my earpiece: "Ground Ops, Outlier."

A steady male voice responded. "Go ahead, Outlier."

"I have visual on Myers thirty feet ahead of me. We're in the ductwork."

"Affirm. We'll inform Agent Smith."

3

"Myers!" I called. He stopped for a moment and turned his head toward me. Evil, bright eyes looked straight at me through the tunnel.

"You." The right side of his mouth turned up the tiniest bit. "You will pay for this, Hill. Mark my words." Then he turned forward and took off quicker than before. Some type of special scooter was tied to his stomach.

So he was rolling through the ducts.

Myers was putting distance between us—I couldn't keep up with the wheels of his scooter. I panicked and pulled the gun from my waistband. Before I thought about the repercussions, I fired two shots into the darkness. The first bullet ricocheted wildly off the sides of the metal tube and whizzed by my left ear, taking a tiny bit of the top off with it. I stopped moving and instinctively pressed a hand to my wound.

"My leg!" Myers grunted in front of me. "You incompetent—Ah! Go back to rookie training, Hill!" He started up again. I heard the wheels speed ahead.

"Go to hell, Myers!" I screamed, but he was already too far ahead. I crawled as fast as I could, my knees filling up with bruises and blisters. I pushed through the pain and soon came to a fork in the ductwork.

Right or left? Right or left?

My gut said right. I rushed down the right path, but not too far in I heard a metallic clang, and felt the duct come unattached to the ceiling.

I started to fall to the ground but held tight to the edge of the duct. One side of the metal tube was swinging while the other side was still bolted in. My feet dangled below me as I tried to pull myself up, but it was no use—I couldn't get a good grip.

Dammit! Myers is getting away!

My fingers slowly slipped down the metal slide as huge beads of sweat dripped down the side of my face. There was no way to get back into the ductwork, so I checked the floor underneath me, looking for a good landing pad.

I was hanging above a tall, oversized room with high ceilings easily two stories from the ground below. I had never seen this part of the CBB the entire time I worked here. Across from me, on the ceiling, hung vast, industrial looking spotlights shining down on what must be an operating room. All sorts of fancy machines, shiny metal sinks, and stark white cabinets housing medical supplies lined the perimeter walls. In the middle of the room sat two operating beds. If I swung the right way, and let go of my grip at the right time, I could probably land safely between all the equipment, and on one of the beds. I used my abs to get my feet in motion and after a few swings I let go. Just like a cat, I landed safely on the left bed. I spotted the exit off to my right and quickly headed to it, but as I approached, I found the door locked from the outside.

"No!" I grunted furiously as I tugged uselessly at the door handles. I had blown my chance to get Myers! How was I going to get out of here? I slammed my fist into the locked doors. Anger built quickly as my breathing felt heavy and fast. Unsure of what else to do, I flipped a medical table holding supplies to the floor with a loud clang.

Damn, that felt good.

I pressed the little button on my earpiece. "Ground Ops, this is Outlier. I lost visual on Myers when the duct broke." I looked out a window to the street below. "I'm locked in some sort of medical room, probably on the fifteenth floor."

"Requesting extrapolation. Hold position, Outlier."

I paced through the room while I waited. On the south wall there was a whiteboard with several notes written on it. Along the top, the numbers one through eight were written in red marker and circled boldly. Names were sketched under three of the numbers and pictures had been attached under the names. Lynette Mitchell, Jody Isaacs, and…Ava Gardner.

I felt my heart drop into my stomach. *Ava Gardner?* I tried to control my anger but it was difficult. I thought Myers's business with Ava was done. Why was she plastered on this wall with these two other women?

Each person was female and looked very similar to Ava—brown hair and brown eyes and seemed to be about the same age. Under each name there was a series of written notes. I ran my eyes over the phrases on Ava. There were details about where she lived and that she had a blue meteor in her house for several years, but it also indicated she was of Cornish descent and that she was right-handed.

What could this mean?

In the lower right-hand corner of the board were three words written in all capitals and circled in black: cure, revenge, vanquishment. Below it stood a date and time—sunrise, November 1st.

My earpiece buzzed. "Outlier, be advised the door will open momentarily."

"Copy that."

I took a picture of the wall with my phone and erased the whiteboard. Then for good measure I trashed the room. Whatever crazy experiments Myers planned on doing to the woman of my dreams would never happen on my watch.

Seconds later the door magically clicked open. "Thanks, Ground Ops. I'm outta here."

A grey hallway welcomed me. I jogged down it toward the stairs while I waited for Op Tech to pull up the blueprints of the office.

Dammit! How could I have been outplayed by Myers again?

I slowed down near the middle of the hallway when an oversized map on the wall caught my attention. It took only a

6

few seconds to realize what was represented, and then an angry fire deep within my body flared up again.

The map of the United States was covered with about thirty little red stars indicating all the CBB offices scattered all over the continent. I was naive enough to believe Myers headed up a small operation central to the Midwest, but I was sorely wrong. Just when I thought taking down this office would render Myers useless, I was flooded with deep and overwhelming defeat.

"Outlier, take the stairs on the north side of the hallway down two floors. Agent Smith is waiting for you there."

"Copy that, Ground Ops." I pulled down the map in anger and ran the rest of the hallway until I reached the door leading to the stairwell. I was about to push the door open when I heard a gun cock right behind my head.

"Don't move, Hill." I recognized the voice as Agent Harper's immediately. Harper quickly grabbed the gun from my belt and tossed it to the floor, sending it sliding away from us down the hallway. I put my hands up and slowly turned around.

"So we meet again." His cropped blond hair and chiseled face looked aged and full of stress. Myers must really be putting the pressure on him. "You know, Nolan, I can't let you out of here alive. Myers wouldn't approve of your attempts at single-handedly destroying our operations."

I knew Ground Ops could hear what was happening, and I prayed my backup would arrive quickly.

"I don't know, Harper," I said, buying some time. "Won't Myers want me alive so he can conduct some kind of inhumane torture methods on me? You better not shoot." I knew I had to make my move quickly. Harper had shot me once before, and I was sure he wouldn't hesitate to do it again.

I had been trained to appear calm, even though furious rage was still burning deep within me. "You know, I have been wondering. Why didn't you kill me last summer when you had the chance?"

Harper's eyes filled with anger. He knew exactly what I was doing and was ready to fight back where it hurt me the most. "She will never be safe, Hill. Myers needs Ava, and some feeble little half-agent wannabe like you could never protect her from his ultimate terminus."

Before he could go on for a second more, I kicked the gun out of his hand and sent a powerful punch across his jawline. He doubled over in pain and tried to pick up the gun, but I was right there seconds before him. I swiftly pulled Harper's right arm tightly behind his back, pushing him up against the wall. With my other arm I held the gun to his head.

It took all that was inside me not to shoot him in the side of the skull right then and there. Through clenched teeth and with rage behind my voice, I loudly whispered into his ear, "You will *never* hurt Ava. She has done nothing wrong and deserves a perfect life."

Harper laughed. "Oh, Hill. It's not what she's done, it's what she is. If you only knew…"

And then I heard a metallic clink on the floor, a hiss, and suddenly my eyes and lungs were burning. Harper broke my hold, and I wildly threw my hand through a cloud of gas and smoke, trying to find him.

Dammit! He escaped!

I bent over, coughing, trying to find my way out when I felt the door.

I pushed my way through and emerged into a stairwell full of clean air. I stopped to take two deep breaths, and then took the stairs two at a time, bursting through the door at the bottom. Drew was there talking on a company-issued cell phone. He hung it up just as I arrived.

"Where'd he go?" I gasped. "Did Harper just run through here?"

"No. No one has come through here."

"Where the hell did he go?" I started to approach the exit door, but Agent Smith grabbed my arm. "Nolan, we successfully brought down the CBB. The building and all its employees have been secured." He dropped his arm since I stopped my forward motion. Then he took his time before he said the next bit of news. "But no sign of Myers. I'm sorry, Nolan. "

I put my hands on my knees, trying to steady myself. "Dammit! No…no!" My breathing was hoarse and quick and my heart was beating wildly. It was all my fault! I had Harper and Myers within my reach tonight and I let them both slip away. I kicked the wall in frustration, putting a hole in the drywall.

"Get me the hell outta here."

Chapter One

Nolan parked his silver Audi near the baseball fields behind the community pool. He pushed the button on the dash to turn off the engine, and then reached over to grab my hand. My insides felt like there were a thousand tiny daggers poking my organs. I squeezed Nolan's hand for comfort. It was his idea to visit the place where our lives drastically changed a bit more than six weeks before, but I wasn't sure if I was ready just yet.

Nolan let out a deep sigh. "Are you ready for this?"

I closed my eyes and took a deep breath, trying to suppress the horror of that night, but I couldn't keep the thoughts from my brain. I was stabbed and left to die right on that rock in the distance. But I knew Nolan was right—visiting Make Out Rock was part of our healing.

Nolan narrowed his eyes with concern and then placed his other hand on top of our already interlaced fingers.

I smiled weakly. How does he always make me feel so safe?

"Yes. Ready or not, let's do this." I let go of his hand and reached for the door handle. I rubbed my stomach—the daggers were still poking.

Was this really a good idea?

Nolan met me around the front bumper with his arms open wide. I walked right into them and they closed around me like safety gates. I snuggled the side of my head into the crook under his shoulder. It was my favorite spot to be.

Nolan lowered his face into my hair, inhaled deeply, and loudly exhaled. I knew he was smelling my hair—a habit of his that I treasured. "Let's go over there before I chicken out," he said.

Ah ha. So he felt a little nervous as well.

Nolan let go of my back, grabbed my shoulders, and held me at arm's length. "Ava Gardner, you are the reason for my existence. I swear to heaven above that I will do everything in my power to keep you safe from evil."

I giggled a little. "Safe from evil? Sounds like a comic book line."

"You'd be surprised how much this life resembles the world of comic books." He gently kissed my lips, making my knees wonderfully weak, and then grabbed my left hand and led me off in the direction of the train tracks.

Today the sky was a brilliant blue backdrop to the fluffy white clouds. A gentle breeze with a tiny bite of cold Wisconsin air blew the hair from my shoulders. It was a beautiful fall day by anyone's standards. The trees' leaves were just beginning to display their gorgeous colors, and I could faintly hear a tour boat chugging its way down the Wisconsin River off in the distance.

As we crossed the train tracks, I could feel Nolan's hand begin to shake in mine. He was the one who stabbed me, but it was a warranted part of a desperate plan to save my life from a sinister man who thought I was a hardened criminal. Messed up? Yes, I knew. But even so, last summer was a chapter of my life that I wouldn't change for anything. It was one that helped me find the love of my life. I wanted nothing more than to be with Nolan Hill for the rest of my days, and I was pretty sure he felt the exact same way.

The thick, green screen of trees and bushes that hid the entrance to Make Out Rock in the summer was now lying in heaps of red and yellow leaves at the foot of bare branches, leaving the entrance exposed and open. We easily found the deep-cut pathway and scaled our way down to the top of the towering rock ledge.

Partway down I stopped dead in my tracks as my mind quickly flashed back to that dark night. Nolan felt me draw back, and stopped his momentum to wrap his arms around my body. My knees began to shake and my stomach turned over, but at the same time I knew this was a mental hurdle I'd have to jump over.

Nolan began to rub the side of my arms and kissed my forehead sweetly. "Maybe I was wrong. Let's get out of here. We can visit in a few months."

I looked up through the tears forming in my eyes. How was I lucky enough to love someone who loved me even more in return? I wanted him to understand. "No, Nolan. I want to do this." I looked down at the ground, gravity pulling a tiny tear out of my eye. "Although that was the worst night of my life, I need to be here with you now. To prove to myself that I can move on." The daggers were still dancing in my stomach.

Nolan's blue eyes glittered in the autumn sunlight. He placed his fingers on my jawline, stroking my chin with his thumb. I felt like melting right into his hand. He opened his mouth to speak a few times but said nothing.

Finally he said, "I would feel humbled and gracious if you could find it within yourself to someday forgive me and trust me once more. I know it will take time, but I am willing to wait as long as it takes."

Then before I could answer, he slowly pulled me in and held his lips half an inch from mine. His warm breath lingered on my mouth, and I wanted so much for him to go the rest of the distance, but he held his position, teasing me carefully. Right as I was ready to go in for the touchdown myself, he sensed my impatience, and kissed me with a lot of emotion.

I led Nolan by the hand to the middle of the rock ledge, and we both sat down. The familiar beauty of the Dells had calmed my breathing, and I could feel the daggers backing off. A deep, cleansing breath of the natural air refreshed my lungs. I watched the gentle, swirling brown water flow down river and my mind was flooded with memories of a summer filled with adventures with Nolan. Falling in love with him had been easy and natural.

Nolan looked upriver toward the docks. "I realized that night that you were the most important person in my life. I knew I needed to do whatever I could in order to protect you, even if that meant harming you in the process."

Did he know I felt the same way?

"That day," I began, "when I knew something was wrong and I was sure you were going to break up with me, I felt like my life was over. I had been through heartbreak before, but nothing compared to the pain I went through that night. That's when I knew, I had given you my heart."

I leaned my head onto his shoulder and we continued to look around, taking in the beauty of the environment around us. I looked down toward the end of the rock ledge and couldn't help but imagine the exact position I was in when I lay here waiting for death to take me away that night. Then I noticed a dark stain on the rock where I had lain.

My blood.

Of course, my blood had stained the rock. All of a sudden I flashed back to that moment when I truly thought my life had ended. When someone I loved and trusted purposely shoved a knife into my belly.

I stood up, shaking. "Let's get going. I think I've had enough for one day."

"Absolutely." Nolan rose and turned to leave. "Are you alri—" He stopped abruptly, made a weird face, and scanned the area around us.

"What's wrong?"

He put two fingers over my lips to silence me and whispered eyes on heightened alert. "Shh...Listen."

I heard it, too— a very faint beeping noise. Its high-pitched warning tone was rapidly getting faster and faster.

"Run!" he screamed, and pulled my arm toward the railroad tracks. I begged my feet to go faster but I couldn't seem to make them keep up with Nolan's. A wild scream escaped my lips as he leaped over the tracks and dove into the ditch behind them. I followed his lead and right as I landed, Nolan rolled over my body and an ear-splitting BOOM echoed out over the river and through the baseball fields. My hands instinctively covered my ears and I screamed again.

Nolan waited a few seconds and then rolled off of me. We sat up on our elbows and looked toward the rock. The whole cliff top had been blown away. Thick, angry smoke took over the air, and fire began to eat the bottom of the trees. My jaw was stuck in the open position.

My Dells! My beautiful Dells blown away!

Nolan stood up. "Are you okay?"

My ears were ringing but I could still hear Nolan. I took a quick inventory of the rest of my body, running my hands up and down my legs, torso, and arms. All parts were accounted for and I could see no blood. "Yeah. I think I'm fine." My head stayed focused on the scene before me.

"We have to get out of here!"

Nolan held out his hand to help me up, but I was still in awe of what had happened. My shock prevented me from realizing that Nolan was right: We had to get away from there immediately.

I couldn't take my eyes off the scene at hand. "We have to call 911."

Nolan began yelling, "They won't be far away! We have to go *now!*"

"Who won't be far away?"

Nolan yanked me onto my feet and pulled me in the opposite direction of his car, toward a grassy pathway parallel with the train tracks. I kept looking over my shoulder, causing my body to twist and my legs to flail, not being able to keep up with my top half.

Nolan stopped and grabbed my face in his hands. He looked deep into my eyes and said with great authority, "Ava Gardner. You have to trust me. We need to run down this path as fast as we can. *Now!*"

I stared with disbelief. Was I dreaming? It wasn't until I heard the police sirens behind us that I snapped out of my trance and began to run.

Nolan led the way, sprinting through the forest. My heart was beating out of my chest, and I didn't think I could go much farther. We must have been running at full speed for at least five minutes. I was not used to such nonsense.

Finally he stopped and surveyed the scene. "This will do," he said.

I bent over with my hands on my knees, breathing like I had just given birth right there on the forest floor. He told me to climb halfway up the tree and sit on a sturdy limb.

"No! Not until…you tell me…what's going…on!" I could barely get the words out between my heavy breathing. I was beyond frustration.

Nolan quickly walked over to me. He pulled me up from my crouched position and stared deeply into my eyes. "My sweet Ava. Please. I know this must be hard, but you have to trust me. Do as I say and this will all be over in a few minutes." Then he kissed me passionately but quickly. "Please."

I wanted to protest, but instead I surrendered to those damn baby blues. I was helpless against their power.

I turned around and climbed the tree up to the third limb. I was lucky my sister and I had had trees to climb in our backyard

15

as kids. Who knew that skill would come in handy as an adult? I looked down. I was probably about forty feet up the tree and glad that heights didn't bother me.

Nolan nervously paced the forest floor under my hideout tree. He took out his cell and dialed a number. Then he turned his back away from me. Normally I would be able to hear what he was saying, but my ears were still ringing from the blast. My stomach had turned inside out again. I was nervous and anxious and sure of one thing—I would *never* go near that rock again.

I could see the smoke rising from the site a few hundred yards down the pathway. There was a fire truck there now, with men pointing long hoses at the fire.

Nolan's voice grew louder. "Dammit! I need a reconnaissance team in here now!" He began to pace quicker. "What do you mean my field rating is unsatisfactory?" He paused and I could tell he was angry. "A civilian's life is at risk!"

Nolan suddenly slammed a finger at the phone's screen to hang up the call, letting out a grunt of frustration. He quickly and intensely scanned the tree line. Had he heard something I didn't? Then out of nowhere the crack of a gunshot echoed through the woods, and Nolan dropped to the ground with a groan.

I gasped. *No…no…no…no!* My mouth opened to let out a scream but nothing came out.

Nolan rolled over to his side, looked up at me, and said in a raspy voice, "Greeeeeeeeen. Trust green."

I whispered back through my tears, "What? Sweetheart…?"

I was about to jump down from the tree when I heard footsteps. I looked out into the forest and saw three men in dark suits carrying guns. They ran towards the unmoving Nolan. I held completely still. They hadn't seen me up in the tree yet.

One of the men pressed something in his ear. "We got him. No sign of the girl."

They knew I had been with Nolan. Chills sped down my spine. Another man picked up Nolan and threw him over his shoulder, and then they all ran out of the forest the same way they entered.

Uncontrollable tears began to fall from my eyes. What just happened? This couldn't be real! A nightmare, this had to be a nightmare.

Wake up, Ava!

I slapped myself in the face, but lost my balance on the tree limb and fell backwards, narrowly missing all the branches on the way down. My body landed with a thud on the grass and weeds below, and I let out a groan as I rolled to my left. My right arm radiated intense pain.

Oh no! I probably broke it.

I knew I had to get out of there before someone else came. But should I run after Nolan's captors or toward my parents' house? I wasn't prepared for any kind of fight, so I painfully set off in the direction of Capital Street. I scrambled about four steps forward before I heard a loud crack and felt a sting in my back, sending me instantly to the ground.

I'd been shot, too. What kind of evil world would bring us together only to rip us apart time and time again?

Well, at least I could join Nolan in heaven.

Chapter Two

Sunlight streamed onto my face, gently coaxing my eyelids to lift. My eyebrows wrinkled as I slowly looked around the room. An unfamiliar fog flooded my brain—where was I? My fingers rubbed my eyes and when I opened them, the fog had lifted somewhat. I was in bed at my college apartment on the campus of the University of Wisconsin in Stevens Point.

Was I late for class?

The clock on the bedside table read 9:30 and there was noise down the hall—sure signs it was the weekend. I knew I should get up and see what my roommates were doing out in the living room, but the warm blanket cocoon was too nice to part with.

My college friends and I had formed great friendships our freshman year, and it was weird not seeing them for three months last summer. Kasie had barely any money saved up for tuition, so she spent her summer working double shifts lifeguarding at the local pool and waitressing at a supper club at night.

Elaina and her family always spent the summer months staying cool by the lake at their northern Wisconsin cabin—no obligations and no cell phone service.

Sharon had a chemist uncle who needed an assistant to help promote his product overseas for the summer. She spent ninety days whirling through the countries of Europe peddling Zit-B-Gone to red-faced teenagers.

Clara was a Natural Resources major and she and her boyfriend much preferred to spend their summers camping deep in the forests of northern Wisconsin studying animal tracks and constructing beaver traps out of all-natural materials.

Last semester we decided to rent a house for our sophomore year. We settled on a basement apartment right across the street from the Student Center on campus. That way we could drag our butts out of bed last minute and stagger our way into class when we needed to. We tended to stay up too late talking, laughing, and doing dumb things like riding large pieces of cardboard like sleds down the stairs.

The basement seemed fine when we toured the house, and the price was right, but as I was lying in bed I realized it was a mistake. I could hear what could only be described as elephants walking in the apartment above me and it was beginning to make my head hurt.

I shoved the blankets off me and sat up onto my elbows, but a pain shot up my left arm. I took the weight off and rubbed it with my other hand. Upon inspection, I noticed oversized yellow and brown areas.

Old bruises. Curious.

I didn't remember banging up my arm. I inspected it again and noticed an unexplainable scar over the bone. Strange. I'd never had arm surgery. I looked closer; maybe the lighting was in the basement bedroom was poor. It did feel pretty tender; I must have injured it somehow.

Slight panic began to set in as I racked my brain and could not remember one detail about the day before. Had I been drinking the night before? That didn't seem like a likely scenario, although I couldn't remember what we had been up to.

"Wake up, Ava," I said out loud.

I got out of bed still rubbing my arm, and gave a stretch before waking my computer up. No new messages. I grabbed for my phone which was sitting on the ledge of the small window above my bed. Another reason the basement apartment was possibly not the best idea we've ever had—this was the only place my phone could get any reception. No new messages on my phone either.

Disappointing. No clues to the previous night's events.

I threw on a bra and left the room in my pajamas. Kasie's door was closed—she was still sleeping. Kasie was an adorable, petite blonde sorority girl who became one of my best friends last year. She was a hardworking Dietetics major who dreamed of being a personal trainer and dietician to the stars. She was always reading *US Weekly* and *People Magazine* to stay on top of the A-List. I knew that dream was a bit out of her reach. We were three thousand miles from LA! How could a little Midwestern Dietetics major find her way out west and "make it" in the craziness of Los Angeles? I never had the heart to tell her I thought so, of course.

The next bedroom down the hall belonged to my freshman year dorm roommate, Elaina. The door was open, so I assumed she was out in the living room. Last year we were randomly paired up and we got along great. Well, except for the time when Elaina had decided to hit a house party, returned home drunk as a skunk and puked inside my backpack. I had been less than enthused the next morning when I was greeted by an offensive smell and ruined homework. Elaina was truly embarrassed and apologized profusely. The next day she bought me a new backpack, and swore she wouldn't go to any more house parties.

Elaina was a French major. At first I found that rather strange, but she was very good at speaking French and really enjoyed learning about foreign cultures. As I got to know her more, I found out she had dreams of becoming an international spy one day, and when she had Googled it, she learned that being fluent in a foreign language is an expected quality in the world of espionage.

The last bedroom was Sharon and Clara's. They were roommates in the dorms freshman year and had volunteered to share a bedroom again. We let them have the biggest bedroom as a consolation prize.

Sharon and I bonded over education. She was studying to be a Special Education teacher, and although we had no classes in common, we could discuss politics and methodology. Well, only when a serious mood struck us, of course, which wasn't very often.

Sharon pledged Delta Nu during the second semester of freshman year, and so she and Kasie were always together. Sharon was usually the instigator of all the crazy stuff we did and we loved how she could make us laugh until our stomachs hurt.

She invented Exercise Ball Rodeo, a game in which you try to wrangle one of those oversized workout balls through various obstacles. The game was really challenging, and although it was hilarious, someone usually got hurt in the process. Nothing major, until Clara broke her foot rolling into a wall-mounted fire extinguisher, and then the game was dead.

Clara was a sweet, petite girl who truly loved being one with nature. She was an avid hunter and spent most of her time out of the house and in the woods somewhere. We really didn't see her too much.

Their door was open too, and I could hear Sharon's boisterous voice in the living room, which was open to the kitchen. Sharon was frying eggs at the stove and Elaina was reading her French textbook.

"Mornin' Lady! Long time no see!"

"What do you mean?" I looked to Elaina for an answer.

Elaina seemed concerned. "You must have got in really late last night!"

"Oh, right...yeah...got in late." I rubbed my head. What was going on? A tiny radiating headache was starting behind my right eye. Why couldn't I remember last night?

21

"How was your long weekend?" Sharon asked. There was some type of inflection in her voice I couldn't quite read. It was like she was suggesting I did something special.

"My long weekend?" I had no idea what she was talking about. "What did we do last night?"

Elaina looked over at Sharon as if neither knew what to say. Finally Sharon broke the silence.

"Um, honey...." She walked over to me and put her hand on my shoulder. "We don't know what you did last night." She led me over to the couch and sat me down. Then she returned to the kitchen and poured me a cup of coffee. "Remember? You left Thursday morning for the Dells, and you only would tell us that you were meeting a mysterious special friend you met this summer. We all thought you had some secret boyfriend!"

"Yeah! We figured you snuck in last night when we were all sleeping." Elaina moved from her spot on the loveseat over to my side on the couch. "Are you sure you're feeling okay?"

I had no idea what she was talking about, and my head was beginning to pound. "Secret boyfriend?" I said under my breath. "What day is it?"

"It's Sunday the 14th." Sharon had poured herself a cup of coffee and joined us on the couch.

I tried to make sense of the calendar in my head. "May 14th?" I took a sip of my coffee, concerned that that didn't seem right. Or was it summer? Why was I with my college friends?

Wake up, Ava.

"No, honey," Elaina said slowly. "October 14th." She looked quite worried now. "Why don't you head back to bed for a while? I don't think you're all the way awake yet."

October 14th? October 14th! What happened to summer?

The room began to spin and my arm started to ache again. I handed off my mug of coffee to Sharon and stood up. "I think I'm going to head back to bed. I'll see you guys later."

22

I rushed down the hallway to the room on the end. I shut the door to my bedroom and leaned up against the back of it. What was going on? Why couldn't I remember anything? I had been going to school for a whole month already? I couldn't seem to pull any memories of sitting in classes this year. Confused, I lay down on the bed and pulled the blankets over my head. I let out a frustrated grunt and wondered what I should do next.

I rolled over and picked up my phone off the rectangular bedside table, turning it in my hands for a moment, and then dialed my mother. Leaning far over into the wall to find the perfect spot, I listened to the phone ring.

"Hey, hon! How are you?"

"Hi, Mom. I'm alright." I was hoping she wouldn't hear the concern in my voice.

"What are you and the girls up to today?" Dishes clanked in the background.

"I'm not sure. I think I have a paper to write," I lied. "We'll probably just hang around here and do our homework."

"Well, that's no fun!" My mother laughed. "Naw, actually, I'm really proud of you, Ava. This will be your best semester yet."

I had a feeling getting good grades was extra important to me, but I couldn't quite remember why.

"Hey, Mom." I wasn't sure how to ask this without giving away my problem. "What have you and Dad been up to lately?"

Come on Mom, help me out. I'm going insane.

"Let's see. After you left the house Saturday afternoon, your dad and I went out to the farmer's market and then to dinner at The Wilderness. They have the best shrimp and steak special in October. We just couldn't resist!"

So I was at home this past weekend and it is October.

Dammit, what was going on in my head?

My mind was still very cloudy, and I just couldn't put anything together to make sense.

"Did you miss me already, hon? I just saw you, you know!" My mother laughed her wonderful laugh, inducing a homesick heartache in my chest. "Well, here's a kiss for ya—muah!"

"Thanks, Mom. Yes, that's exactly why I called," I lied again.

"Well, I've gotta get going! Dad had to run to work, but I'm off to church. Love you!"

"Love you too, Mom." Then she hung up and I held the phone to my ear for another few seconds, staring up at the ceiling. A tear flowed from under my eyelid, down my cheek and into my ear. Maybe I did need some more sleep. I hung up the phone, put it on the table, and rolled over toward the wall. I prayed that when I woke up my mind would be clear and this strange nightmare would be over. Soon my breathing was slow and even, and my eyelids began to feel heavy. I knew I'd be out in a matter of seconds.

Chapter Three

My phone's alarm woke me up. I rolled over to turn off the annoying sound.

7:30…7:30! In the morning?

I jumped up on top of my bed and looked out the tiny window near the ceiling. The sun was rising off to the right. I had slept through the entire day and all night?

My stomach ached with hunger, so I grabbed a granola bar out of the box on my bookshelf. As I chewed, I thought about yesterday morning's events and scanned the room for some clues to jog my memory. I saw framed pictures of my family and friends, and remembered everything about when those pictures were taken. I could remember last year and events from when I was a younger.

I grabbed my silky green robe off the hook on the back of the door, and headed down the hallway. All the bedroom doors were closed.

Yes, right. I was the only one who had an eight o'clock Monday morning. Eight a.m. Monday morning…hmmm…Bio 101. I smiled. Were things starting to come back to me? I could picture myself sitting in the lecture hall in the science building. I was still smiling as I turned the water on. The cloud hanging over my head was lifting as I woke up, and the pain in my arm had pretty much gone away.

What was my problem yesterday?

I knew exactly how to get to my biology lecture, and felt strangely proud of that fact. Biology was a bore, as usual, but being the serious student that I for some reason felt I wanted to be, I took notes and tried to pay attention. I couldn't help my pen from making random doodles on the margins of my paper, however. About halfway through the lecture I had drawn a beautiful tree up the left side of the notebook and extended the branches over the top margin. I added some fall leaves turning colors all over the branches. Then I sketched myself sitting on a limb part of the way up the tree. Standing near the trunk I drew a very handsome man with dark hair and sideburns talking on his cell phone. It was an odd thing to draw, but perhaps my pen was listening to the lecture on the biological classification of trees. And the man? Well, I always thought I'd meet my husband in college. Maybe he'll have dark hair and sideburns and, of course, be as handsome as a movie star.

After class I took a detour to the Student Center instead of going straight home. I wanted to stay away from the house for a while until my memory returned to me a little more. I couldn't confront my roommates until I knew what was going on with me.

The Student Center at UWSP is basically a hodgepodge of institutions that don't fit anywhere else on campus. It's home to the bookstore, a cafeteria, a large banquet hall, meeting rooms, the gift store, student lounges, Greek Headquarters, and the Cardio Center. I found a nice comfy couch on the second floor lounge by the fireplaces and took a seat all the way to one side. Any luck and some hottie would take the other half of the couch. I let my dark blue backpack sit on the floor at my feet, and decided to people watch for a while.

There was a lot of action this time of day, and I had plenty of people to observe. Although the weather had turned pretty brisk, many of the guys were still wearing their summer shorts. It's a Wisconsin thing—we try to hold onto summer as long as we possibly can because an undoubtedly long and cold winter is always on its way. Alternately, many of the women were still wearing their warm-month flip-flops. My toenails were painted red and peeking out of the toe of my sandals. They wouldn't see socks until the snow flies...which could be any day.

I casually scanned the room and this time someone caught my eye. Sitting all the way on the other side of the room on a couch near the exit was an extremely handsome man. He stood out among the college crowd wearing a fancy suit. Only a professor would be wearing a suit on campus, and he seemed too young to be a professor.

I took a good look at his face and felt mild pain behind my eyes and an uncomfortable pinch in my heart. He was staring straight at me—smiling an adorable, sweet smile. The headache got worse, but he was drop-dead gorgeous and I couldn't take my eyes of him.

He smiled and I was suddenly overcome with embarrassment. Panic forced me to quickly avert my eyes to the floor and try to calm my heart drilling out of my chest. Perhaps if I pretended to dig in my backpack for something, I could steal another look at his perfect face. My tiny brown eyes peered through the space under my upturned elbow, but the couch was empty. He was gone. I popped up and whipped my head around, checking all the chairs and couches in the lounge.

No suit anywhere.

Suddenly something purple smushed into my face. A large torso wearing a UWSP T-shirt had tripped over my backpack and landed half on top of me and half on the open space of the couch. Sharp pain radiated from my curiously injured arm, and I grunted as I tried my best to push the big lug off of me.

People around us laughed as the guy struggled to get unwrapped. His legs and feet were still tangled within the straps of my backpack. "Sorry, sorry! Oh bugger!"

An overpowering British accent forced me to assume he was an exchange student. The guy reached down and finally unwrapped my backpack strap from his ankles, but stepped on my bare toes in the process.

"Ow!"

"Oh bloody hell, so sorry!"

Finally free of me, he sat down on the empty spot of the couch. The guy looked older than the average college student, and had buttery blond hair that lay longer than his ears. A hideous, large cowlick flipped right above the middle of his forehead. I imagined a tiny surfboard with a little Hawaiian dude sliding through the middle. I wanted to tell him that seat was reserved for someone with better hair, but didn't have the heart to.

"Are you okay?" His awkward hands were all over me like I was being frisked by airport security. I slapped his paws away and he pulled back considerably.

"Yeah, I guess," I said, sarcasm laced through my voice. My fingers brushed the brown hair out of my eyes, my heart wanting this loser to leave.

I scanned the room. Where did that handsome, fancy guy go?

But the creep kept talking. The accent was already starting to get a little annoying. It was like I had to strain my ears to determine what he was saying.

"Are you sure you're doing alright? Looks like I got your arm," he said pointing. It took me a second to understand what he was saying and then I looked down. I hadn't noticed I was rubbing it, so I stopped abruptly.

"Look. I said I'm fine." Then for the first time since I got trampled, I looked the guy straight in the eye. He radiated an average, very ordinary vibe. I flashed him my best "scram" look.

Ah, there!

In my line of sight, right past the guy's kind of large head, I thought I saw someone wearing a dark suit near the exit. I leaned over ever so slightly to see past, but that put my head to rest on Mr. Creep's shoulder for half a second.

Shoot.

He got the wrong idea and slid an arm around my left shoulder. Apparently my "scram" look needed a little work.

That was enough foolishness. I stood up quickly and grabbed my backpack, peering at my pretend watch. "Hey, look at the time! I gotta go to class."

"Wait!" he yelled a little too loud and half the room stopped to look at us.

I have to get out of here, and fast!

But against my better judgment, I faced him once more. "What?" I asked impatiently. I had a bad feeling he'd follow me if I fled the room.

"Do you know how much a polar bear weighs?"

"Excuse me?" This guy was unbelievable.

He stood up and held out a hand to shake. "Enough to break the ice. My name is Adam Greene, and it was a great pleasure bumping into you."

Wow, two horrible jokes in one breath. A laugh and a smile snuck out beyond my control. He reminded me of my dad— always a joke. Always a bad joke.

I guess I may have reacted a little harshly. I shook his hand cordially. "Nice to meet you, Adam. I'm Ava Gardner. See you around campus." I tried to let go of his hand, but he held on tight and stared deep into my eyes.

"I certainly hope that is the case, Ava Gardner." His ordinary smile pulled back to display some actually handsome teeth. Adam pleasantly held my gaze for a few seconds. Suddenly this guy was in fact quite charming and seemed to remind me of someone, I just couldn't think of who. He let go of my hand, winked at me, and turned on his heel to walk off toward the front exit.

29

I watched Adam stroll away without looking back. Somehow I couldn't take my eyes off him until he was out of my sight. What just happened?

I had intense feelings of hatred toward my molester and then in a matter of minutes he somehow brainwashed me into feeling a little gooey inside. I shook my head, trying to clear it like a magic eight ball. "Outcome unclear," I said out loud as I turned and walked toward the opposite door.

The walk home should have taken approximately forty-five seconds, but it was such a nice day outside I decided to take a detour around the backside of the block, breathing in the brisk autumn air. I finally descended down the steps and through the door to our basement apartment, where I was greeted by the delicious smell of grilled cheese the instant I walked in the door.

Kasie was at the stove. "Hey, sleeping beauty! We missed you yesterday." She smiled as she flipped the golden brown sandwich in the pan.

"Yeah, I can't believe I slept that long!" I opened up the fridge and took out a Diet Coke. "And I can't believe you guys didn't wake me up!"

"The girls said you just weren't yourself and thought you probably needed to catch up on some sleep." She got the ketchup from the fridge. "Are you feeling better?"

"Yes. Absolutely." I took a seat on the couch and turned on the TV. It was quiet around the apartment. "The others at class?"

"Yup. Do you want a sandwich?" Kasie plated her grilled cheese and squirted a blob of ketchup on the side for dipping.

"No thanks. I can make myself something in a few minutes." I absentmindedly flipped through the stations. Two hundred channels and never anything to watch.

Kasie brought her plate over to the living room and took a spot on the loveseat across from me. "So, how are things?"

Hmmm. That might be girl code for, *What the hell was up with you yesterday?*

"Listen, I just had some weird headache thing going on. I promise, I am much better today!"

Half-truth. I was better, but still not the Ava I was used to.

"Good, because it's Monday and you know what that means?"

Then we both said at the same time, "Karaoke Night!"

Partners, a bar strategically placed right in the middle of a two-block radius of student housing apartments, hosted underage night on every other Monday—a night when students under twenty-one were admitted into the bar to sing karaoke and play pool. We all had to wear bright orange wristbands to indicate our legal status, and the place was always crawling with police. My friends and I didn't care. We weren't there to try to drink beer, only to sing and hang with friends. If there was one bar activity I was good at, it was karaoke! It must have been all the summers at the boat tours.

My thoughts slowed down for a second. Yes...I was a singing tour guide for the Lower Dells Boat Tours.

All of a sudden it was like my brain's filing cabinets were slowly opening and someone was filling them up with memories of working at DBT.

"Jack..." I said under my breath. My eyes stared at the wall above Kasie's head as I searched for more memories.

"What?" Kasie asked through a mouthful of sandwich.

"Oh nothing. Nevermind."

Curious. Very curious.

Chapter Four

"Well, Miss Gardner." My academic advisor, Mr. Weigel, tapped a pen on his desk calendar as he read his computer screen. "Last semester was, shall we say, less than stellar?"

My grades? What were they?

"Oh really?" I replied. I tried to remember how last semester checked out, but my mind was blank.

Mr. Weigel removed his reading glasses from his nose and pointed them in the air at me. "If you're serious about entering the teaching profession, young lady, you'll have to change your priorities, your study habits, your efforts, and mostly your attitude."

Oops. I came off as sassy when in reality I just couldn't remember.

"I understand, sir. I'll change."

Bad grades? How could I have...but my mind shifted gears as I began to recall my crappy freshman year.

"You'd better change," Mr. Weigel said. "It'll be almost impossible to apply to the School of Education at the end of this year if you don't turn things around here."

My advisor's tone threatened tears deep behind my eyes, but I took a deep breath and pushed away the feeling. No school of Ed? This was all Aaron's fault. No, I allowed him to distract me. I made this happen; I had to get myself out of this mess.

"Is there anything I can do?"

Mr. Weigel put his glasses back on and glanced at the computer screen. "You're in luck. Thursday is the deadline to add courses for the semester. If you're really serious about your education, I would retake the history course you failed last spring, and I might even take the psych class over as well. There are a few seats open in the online version of the course."

I exhaled loudly. Adding more credits to my already tough semester seemed impossible. The tears threatened an appearance again.

Mr. Weigel sensed my uneasiness and his voice softened. "It won't be easy, but I'll tell you this—if you work hard and get acceptable grades this semester, the School of Education Committee will be impressed with your improvements. This could really help you."

I nodded, visualizing how any second of spare time I had this semester would be spent reading, writing papers, and studying.

"Thank you, sir," I said politely.

He handed me the paperwork I'd need to sign up for the extra credits. I grabbed my backpack and left his office, wondering what my grades were last semester. No matter, I was determined to dedicate myself to my studies this semester. There was no way I was accepting defeat.

I signed up for both of the courses and for the rest of the week, I continued my daily routine of attending classes, completing homework, and studying, but something inside me felt very off and I had an unexplainable and very overwhelming feeling of loneliness.

Memories started to slowly creep back to me in quick flashes throughout the week, but each time I saw a new memory in front of my eyes I experienced a strange and very intense pain in my head. It usually would go as quickly as it came, but unsettling just the same.

I went through my schedule as best I could, focusing on studying, but it still bothered me that my memory seemed to dart in and out. I was beginning to wonder if I should alert my parents, or see a doctor, but I didn't want to worry my mom and it wasn't like I couldn't get through the day normally. So I decided to ride it out. If memories were coming back to me every day, then perhaps they'd continue to do just that as time went on.

On Friday, I decided to head over to the library after my Intro to Algebra class. The university library was a rather large and sterile feeling concrete building. At six floors tall, it overlooked all of campus. I was proud to admit that I had actually visited all six floors, and was most impressed with the movable stacks on the third through fifth floors. The long bookshelves were attached to a track on the ceiling and hung off the floor. They all stood together until a push of a button on the wall separated as many shelves as you needed until the book you wanted was exposed. Although I thought whoever engineered that system was a genius, I was always apprehensive to use the moving shelves because I was afraid someone might push the button while I was browsing and squish me flat as a pancake between the shelves. Death by books was not how I wanted to leave this world.

The first floor hosted a small natural science museum, the circulation desk, a large computer lab, and study lounge. Although the library was very populated this morning, it was also expectantly very quiet. I took out my math methods textbook and set my open notebook right next to it. I wanted to get my homework done before I headed home. It was Clara's birthday and I knew there wouldn't be an ounce of quiet all evening.

Just as I settled into the second paragraph on the math textbook page, my phone loudly announced someone was calling. All eyes in the room were quickly turning toward me.

Hurry! Turn it off!

But as I bent down to retrieve the darn thing from my backpack, my elbow slammed into the edge of the textbook, flipping it to the floor and sending my graphing calculator and pen flying through the air.

I winced when I heard the smack and felt the eyes of the entire room on me.

"Ow! What in the—?"

"Oh no," I said under my breath. I thought about bolting out of there, but I heard my name.

A tall blond guy got up from his chair and approached me. I let out a groan when my eyes confirmed what my ears had recognized.

"Well, now we're even!" he said.

Adam. What were the odds?

He continued, putting his hand to his chest. "Adam. Remember? I clobbered you in the Student Center lounge last week?"

"Yes…right, I remember." The big purple blob with the British accent. There was no forgetting that. "Right, Adam. Now my calculator clobbered you. I guess we are even."

"Exactly," he said, smiling.

"I'm sorry, Adam. I'm a bona fide klutz." It was true. There wasn't a day that went by that I didn't accidentally knock over something or trip and fall. I suddenly had a memory flash of brochures flying through the air. My eyebrows furrowed in confusion as the vision left as quickly as it came on.

"We've got to stop meeting this way. Soon enough one of us will end up in the hospital!" Adam pulled the chair out from the table and sat down.

Today his accent didn't seem quite as annoying. Something was different about his appearance, too. I scanned his face and noticed his hideous haircut had changed. It was much shorter now and the large wave in the middle was gone. He looked much younger. It was quite an improvement from the other day.

Although my first impression of the guy wasn't that great, he seemed a little more tolerable today.

I was not sure what possessed me, but I said, "My friends and I are going to the Homecoming game tomorrow. Would you like to join us?"

"Thanks for the invitation, but actually I'll be there already. The Theta Sigs are hosting a fifty-fifty raffle. You should stop by the booth."

Theta Sigs? Oh no, I usually tried to steer clear of those fraternity types.

"Oh. A frat boy. I thought you guys only fraternized with girls bearing big boobs and curly blond hair."

He smiled as if he'd heard that one a thousand times before. "We all make exceptions for truly beautiful women." I gave him a snarky smile before I realized it was a compliment. Then he leaned over and whispered, "It's in our secret brotherly code." He smiled as he watched it all sink into my face.

He was hitting on me.

I blushed a little bit and looked down at the table. I needed to change the subject off of me and back onto him. "So, Adam, when did you join the fraternity?"

"Believe it or not, I'm not from around here." He paused to see my smile. "I arrived at the beginning of summer, and will just be here for the term. I've come from the University of Greenwich in London. I always thought I should get the real American college experience, so I joined a fraternity. We don't have those in the UK, you know."

"Really? I had no idea." I awkwardly pushed a pen around the table. "What are you studying while you are here?"

"Communications. Someday I aim to anchor the London evening news! Do you think I have the voice for it?" He cleared his throat before I could answer. His voice dropped an octave and he had a very cheesy smile on his face. "And tonight on the BBC evening news…"

"Very good," I admitted. "Actually, I have a lot of experience in public speaking. I could give you some pointers if you wanted."

"Really?" He laughed. "Wait, you aren't a radio personality or anything, right?"

I snickered. "No, no. I'm from a tourist trap in the middle of the state called Wisconsin Dells. I've been working as a tour boat guide for the last four summers."

"A tour guide? I would have never guessed! That's brilliant!"

"Yeah, it's a pretty great job. Last summer was…" I was drawing a blank. "Last summer was…" I could not picture a moment of last summer. A small irritating pain began to form behind my right eye. I rubbed my eyes instinctively and scrunched up my eyebrows and forehead.

"Are you okay, Ava?" I felt Adam's fingers on top of my left hand, which was resting on the table top.

"Yeah, sorry. Sometimes I get these weird headaches. They come on out of nowhere." It was a complete lie, but I didn't have a plausible way to explain what I was going through. I stared at Adam's hand, which was still lying on top of mine. He followed my stare and moved it quickly.

"I think I better head home and lay down for awhile."

What was happening to me?

"Right, right. I hope you feel better soon. Oh, and don't forget to stop by the booth tomorrow at the football game if you're feeling better. I'll be looking for you."

His smile was warm and friendly. Maybe he was a rare breed of frat.

Then again, perhaps he just wanted to try to sleep with me.

"Okay. Bye, Adam." I started to pack up my textbook and things, wondering what to think.

"Cheerio, Ava." He grabbed his books off the table nearby and headed out the side door.

Clearly he had interest in me, but a frat boy? I didn't think I wanted to go there. The partying, drinking, and promiscuous sex was seriously not for me. And he was an exchange student! I thought I would find the man I was going to marry in college, and I had no plans to move across the pond for the rest of my life. He did seem like someone fun to hang out with, though. Perhaps I'd find a permanent spot for him over on my friend list.

Chapter Five

I got up extra early Saturday morning and spent three hours working on schoolwork. I had to stay on top of my assignments knowing that I wanted to go to the football game later.

"You ready, Ava?" Kasie asked as she knocked on my partially opened door.

I closed my history book and happily set my pen down. "Yeah. I need a break."

Kasie entered my room holding a homemade purple scrunchie.

"What is that?" I asked.

"It's for your hair, silly! Come on, we're all getting ready in the living room." I followed Kasie out of my room and found my friends all decked out in Pointer purple, doing each other's hair and makeup.

Kasie, with sorority spirit running through her blood, made us all wear face paint and added the homemade purple scrunchies to our hair. We looked seriously ridiculous, but Kasie assured us we would fit right in when we got to the game.

We walked the short few blocks over to Gerke Field and waited in line to show our student IDs. Before we even got through to the field, I spotted Adam. He was standing at the Theta Sig fifty-fifty raffle booth, as promised, right near the front gate. I couldn't even get through before he left the booth and over enthusiastically ran to me.

"Hey Ava!" he yelled, and then stopped suddenly, dropping his voice a little. "Wow. You are...drenched in school spirit."

Great. We did look ridiculous. My cheeks turned pink with embarrassment. "Yeah, it's all Kasie's fault." I turned to Kasie and she stuck out her hand to shake Adam's.

"Adam, right? I saw you were recently added to the Theta Sig roster. I'm a Delta Nu."

"My pleasure, Kasie."

"And these are my other roommates, Elaina and Sharon."

"Hello ladies! Anyone up for a raffle ticket?"

Kasie said she'd buy a few, so we all walked over to the booth. When we got there Adam introduced me to his friends as the girl who smacked him in the face with a calculator.

"Nice one, Ava! Someone had to put our little Brit in his place!" One of the hot frat boys pinched Adam's cheeks as he spoke the way a grandma might do to a little child. Adam quickly swatted the guy's hands away as a tiny bit of pink showed up on his face. It was kind of cute.

Soon the band blasted our school song as the football players ran onto the field. Cheerleaders jumped and yelled, waving their pompoms on the track outlining the grassy field. The bleachers were filled with students soaked in Pointer pride and the air was electric with school spirit. I suddenly didn't feel so ridiculous in my getup.

"See ladies? I told you we look awesome!" Kasie led us up the broad metal stairs to some bleacher seats in the middle of the stands, then turned and screamed obnoxiously over our heads, "Go Pointers!"

"I love Adam's accent, and he's pretty cute," Elaina said, hinting at the obvious. "Don't you think so, Ava?"

I shrugged my shoulders. The truth was I didn't know how I really felt about Adam. I had just met him. Plus I just didn't feel like a relationship was that high on my priority list right now. And there was some strange force in my brain telling me that I had to focus on my grades. Was it this year that I could get into the School of Education?

Sharon jumped in when I didn't take the gossip bait. "So are you going to date him?"

"I don't think so." They stared at me in disbelief. "I don't like him that way." No one said anything for half a minute. "What?" I asked, as their silence burned my ears.

"Fine, I'll say it," Kasie said. "Ava, you're crazy. That man is adorable!"

Unexpectedly, the announcer came over the loudspeaker to declare the start of the game and introduce the players, saving me from dodging any more questions.

Why did my friends want me to date Adam so badly?

It was an exciting football game, but as much as I tried not to, I found myself thinking about Adam most of the time. Were my friends seeing something I wasn't? I involuntarily glanced back at the booth several times to see what he was doing, but each time I made sure to turn back around quickly. I didn't want to get caught by my friends—they'd heckle me for sure.

Before the game ended Adam found me up in the stands and sat down to chat for a few minutes. My roommates thought his accent was completely charming and spent most of the time asking him to say certain words so they could hear them with his accent and laugh. Adam was a great sport about it all.

"Well, I should get back to the booth before the game ends. We'll have to tidy up." Adam stood.

"Wait, I'll walk with you. I have to use the bathroom anyway." I followed Adam down the stairs and across the bleachers. He stopped at the bottom so we could walk together.

"Did you know I played football at University in Greenwich?" He kicked a rock with his left foot.

"You did?" We walked along the chain link fence separating the field from the bleacher area.

"I did. But football is played a lot differently in Europe."

"What you call football is what we call soccer, right?"

"Exactly." We were almost to the bathrooms. "You are one smart cookie, Ava."

"Thanks, but I don't always feel like it. I have a crazy Bio exam on Monday and I'm doomed to epically fail."

"Biology? I'm a pro. Can I help you study?"

"Actually, that sounds nice. Are you doing anything later today? We could meet at the library."

"Yeah, let's give it a go." I detected a hint of excitement behind his eyes. "I'll see you in the lobby around four?"

"Thanks so much, Adam. You're awesome!"

Adam laughed.

"What?"

"That is the most ridiculous and overused American word." I smiled at him, waved good-bye, and then turned into the ladies' room.

*　*　*　*

On the walk home my roommates and I ran into a friend that used to live across the hall from us in the dorms. She was holding hands and making googly eyes at some guy walking with her. I could almost see little pink hearts floating up from their heads.

"Hey, Molly!" Kasie yelled.

The brown-haired beauty turned toward the sound. "Hey, ladies! How's it going? Oh, I should introduce you to my boyfriend. This is Nolan Williams."

Nolan? Nolan...where have I heard that name before?

My brain suddenly flashed an image of a very handsome dark haired man with the most beautiful blue eyes I'd ever seen. Then he was gone as quickly as he was there.

No! Come back! Who is that?

My heart felt like it stopped beating. I put my hand on my chest and my breathing sped up. I thought I might collapse, so I bent over and put my hands on my knees, waiting for my lunch to make a second appearance right there on the sidewalk.

My head throbbed like someone had whacked my skull with a baseball bat. "Ow! My head!"

All at once everyone was all around me and I was lowered to the ground, Elaina letting my head lay in her lap.

"Ava! What's wrong? Is it a headache?"

"Do you know who we are?"

"What is today's date?"

The whole group bombarded me with questions as if I had gotten tackled by a linebacker.

"Wait! Wait! Stop freaking out! I'm fine!" I sat up slowly and faced a crowd of concerned eyes, my headache subsiding a little.

Out of nowhere, Adam pushed his way through the crowd and was somehow there next to me on the sidewalk. "Ava, tell me exactly what happened," he said calmly, grabbing my hand. "Are you alright?"

"Adam?" I said, my cheeks flushed. "Where did you come from?"

"I saw you go down." He looked deep into my eyes, concerned. "How do you feel?"

"Completely embarrassed," I said quietly.

Adam put two fingers on my wrist and looked at his watch.

"What are you doing?" Elaina asked. "Are you a Med student or something?"

Adam dropped my hand instantly. "Oh, I don't know. They always do that on TV. I just...nevermind."

"Sorry, everyone. I'm fine," I sat up slowly. "I just had a quick moment of nausea. I just need to sip some water and lay down at home."

Adam hooked his arm under mine and helped me up. I really did feel better, except for the fact that I craved the beautiful face from my vision to fill my mind again.

"If your head continues to hurt, make sure to take something for it." Adam administered some fatherly advice. "Stay hydrated this afternoon. It'll, um, help your headache. I'll see you later at the library, if you're up to it."

"Thanks, Adam."

"Here," he put his hand out, palm up, "let me punch in my number in case you need to cancel."

I handed my phone to Adam.

"I hope you're feeling better so we can get together later," he said, while typing on my phone. "But if not, no worries. You might need your rest. See ya, Ava."

My friends were incredibly silent on the rest of the walk home. I knew they were all worried about me, and to be honest I was starting to get worried, too. What was going on with my head?

When we got home I was feeling much better, but decided to lie down for a while anyway before I had to meet Adam at the library. A short nap would make me feel brand new, I was hoping. I got myself a glass of water and then set the alarm on my phone just in case I did fall asleep.

A few deep, cleansing breaths and the dark room helped to relax me. In the silence, I tried so hard to pull that beautiful man's face back to the front of my mind, but I just couldn't get it. I felt it stuck stubbornly far back in my brain, not wanting to move to the front of the filing cabinet. I tried hard to focus on any part of his face, his hair, his neck...but it seemed like right when I focused in on a detail, it faded quickly away.

For many minutes I tried to retrieve any visions I could, but only frustrated myself in the end. Soon my alarm blared, reminding me it was time to head over to the library and start studying for my test.

Adam was already there sitting in the lobby lounge waiting. He reading some type of textbook, but looked up and smiled when he saw me.

"Feeling better? I've been worried about you."

He's been thinking about me all afternoon?

"I'm feeling much better, thanks."

Adam and I found a private study room upstairs. Adam was very patient, quizzing me for over two hours on the flashcards I had made. I needed to memorize fifty different scientific names of plants and animals, and memorizing was not my strong suit. Even so, he was encouraging, he was helpful, and when I felt like quitting he would take a break with me, telling me jokes or sharing stories from home.

We went over and over those notecards until Adam felt confident I'd do great on the test. I couldn't believe someone I had just met would be willing to spend an afternoon helping me out. Although I appreciated his friendship, I couldn't help but be on my guard. What were his intentions true intentions?

I never felt that Adam was anything but authentically friendly. Studying with him made it seem like not such a horrible task and by the end of the two hours, I did feel more prepared than I ever would have felt studying on my own.

Adam and I split ways outside the front door. "Thanks again, Adam. I think I'll be ready now for that test."

"Not a problem. I enjoyed studying with you." His smile was sweet.

"I owe you one."

"I won't forget." We stood there smiling at each other for a few seconds before he said, "Later, Ava," and turned to walk down the sidewalk toward his house. Perhaps this guy was just looking for a friend.

The walk home was refreshing. I had a happy feeling in my heart, and a simple smile on my face.

*   *   *   *

Later that night I was in my room studying when my cell phone rang—*mom and dad.*

"Hi!"

"Hi hon!"

"What are you up to?"

"Oh, your dad and I are just finishing packing for our trip. Remember we might not be able to call you while we're abroad, but you can always email. Anyway, how are you doing?"

Mom didn't necessarily sound concerned, but I wondered if she could somehow know about my recent episodes. "Oh, I'm doing alright, Mom. Staying really busy."

"Great. How's school?"

"Exhausting. All I do is eat, sleep, and work on homework. I met with my advisor last week. He said I could probably apply to the School of Education next semester." I wasn't sure if my parents knew the academic trouble I was in. If my mother was aware, she wasn't leading on. "If I don't get in, I'll only have one more chance, and then I have to change my major, or transfer."

"Oh, honey. That would be horrible. I know how much you want to be a teacher."

"Yeah, well, I'll just make sure I pass all my classes and get a great score on the PRAXIS exam next week. I've done a lot of volunteering in the elementary schools here lately, so that's gotta help, too."

"Looks good on an application, anyway." A silence followed that seemed to be filled with motherly questions.

I decided to ask her before she could ask me: "Is everything okay with you, Mom?"

"Sure, sure. Ava…I don't know how to say this, but…how come you haven't mentioned anything about Nol—" The phone cut off abruptly.

"Mom?" I pulled the phone away from my ear. It seemed to still be connected. "Mom? Mom?" There was only silence, so I pressed *end* and was about to call her back when my phone rang again.

"Mom? We got cut off."

"Yeah. I don't know what happened there. Anyway, I was saying, did Nol—" Then the phone cut off again.

Jeez, her phone was awful. What was she trying to say?

I dialed once again but this time a nice little automated voice greeted me. "This number cannot be completed as dialed."

Oh well. If it was important enough my mom would call back later.

Chapter Six

Sunday morning brought some really beautiful fall weather—brisk, fresh air and golden sunlight shining through colored leaves. I wrote a history paper I was really proud of, did my Algebra homework, completed some posts for my online class, and then Kasie and I decided to get out of the house and take a jog through Iverson Park.

I pulled my baby blue Cutlass Ciera Oldsmobile between two handsome grey, stone pillars standing guard at the entrance of the driveway and parked a quarter of a mile down the way. We were the only car in the lot.

Kasie and I were the athletic ones of my group and couldn't talk anyone else into exercising today. We started out on a slow jog down the wide dirt pathway. After we warmed up, we picked up the pace and wound around a few playgrounds, a soccer field, and then a picnic pavilion. We jogged over rustic stone bridges spanning the swift-flowing Plover River and past the abandoned swimming area. A nature center and fireplace lodge sat quietly on the land to our right. Running felt so great, and spending time within nature was just what I needed to relax.

Soon the pathway turned into a forest area with no park structures. Tall, Wisconsin pines lined each side and I instantly felt at home. The smell of the crisp fall Wisconsin air was alluring. Wisconsin Dells was one of my very favorite places on earth, and one of the many reasons was because of the beauty of the nature there. I could find these exact same trees near one of my favorite places in the Dells—Make Out Rock.

Suddenly my brain jolted another unfamiliar picture in front of my eyes. I was on the rock cliff in the darkness, crying and lying in a pool of blood. It was really disturbing and I stopped running for a second to rub my forehead as a sharp pain jabbed at my head.

"What's up? You okay?" Kasie slowed down her run, but kept jogging in place while she questioned me.

The pain was almost gone, so I stood up and started to jog again. "I have to be honest with you, Kas." I couldn't keep my secret much longer. "I've been having these massive headaches and weird visions lately."

She looked at me strangely. "Do you mean like nightmares?"

"Well, kind of. But it's just for a quick second and then they disappear. And it's only happened during the day when I'm awake. Sometimes they really catch me at odd times and they are more confusing than frightening."

We kept jogging and Kasie said nothing but looked at me with a concerned stare.

"Kas, I know this sounds weird, but please humor me." I continued cautiously. I didn't want Kasie to think I'd gone insane, although I wasn't entirely sure that I hadn't. "What have I told you about last summer?"

Please know something.

"Um, not too much. You said you made some good money with Jack but that was about it. Why, don't you remember?"

"See, that's the scary part. I can't remember anything about last summer." I shook my head with disbelief. "God, I feel like I was high on some street drug for three months or something."

"Ava, I don't know, involved in drugs? That just doesn't sound like you. Plus, if you did, wouldn't you think you'd still be addicted? I think we would know."

"Yeah, I guess. I just can't find an answer." We arrived back near my car and sat on the grass to stretch. "I feel like a whole chunk of my life is missing."

"Have you said anything to your parents? I mean, they were there with you all summer. You think they'd know if something weird was going on." Kasie reached for her toes.

"No, I haven't said anything. Oh wait, it's October 19th, right?"

"Yeah."

"Well, now I can't ask. They left for their trip to Ireland. They'll be gone for fourteen days." I grabbed my left arm above the elbow and stretched it across my chest.

"And you can't get ahold of them at all?" Kasie switched legs and reached for her other set of toes.

"They said they might check their email a few times during the trip and they left the number of the hotel they're staying at in case of emergency, but I don't want to bother them with this."

"I guess. Hey, what about Laura? Call her up! She was home last summer, right."

"Oh, didn't I tell you? That's why my parents are going to Ireland. Laura is studying abroad this semester."

"No! You didn't tell me. That's awesome!" Kasie laid down on the grass and extended her arms over her head for a full body stretch. "Well, I'm sure you'll solve your mystery soon enough. Hang in there, girl."

"I hope you're right." I stood up and grabbed one of my ankles, pulling it up near my hip to stretch out my thigh.

"Thanks for the run, Ava. This was fun." Kasie stood up and then bent over at the hips to touch the grass without bending her knees.

We continued stretching for a few more minutes when suddenly a sleek black car zoomed down the gravel hill a little too fast and pulled up a few spots down from my Olds.

The door opened and Adam got out.

"Oh, seriously," I said under my breath.

He shut the passenger door and stayed facing the car. I could hear the clicking noise of someone sending a text.

"Well, well. Who do we have here?" I couldn't hold back a smile as Adam slowly turned around. He was dressed in black warm-up pants with a white stripe down the side, a long-sleeved grey T-shirt that said "Fulham Football Club," and a pair of athletic shoes.

"Ava! You know, this town isn't that small. How do we keep ending up in the same place?" He put his phone back into his pocket, smiled widely, walking over toward Kasie and me.

"I just don't know, Adam. It's almost like someone is stalking me." Then I gave him a little playful punch on the shoulder.

"Ha. You wish." Adam's eyes drifted toward Kasie.

"Adam, you remember my roommate, Kasie?"

"Hey, Adam."

"Yes. Right, right. Hello, Kasie. Nice to see you again." Adam leaned against the bumper of my Olds. "So, judging by the deep shade of red on your faces, I'm guessing you girls just finished a jog?"

Oh gosh, how ridiculous did I look right now?

"Yeah, just finished." I brushed my cheek with the back of my hand as if that would erase some of the red. "Isn't it a little early for you frat boys to be out and about? I thought you couldn't leave the house before noon."

"Many don't," he laughed. "That is true." He paused and looked around the area. "A friend recommended I take a little jog through the park."

His accent was particularly adorable this morning.

"You wouldn't want to join me on a little jaunt, would you? I'll need a proper guide since I've never been here before and I'd hate to get lost in the woods." He hit me with pleading eyes. "You do owe me, remember?"

It's true I barely knew the guy, but something inside me urged me to trust him. "Yeah, I guess I could go back out for another jog. As long as we don't go for too long."

I looked over at Kasie and she mouthed, "Are you sure?" I nodded, and handed her my car keys.

"You can give me a ride back to my house later, right Adam?"

"Absolutely! I'd love to see where you live." He leaned up against the side of his car, smiling.

"Okay. Well, don't work her too hard, Adam." Kasie gave a menacing smile and Adam laughed out loud. She took my car keys, opened the passenger side door, and then leaned over and gave me a hug. "See you later, Ava." Then she whispered "be safe" in my ear.

"I will. Bye Kasie. See you soon." And then she got in, started it up, and drove off with a bang when the transmission shifted.

I giggled, embarrassed. "I gotta get that car looked at." I looked over at Adam's ride. It looked very expensive. How did he get such a nice car—let alone any car—as a foreign exchange student? But before I could ask, Adam took off running down the pathway.

"Come on, local. I need a guide!" He yelled over his shoulder.

I jogged after him with a smile on my face. Very quickly my body started aching. Why did I decide to go around again?

"Brilliant. It is beautiful here," Adam commented.

"If you like this, you'd love the Dells." I wiped a few beads of sweat from my forehead.

"What's it like in the Dells? You keep telling me how great it is."

"The Dells is the name for a seven-mile series of sandstone rock cliffs that line the Wisconsin River. I can't even explain how gorgeous they are. You should come back with me some weekend and I'll show you around town."

What did I just say? Was I inviting this guy I barely knew back home? I had never taken a boy home to my parents' house before, besides my high school boyfriend. I was about to take it back, but Adam already accepted.

"That'd be, as you Americans say, awesome!" He was smiling at me, excitement in his eyes, when it hit me again.

"Ow! My head!" I was struck with blinding pain, and didn't see the tree root sticking out of the dirt. I tripped and rolled onto the ground, laid out flat. Suddenly I saw a vision of a very handsome man kissing me in a very small room that looked somewhat like a bedroom. He was caressing my lower back and slowly dancing with me. It was so real I thought I might actually be in the room with that man—until I heard Adam's voice.

"Ava...Ava, dear. Take a deep breath." I could barely hear him. I pushed his voice out of my head—I wanted to keep the vision in front of my brain. My heart was aching for whoever was in that room with me.

"Ava. You're far away."

The man in my vision was incredibly handsome and his beautiful blue eyes were mesmerizing.

"Ava...come back to me. Open your eyes." Adam's voice sounded miles away.

But then my vision became hazy, like someone slowly turned down the color.

No! No...no...

Adam had crouched down next to me, gently coaxing me to sit up, eyes right at my level. He kept very calm, speaking to me as he placed his hand on my upper arm, rubbing slowly.

"Ava.... You're safe. You're here in the park with Adam." He continued to comfort me. "Come back to me, Ava."

I shook my head a little as the vision faded away. My breathing was heavy and fast. I looked up at Adam's brown eyes with hurt and concern on my face. But he did not freak out. He did not overreact. He was perfect. He said nothing, but grabbed my hand to pull me into a sitting position. A tiny smile of disbelief slid onto the corners of my mouth and I let out a sigh.

"Welcome back, Ava. I thought I had lost you there for a second." He took my hand in his and it felt wonderful, like a tiny blanket of hope wrapped around me.

"Adam, why are you being so nice to me?"

"We have an old saying in England: 'You can't judge a book by its cover.'"

I snorted. "We have that saying, too.

A look of surprise took hold of his face. "Blimey, you do?"

"Yes! Of course! But what does that have to do with me?"

"I see what's inside you, Ava. I can tell you are a good person, and a strange outburst here and an odd headache there won't turn me away from being your friend."

Adam felt somewhat like a father figure to me, and even though I just met him, he was proving himself to be a good friend and I was thankful I had him in my life.

He stood up from the ground and extended his hand to help me up. "I think you've had enough strenuous exercise for one day. What do you say we take a pleasant stroll through the rest of the park?"

"That sounds great."

How did he do that? He turned me from a crazy mess to calm and comfortable. Was Adam a great guy or just good at deceiving innocent girls like me? Either way, he somehow made me feel secure and safe next to him.

We approached the summer swimming area and I explained how the Plover River brought tons of people to the beach each summer. "They even employ a few seasonal lifeguards, and there is an old red brick bathhouse behind the beach."

"That antique stone on the building is so beautiful—reminds me of home." He took a deep breath, staring out over the pool and bathhouse. "Do you like swimming?" he said without looking back toward me.

"Love it! I was on the Dells Dolphin swim team when I was a little girl."

"Really? A little fishy, huh?" Adam played the part of big brother, playfully teasing his little sister. I liked it.

"How about you?"

"I love it as well. Just don't get to do it that often. Greenwich is right on the River Thames, but you won't catch anyone swimming in there. All that passes by these days is rubbish barges and empty lager bottles. But, ah, the Thames is part of my home."

"Do you miss it? I mean, being at home?"

For the first time I saw a little distance in his eyes. He turned to me and said very sincerely. "I do. I miss my family and mates. But I've had so many wonderful experiences here and I've grown so much in only the short time I've lived in the US. I wouldn't trade it for anything."

"I've always wanted to visit Britain. Tell me about London."

It took us almost forty minutes to finish the walk and he spoke of home the entire time. He told me about his family's cottage just outside of Loughton, northeast of the heart of London, about his brother and sister, and his favorite travels. It was all very interesting and I loved hearing about a different culture.

We finally arrived back at the parking lot. "So, Ava. Do you remember every single one of those blasted notecards from yesterday?"

"Oh gosh. I haven't thought about those all day. I hope I remember them."

"You'd better, after all the time I invested in you!"

"Don't worry. I'll study again later today and a bit tomorrow before class."

He leaned his backside on the hood of the car while I took a seat nearby on a bench at the edge of the parking lot. "So, Miss Ava, what are your plans for the rest of today?"

I cautiously answered, "Well…" *Oh no. Is he going to make me study for hours again?* "Not too much," I said hesitantly.

"Brilliant! Then you're spending the day with me!" He reached into his pocket and pulled out his car keys. I heard the locks click open.

"Oh really?" Excitement stirred in my stomach. I tried to hide it, not wanting to look too eager. "Well, okay then. What are we going to do?"

"Just get inside, little lady!"

I curiously walked around to the passenger's side door and slid into the seat of the car. I was immediately impressed. I didn't know a thing about cars, but this one looked like it had all the extras. The interior was sleek beige leather and the dash was basically a fancy computer. Adam put the keys in the console between us and then pressed a button on the dash to start the engine.

"Where did you get this car?" I reached out and ran my fingers over the temperature controls by my side. It put the tape player in my Olds to shame.

"Well, there's something about me you don't know." He started the ignition, but then stared out the windshield and said nothing.

The silence ate at my patience. *Come on! Say something!* My heart began to race, and an anxious feeling snuck into my stomach. Was getting in a car with this man completely unsafe?

56

He had successfully backed up the sophisticated car, using the rear camera display in the dash, and then said, "I'm royalty."

My jaw dropped.

"What do you mean, 'royalty'? Like a prince?" He didn't seem handsome enough to be a prince.

Suddenly Adam burst into wild laughter. "Oh good God! To see your face! That was hilarious!" He put the car in drive and headed up the hill, continuing to laugh as I felt my face turn red with embarrassment. "No, I'm not royalty!"

"That is not funny." I told him, half laughing, half serious, but he kept smiling. "Okay then, Your Highness. Where did you get this fancy car?"

"Would you believe I won the lotto?"

"No." I looked out the window as he drove past the baseball fields.

The corner of his lips turned up as he searched for another answer. "Quiz show champion?"

I couldn't hold back a smile. "Absolutely not. Try again."

"You're a tough audience...hmmm...well, I don't think you'd actually believe the truth, so you'll have to settle for...pop star!" He turned the car left onto Main Street.

"Yeah, right. I like royalty better."

He looked out the windshield smiling curiously. "Fine, royalty it is. Just call me Prince Adam."

We drove through some residential areas and drifted into UWSP territory. I watched Gerke Field pass on our right. I knew something suspicious was brewing, but I wasn't about to push it. I barely knew Adam, after all. "Alright, Prince Adam. Where are you taking me today?"

"Back to your house."

"I guess I set my bar too high."

"No offense intended, but you need a shower first."

I laughed out loud. That was not what I expected to hear but it was probably true. I did need a shower. "I thought Europeans didn't shower everyday."

He shook his head. "Nasty rumor. The French don't bathe for days. Londoners, if we stink, we shower."

"Fair enough. Turn here on Fremont." Adam turned his fancy-schmancy car down the street.

"I'll drop you off. Could you be ready in forty-five minutes?"

"Now turn here on College Avenue." I pointed through the windshield. "Sure, I'll be all clean and fresh for your olfactory nerves. We're the last house on the block."

"Oooh…did you look ahead in your biology textbook, Dr. Gardner?"

I gave him a fake angry face and Adam chortled gleefully. He pulled to a stop in front of the two-story, creamy yellow house. A dark, screened-in porch hung off the top floor.

"See you later, Your Highness." I flashed a smile from the lawn, and he called, "Cheerio, Ava!"

Inside, Elaina and Sharon were sitting around the living room playing one of our all-time favorite board games, Sequence. Elaina was kicking Sharon's butt, like always.

"Hey! There she is!" Sharon's face lit up when she saw me.

"Kasie told us we may have to send a search party after you!" Elaina played a blue poker chip on the board.

"Naw, Adam is pretty cool. I totally trust him." I took a seat on the couch for a quick second. "Actually, I'm just home to shower and change, and then I'm going back out with him again."

Elaina put down her cards and sat forward. "Really? So are you ready now to admit you like Adam as more than a friend?"

"No," I said quickly. "I mean, I don't think so."

Oh no, my cheeks were burning pink!

"At this point he has just been really great company. He's easy to talk to and I feel comfortable with him, but I'm pretty sure there isn't any physical attraction between us."

Sharon seemed to be studying my face for the truth. "I guess I'll believe you. But are you sure he feels the same way? You don't want to lead him on and then break his heart, do you?"

"Of course not." Maybe Sharon was right. "I promise I'll be careful. If he ever gives me a signal that says more than friends, I'll get the heck out of there right away!"

"Good plan." Sharon placed a red chip over the king of spades.

"Okay, I'm off to shower. He's gonna be back in forty-five minutes." I left the living room and headed for my bedroom. I checked my phone sitting on the window ledge above my bed— *no new messages*. I undressed, pulled my silky green robe off the hook behind my door, and then grabbed a white towel and some clean clothes from the laundry basket on the floor.

The hot shower massaged my sore muscles and refreshed my sweaty skin. After the quick shower, I dressed and blow-dried my hair. I was applying makeup when I heard the doorbell ring and my friends calling for me.

"Ava! Adam's here!"

"I'll be right out!" I yelled from the bathroom. I felt a quick flip of nerves in my stomach and smiled involuntarily. I suppressed it quickly—*he's just a friend*, I reminded myself. I spritzed a bit of perfume, took another look at myself in the mirror and then opened the door.

Adam was sitting on the couch chatting with my friends, but stood up when he saw me. He was wearing a brown sweater with a dark green T-shirt collar peeking out. His jeans fit perfectly, and on his feet were casual brown loafers. He looked preppy-cool with his gelled and carefully styled hair.

"Ava!" He gave a big show of sniffing the air. "That's much better! You ready to go?"

"Sure. Let me just grab my purse," I said laughing. I ran down the hallway to my room on the end and grabbed my phone from the ledge, slipping it into my bag. Nerves crawled around my stomach. I took a deep breath and let it out loudly, trying to force my gut to settle down. The sound of my girlfriends laughing on the other side of the apartment interrupted my momentary freak-out moment.

"Everything is fine," I told myself.

I pulled on my brown, heeled boots and then left the room. When I arrived in the living room Kasie was laughing so hard she was crying.

"What the heck is going on in here?" They all turned to see me standing in the hallway and toned down the laughing immediately.

Were they laughing at me?

Adam stood up quickly and came over to my side. "Your flatmates are a riot!"

"Yes, they are." I looked from face to face trying to get a clue from someone. No one gave me any kind of hint as to what they were talking about and I began to feel a little hurt. *What secrets were they sharing with Adam?* I gave the girls a "shame on you" look when Adam turned and headed for the door.

"Have fun, you two!" Elaina hollered after us.

"We will!" Adam and I both said together.

"Cute. That was very cute," I said as I opened the front door. We walked up the stairs and down the sidewalk to where Adam had parked his black car. He opened up the door for me.

"I guess chivalry is not dead in the UK?" I sat down, smiling, and then watched him walk around the front and get in his side.

"No, it's not. We are taught to treat our women with kindness and respect." He started the car and pulled out onto Fremont Street.

"How wonderful." I wasn't used to being treated like a lady. "So, Prince Charming, where are we headed off to now?"

"Surprises, surprises." He smiled sweetly as he pulled onto Clark. "Are you hungry? I thought we'd do lunch first."

"Starving." We passed Iverson Park and the morning's jog replayed in my mind. A little farther up the road sat my favorite restaurant in Steven's Point—Hilltop. To my surprise, he pulled the car into the driveway instead of passing by!

Lunch was delicious and the conversation was wonderful. Adam asked me all about my interest in teaching and then shared with me how he decided to study communications. He graciously offered to pick up the check, but to me that felt too much like a date, so he allowed me to pay for half. With full bellies, we made our way out to the car.

Adam drove back down Main Street toward campus. "Alrighty, Miss Ava. I did my research and found a place right here in Stevens Point that will make you feel right at home."

"Really? That sounds exciting. Where is this mystery place?" The car made its way around the mall and over to the riverfront.

The riverfront!

He was taking me to see where the Wisconsin River ran through Stevens Point. I suddenly felt very excited and a large, toothy smile struck my lips.

"Brilliant! You've figured it out. I can tell by the look on your face." He drove past Pfiffner Park and over to a parking lot lining another grassy area. I could see the river from the road and my heart began to leap with joy. I barely let the car stop before I jumped out.

"Hold on! Wait for me!" Adam shut off the car engine and jumped out after me, laughing. I could hear him yelling as he

caught up. "I knew you'd be excited, but wow!" We ran across
the empty field, over the sidewalk and past a row of tall trees. We
didn't stop until we were all the way to the riverbank, where
Adam slowed down and let me go on ahead.

I ran right up to the place where the rocky shore met the
water's edge. There I stood before the grand and glorious
Wisconsin River. It took my breath away like seeing a great old
friend I'd been apart from for many months. The river's deep
brown water flowed swiftly past me, and I imagined that same
water reaching my beautiful Dells by the time the sun set.

I took a deep inhale through my nose and recognized a smell
I knew only as river water—a scent that filled my soul with hope
and calmed my heart to contentment. The only sound was
something I'd heard a million times before—tiny waves lapping
up on the rocky shore, a lullaby to my ears.

Although I felt at peace, I suddenly felt incredibly homesick.
The lump in my throat showed up just before the small, salty tear
fell from my eye. It gently rolled down my cheek and dropped
into the water below me. I looked out over the broad, brown
river and wiped my face as another tear escaped.

A hand landed on my right shoulder and a voice came from
behind me. "I'm so sorry, Ava. I didn't intend to make you cry."

And then a dam burst inside me. Overcome with emotion, I
turned into Adam and surrendered to my tears. He pulled me in
for a tight hug, assuring me that everything was going to be
alright. I had no feelings of embarrassment, only a sense of
comfort from my new friend. He was so patient, just letting me
release my tension on the sleeve of his shirt. He held me tight,
slowly rubbing my back.

Soon the clouds above us began to cry, too. I felt a water
drop from the sky land squarely on my forehead. The sound of
the raindrops quietly landing on the surface of the river was
soothing. Adam broke the hug, and although I wanted to go

back in for another one, I thought of the conversation I had earlier with my roommates—*Don't lead him on.*

The rain's pace picked up, raindrops coming down faster, each one a bit bigger and fatter than the last. I tried to stop the tears. I knew most guys never liked blubbering girls as company, but Adam was very patient, standing next to me, staring off into the water patiently.

Finally I found my voice behind the lump in my throat. "Oh, Adam. I feel like there's a hole inside of me."

He looked deep into my eyes and gently placed his hands on the outside of my upper arms. "In three words I can sum up everything I know about life: it goes on.' " His words were beautiful and a bit pretentious, but somehow comforting.

A tiny smile poked through my somber face. "Did you make that up yourself?"

"I'm sorry, I cannot take credit. Those are the words of the famous American poet Robert Frost."

"Studying American Lit, are we?" The rain continued to drizzle on our heads.

"Nine o'clock every Monday and Thursday morning," he confessed.

We both took a deep breath and exhaled at the same time. I could feel Adam's eyes carefully examining my face, but I kept my gaze on the river and my imagination followed it all the way to the Dells. A vision of Jack smiling showed before my eyes and then left as quick as it came. There was something big that happened this summer, I could feel it in my bones, and I felt like a complete idiot for not knowing what it was.

"Ava. My heart aches for home, too. But you have to remember this: You cannot discover new oceans unless you have the courage to lose sight of the shore."

"More Frost?" I said, sniffling my runny nose.

"Nope. That one is anonymous, but it's sort of been my credo this term."

A gust of wind blew the brown hair from my shoulders, and a shiver ran down my spine. "I like it." I looked up to the sky and felt a few light raindrops on my face. "Can I use it, too?"

"Absolutely." Then a sharp crack of lighting and a loud boom of thunder interrupted our pair of aching hearts.

"Uh-oh." The clouds opened up and the rain fell down harder than before. "I hate to pry you away from your river, but I think we better head back to the car park now," Adam took off his jacket and held it over our heads as an impromptu umbrella. We dashed across the grassy field with little rain on our heads, although the storm continued to rage above us.

We quickly got inside the car and slammed the doors. Adam reached to the dash to press the ignition button, but I grabbed his hand before he touched it. "Wait. Listen…. I love this noise." I dropped his hand and closed my eyes, tipping my head back against the headrest. The sweet sound of fat raindrops gently hammering on the metal roof of the car filled me with comfort. I breathed in a cleansing breath and slowly let it out.

Adam leaned back against his seat, eyes closed, listening carefully. "Laughton…" he whispered. "I love this noise, too. Reminds me of lying in my bed as a young chap listening to the rain beat against the tin roof of our house at night."

We sat in the car for several minutes, pleasantly listening to the storm until Adam's cell phone buzzed in the console. He quickly grabbed his phone, looked at the screen, and then stopped the vibrating.

"It's my mom. I can call her back later," he said, putting it down.

"Your mom? From London?"

He nodded his head.

"You should probably call her back!"

"Nah. It's okay." Lightning streaked the sky just before a loud thunderclap struck above our heads. It startled me so much I jumped in my seat. Adam softly laughed as he pressed the ignition button on the dash and waited for my permission to leave.

"You're right," I commented. "We better get going and out of the storm."

Adam backed up the car a little quicker than I thought necessary, and followed the tiny roadway leading out of the park.

A thought suddenly occurred to me. "Is it hard to get used to driving on the right side of the road?"

"Huh?" He looked over at me, and I saw the light click in his eyes. "Oh right. Yes, it was difficult at first, but I've got it down, now."

We both laughed sort of awkwardly. A long pause followed, and I noticed Adam kept looking in his rearview mirror. Perhaps I freaked him out and he was paranoid of driving the wrong way.

I moved a hand over to pat him quickly on his forearm. "You're doing fine."

"Thanks."

A few more seconds of silence followed as he continued to drive toward my house. I figured I better apologize for blubbering all over his sleeve earlier.

"Adam. I'm really sorry for overreacting back at the riverbank. I've just had a crazy week. Stressed out, you know."

"Don't apologize, Ava," he said sincerely. "I'm happy to be a shoulder to cry on."

"Thank you, Adam. I wish I could repay you for your kindness."

He smiled but kept driving, saying very little.

A few minutes later we arrived back in front of my house. Adam turned off the car and sat looking out the windshield for a few seconds. Obviously something was bothering him—his

65

demeanor had changed considerably since we got in the car at the river.

Had I said something wrong?

My mind rapidly replayed the afternoon's events as the rain above us pounded down on the roof above our heads.

"Are you okay?" I finally blurted out.

Should I put my hand on his shoulder?

He turned his head from the window and looked me straight in the eyes. Adam held his gaze for a few seconds without saying a word, and it made me feel a little uncomfortable. "I'm fine, Ava." His voice sounded like his own but with some unidentifiable emotion behind it. "Thank you for a wonderful day in your company." Then he smiled a sincere, wonderful smile, and I was pretty sure that whatever was bothering him had nothing to do with our friendship.

"I feel the same way. See you later, Adam."

Chapter Seven

The next morning I woke and got ready for class, feeling nervous. It was quiz day. I revisited the notecards Adam and I made over a bowl of Fruit Loops. It felt like I knew the words, but I was half sure my mind would blank out when that quiz paper appeared on my desk in thirty minutes.

Why had I lost my confidence? School had never been an issue for me. Well, until my freshman year of college.

I scrunched up my eyes, trying to remember what happened last year.

And then it occurred to me that I had considered not coming back to school this semester. The details of what happened were very hazy. A faint pain began to form in the back of my brain as I strained to remember what had happened last summer. I wasn't ready for a full-blown headache again, so I dropped the thought. Almost instantly the pain subsided.

Huh.

I washed the bowl in the sink and then set it in the rack to dry. No one else was awake, so I grabbed my backpack and quietly slid out the front door, locking it behind me.

On the chilly morning walk to class I quickly shuffled through my notecards in a desperate last minute attempt to commit those vocab words to memory. When I arrived at the science building, I nervously drifted through the halls until I found room 210, and sat down at a desk in the back of the room. I put my backpack on the floor and grabbed a pencil from the front zipper pocket.

An hour later I was released from my nervousness and on my way home. Although I should have been overcome with relief, I had an odd sense like someone was watching me as I walked. Several times I peered over my shoulder but saw nothing out of the ordinary, just college kids walking here and there, some texting, some on their phones, some with earbuds in, but all minding their own business.

Weird.

I continued on my way, but the uneasy feeling didn't subside. A few more quick glances around me did not help solve the problem. I pulled out my phone and held it in my hand, not sure what I was going to do with it. There wasn't a real emergency here, just a crazed girl with paranoia and an absent memory.

Finally, I took refuge on a wooden bench near the back of the Student Center and looked up into the trees around me.

Relax, Ava. Your brain is on overdrive.

The leaves were displaying their beautiful fall colors, and the wind was gently blowing their branches. The sun was peeking through clusters of fluffy white clouds, and the brisk autumn air cleared my senses.

I was starting to feel my body relax and had even lost the feeling that someone was following me, when Adam popped out from behind the back entrance of the Student Center and scared me out of my skin.

I screamed loudly, jumping backward.

"Good gracious, Adam!" I put my hand on my chest, trying to slow my hyper beating heart.

His loud laugh filled the courtyard between the Student Center and the student services building. "Oh, Blimey! I'm sorry. Are you okay?"

"I suppose. You better watch out, though. I'll have to get you back, now."

"I guess I deserve that." He laughed again and took a seat next to me on the bench.

"And also, Your Highness, you seriously need to stop stalking me."

"Stalking? You would be so lucky." He smiled. "So, how was the quiz? Please tell me you aced it."

I pulled out the Scantron test sheet from my backpack. "See for yourself." I shoved the paper into his open hands.

Adam looked like an excited puppy waiting to go for a walk. He kept the paper faced down. "It's corrected already?"

"Sure! Haven't you seen those little machines professors have that scan the answer sheets right there in the classroom? Instant grading!"

"Nice!" He dramatically and very slowly turned the paper over to reveal a big red "100%" written across the top. Adam jumped up onto the seat of the bench. "Brilliant! A blinding success!"

I laughed at him, elated and embarrassed at the same time.

"Ava! I'm so proud of you!" He jumped back down and grabbed my shoulders for a hug. "Great job! I knew you could do it!"

I pulled away quickly—people were starting to gawk. "Thanks," I meekly replied. "I'm pretty pumped, too." Although that was the truth, I wasn't necessarily ready to announce it to the world as Adam was.

Adam stood up again. "Well, this calls for celebration. Come on." He held his hand out for me to take. "I'm taking you to Belts."

"Belts? It was just a tiny quiz!" There was something sort of admirable about Adam in this moment. I had never lived my life this way before, but the idea of celebrating all the small stuff seemed pretty exciting. My favorite ice cream shop was starting to sound like a nice way to ruin my lunch.

"It is only 10:30, by the way."

"No excuses. Be proud of your accomplishments!" Adam was still waiting for me, hand stretched out.

"Well okay, Prince Adam. I guess you're right." I accepted his hand to help me off the bench but then dropped it as we began walking down the winding sidewalk lined with fallen leaves. His black car was sitting in the parking lot between the Student Center and the Communications building. The Com building reminded me of Adam's aspirations to be a TV reporter. "So I owe you for helping me study for my quiz. Are you in any need of some tour guide tutoring from yours truly?"

He laughed quietly, unlocking the car door for me. "Oh, I forgot to tell you! I just landed myself one overnight shift a week on," he changed his voice to a deeper and cheesier tone, "WWSP 90FM."

"The University radio? Ohhh, the big time! Congrats!" I slid into the car and then held up my left hand for a high five.

He returned the gesture, saying, "Right! A listening audience of probably twenty-five hammered college kids who are too lazy to get up and change the channel! I'm pretty stoked!"

"Tell me when you are on and I'll stay up one night." I pulled my seatbelt from the wall and clicked it into the fastener below the console.

Adam started the car and then turned around to scan the area before backing up. "You'd better!"

I smiled as Adam drove down Division Street. He was so easy to talk to, and had such a positive outlook on life. He was humming a song while he pulled into the tiny lot. There was only one person at the order window. Not a shocker since it was only late morning and a cold autumn day.

Belts was one of those mom-and-pop seasonal ice cream shops. It was basically a two-room shack with a few walk-up ordering windows on an outside wall. Every November they boarded up the windows for the winter, and then hosted a grand opening each spring where dozens of crazy college kids would pitch tents in the snowy parking lot the night before it opened some cold Wisconsin March morning. For most of the season you could find long lines of locals patiently waiting for their oversized scoops of delicious soft serve.

Adam and I got out of the car and stood staring at the menu signs above the window. They had great flavors, cheap prices, and portion sizes that out-scooped any other ice cream parlor I had ever been to.

"What's your favorite flavor, Ava?"

"Hmmm…probably chocolate. How about you?"

"Well, I'd just about die right now for a Lemon Cornetto."

"A what?"

"Yes. I know. It's a real tragedy. The utterly delicious Italian frozen waffle cone has not jumped the lake and landed over in America yet. You Yankees sure are missing out."

"Well, I'll take your word for it. I'm pretty sure I'll never be in England to sample one."

"Never say never, my dear."

Adam stepped up to the window smiling and ordered two chocolate cones. We sat at a metal round table in the outdoor seating area off to the right. Although it was chilly, the sun was shining on my back, warming it while we ate.

There were a few moments of silence between us as we licked our ice cream. A chill went through my spine and I visibly shivered.

"I guess it's too cold for ice cream. Hold this?" He held his cone out for me. I grabbed it wondering what he was up to. He pulled off his fleece pullover and held it out for me. "Here. It'd be a shame to see your lips and fingernails turn blue." He reached out and took his half eaten cone from my left hand.

"Won't you be cold?"

Adam pushed the fleece closer to my hand. "Naw! It's this chilly every day except about two in London. I've become accustomed."

I accepted the fleece with a smile and asked Adam to hold my cone as I pulled the fleece over my head. It was very warm and cozy and smelled like, well, man. That was the best part, the smell. I shrugged up my shoulders so the neck of the sweatshirt was right at my mouth. I closed my eyes and took a big whiff before I reached for my ice cream back. Adam laughed at me.

"What?"

"You are too cute, Ava Gardner. Too cute." And then he laughed under his breath again and smiled, licking his ice cream cone and shaking his head.

Chapter Eight

I had been spending so much time on schoolwork, I didn't see Adam again until Friday when we ran into each other at the Student Center cafeteria. I had just made my way through the sub sandwich line and was heading for a place to sit when I saw him sitting at a table by the long row of windows. A pretty blond stood up and left when I approached.

"Who was that lovely lady?"

"She's the Theta Sig sweetheart. You know, silly Greek stuff." I wondered if he had feelings for this woman, but I didn't dare to ask. I took a seat across from him and glanced at his tray of half-eaten lunch.

"I'm glad I ran into you just now," Adam said. "I've been meaning to ask you. Do you like jazz music?"

I scrunched up my nose for a moment, surprised at his question. "Actually, I am a big fan. I owe that to my father. When he wasn't off on business he would spend time listening to jazz on an old LP player. He introduced me to all the greats early on in life—Louis Armstrong, Ella Fitzgerald, and John Coltrane."

"Lucky girl," Adam commented before he polished off his Coke.

"That's sort of a strange question, anyway. Why do you ask?" I opened up my small bag of potato chips, pulled one out, and popped it in my mouth.

"I was planning on going to the Riverfront Jazz Fest tomorrow night and wanted to know if you would accompany me."

"Riverfront Jazz Fest?" I dropped my jaw. "How did I not know about this?"

"I have no idea. There are signs hanging all over the place." He grinned at my nonobservance, pointing at a poster hanging on the wall right next to my head. I laughed at myself as I read the info.

"So are you free?" Adam said excitedly.

"Of course! I'd love to go!"

But inside I knew I probably shouldn't. This sounded somewhat like a date, and although I really enjoyed spending my time with Adam, I still wasn't ready to explore any romantic feelings.

I looked up at Adam and he was beyond excited. His brown eyes confirmed just what I was afraid of—he was looking at me with admiration and perhaps even a hint of lust.

"Oh, Ava! It is going to be—" and then he put on his obnoxious impression of an American accent, "—awesome!" He leaned back in his chair laughing and smiling.

I rolled my eyes, but in all honestly, he was adorably cute. I poked a finger in the air. "Don't start with me, mister. There are plenty of ridiculous sayings you Brits use."

He said nothing but winked at me and smiled.

A pleasurable ping in my heart startled me and I looked away quickly.

Uh-oh.

I recognized that feeling. Was this platonic relationship starting to go differently than I wanted it to? I replayed the few times I had spent with Adam in the last two weeks since we met in the student lounge. I couldn't remember a single time I had knowingly led him on.

When I looked back at Adam, he was busy texting. For a split second there was a hint of distress on his face and I thought I heard him say, "Oh bugger!" under his breath. Suddenly he shoved the phone in his bag and stood up, lifting his purple lunch tray. "Well, Princess Ava, I gotta run to lecture." He dumped the contents of his tray in the garbage nearby and returned to the table. Then he picked up his backpack from the chair and threaded his arms through the straps.

"I shall pick you up tomorrow evening at 5:30. Don't eat dinner before. I have plans."

Dinner too? Sounds a lot like a date. I'm in trouble.

"I'll be ready," I said quietly.

Adam walked across the cafeteria and through the door on the far side. I didn't want to let him think I had romantic feelings for him, yet I didn't want to stop spending time with him. He really was a great friend and I especially appreciated the way he reacted differently than my girlfriends to my crazy head problems.

A few seconds before I was excited about Jazz Fest, but somehow I talked myself into feeling uneasy.

* * * *

The next day Kasie and I went for a run, I wrote a stellar paper for my Children's Literature class, studied for a few quizzes I had coming up, and then my friends and I watched a movie. As the day progressed I kept trying to find a way to fix my relationship with Adam. How do you stop someone from falling in love with you, but continue to be friends?

Not possible, my head replied.

Soon enough the sun was setting outside my window and I was stuck staring at my closet, trying to decide what in the world to wear. If this were a real date and I wanted to impress my guy, then I would know exactly what to pull from the closet. But I didn't want to impress Adam; I just wanted to go out and listen to good music with a good friend. I really wanted to pull a pair of comfortable jeans and an oversized hoodie from my dresser, but I was sure Adam would be more dressed up than that and I didn't want to feel out of place. I was still standing in front of my closet wearing only my pink undies and a baby blue bra when I heard knocking on the door.

"Hold on!"

I quickly pulled on my best-fitting jeans and then grabbed a long-sleeved, dark grey cotton shirt. I slipped my arms into my white, puffy zip-up vest. Elaina knocked on my door and slowly came in. I was pushing some fake diamond stud earrings through the holes in my lobes when I looked up at her with agony in my eyes.

"You look nice," she said as she crossed the room and took a seat on the bed.

"Do I?" I tried to hide my nervousness by busily filling my purse with a pack of gum, my cell phone, and wallet.

Elaina patted a spot on the bed next to her, signaling for me to sit down. "Ava, what's wrong?"

Was it that obvious?

I took my black boots from the closet, and then sat down next to her and pulled them on. "I don't look *too* nice, do I?"

What was I going to do about Adam?

"Ava, if you don't like him, why are you going out with him?" Her tone wasn't accusatory; it was laced with care.

There was a long empty pause. I didn't have an easy answer for her. "Elaina, I love hanging out with Adam. He is a great friend to be around. I just don't—"

"Let me just stop you right there."

"What?"

"What is holding you back? Adam is cute, funny, friendly. Why can't you let yourself fall in love with him?"

My heart jumped at her words. Fall in love? Yikes.

"I don't know. I just…." For some reason I felt like my heart wasn't free to be shared, but I couldn't explain why. There wasn't another guy I had my eyes on.

"Is it Aaron?" she asked.

I hadn't thought about Aaron for quite a long time. Although my steady high school boyfriend broke my heart into what felt like a million pieces last year, I couldn't remember the last time I had thought about Aaron.

"No," I said with certainty. "It's not Aaron."

"Then I suggest you go into this *non-date*"—she used air quotes—"with an open mind and heart. Ava, the other girls and I see how happy you are when you're around Adam. Just give him a chance." She looked up at me with pleading eyes. It was almost alarming.

Then instantly it hit me that perhaps I had been a little too obsessed with my heartbreak last year. And the last few weeks had been filled with some strange and somewhat disturbing head problems. Of course my friends wanted to see me happy. Maybe I could give Adam a chance.

A knock on the door interrupted my thoughts. "Ava? Can I come in?" It was Adam. My heart skipped a beat, and I suddenly felt very sweaty.

What was happening to me?

"Yeah, sure, come on in," I yelled to the door, my voice cracking at the end. I half whispered to Elaina, "Thanks. I promise I'll try to open my heart," and then leaned in for a hug just as Adam opened the door.

Adam walked into the room. He wore casual brown slip-on loafers and dark-wash jeans. A button down, dark blue shirt was tucked into his jeans exposing a brown leather belt around his slim waist. The first few buttons of his shirt were left undone to reveal a white T-shirt beneath.

Elaina moved toward the door, calling, "You two have fun!" Then she gave me a wink and left the room with a smile.

Adam took the seat at the desk by my computer and swiveled around to look at me. I guess we were going to hang out here for a few minutes.

"You look smashing."

"Thanks, Adam," I giggled. "You, too."

"So this is your room?" He turned around on the computer chair and checked out my old-fashioned desktop computer with a large monitor that was definitely not a flat screen. "Where'd you get this dinosaur?" He laughed a little bit under his breath.

"Hey, you can't deny free! It works just fine," I said proudly. "My dad upgraded several years ago and for some reason kept this computer in our basement. I took it when I moved to Point last year. It's kind of annoying, though, because he left all his files on there and so there isn't much room for me to save my papers."

Adam's eyebrows rose a little. "Did you clear out all his files to make room for yours?"

"I started, but it takes so long I haven't got much of it deleted out yet."

"I see. A job for a rainy day, I guess."

He got up from the chair and looked around at the pictures on the wall and the books on my shelf. I explained who some of the people were and Adam asked me a few questions about my family.

When silence was upon us, I suggested we get going. I grabbed my purse from the bed and my white mittens and scarf from on top of my dresser. The October nights were getting pretty chilly, and I didn't know how late we'd be out.

Adam and I walked down the hall, and found the girls were sitting around the TV in the living room eating the pizza they had ordered. We bid my friends good night and then headed out the door.

As we climbed the stairs, he patted his jeans pockets. "Hold up! I forgot my phone in your room. I'll be right back."

"Sure."

I stood at the top of the stairs and stared out over the rooftops on the other side of the street. The sun was almost set, and a gentle orange glow was casting its light onto my eyes.

What would tonight hold for me? I knew I would have fun with Adam, of course, but would I allow myself to find more?

Adam opened the door and jumped up the stairs two at a time. He held his phone up for me to see. "Got it."

We walked across the front yard to Adam's car, and I got in after he opened the door for me. I let out a profound sigh as I watched him walk around the front bumper.

Pull it together. Just let tonight happen naturally.

He opened the door and I smiled uneasily at him as he sat down. "You ready, Miss Ava?" He moved his hand over and patted me on my knee. The sight of his face was calming, and I suddenly felt a wave of excitement brush the nerves away.

I returned the smile and nodded my head. Keeping his gaze at me, he started the ignition and I left my worries right there on the curb as we set off into the sunset.

Adam took me to a restaurant downtown that oozed a Midwestern supper club feel. There were deep red linens over the tables and little yellow opaque glass candle holders flickering light onto the faces of the hungry patrons

The menu was full of classic American fare including juicy hamburgers, fresh shrimp cocktails, and ample T-bone steaks. An antique, opaque glass relish tray welcomed our arrival to the table. I loved it all mainly because it reminded me of a place my parents used to take us on Saturday nights when they didn't feel like cooking at home.

Over dinner we settled into our familiar and comfortable dynamic. We chatted about our week at school, and I told him about my nerves for the upcoming PRAXIS test—an exam I had to pass in order to be accepted into the School of Education. Adam assured me I would pass, but I wasn't so sure. There was a lot of pressure associated with the test. If I wasn't successful, I would have to change my major or transfer schools and start all over somewhere else.

I asked Adam more about living in London. It was very fascinating to hear about another world. So many things were different from the way I lived my life, and I thought it would be interesting to someday visit London.

Right in the middle of dinner, Adam's phone rang. He took it out of his pocket and checked the screen.

"Sorry, Ava. I really need to take this one."

"No problem," I replied.

Adam got up from the table and answered the phone as he shuffled past the tables and out the front of the restaurant. I wondered who was on the phone and why he had to go all the way out the front door to have his conversation.

While he was gone, I finished my chili and sipped on my Diet Coke. I replied to a text message from Elaina, and then looked at the dessert menu for almost ten minutes before Adam came back to the table.

"So sorry, Ava. Please forgive me. It was my mother and I just couldn't get her off the phone."

"Is everything okay?"

"Yes, she was just complaining about—" Then he paused a moment. "You know what? It's no matter. Anyway, I'm back here now with you and off the phone."

"I guess I'll forgive you. Just don't do it again." I winked and took another sip of my soda, my eyes still holding his.

"Ava, I'd love for you to meet my family."

I almost choked on my drink.

"You need to come back to London with me sometime. You haven't lived life until you've taken a turn on The Tube."

"The what?" I said, picking up my napkin and wiping the dribble from the corner of my mouth.

"The Tube. The London Underground."

"Is that a band?"

He snorted. "The Tube is the oldest underground railway system in the world!"

"Really? And it still works?"

"Well yes, but they've been working on updating it for the past few years. It's quite slick, actually."

He paused and pushed some food around on his plate. Was he nervous about something?

"You've been on a subway, right?"

"Yeah. When I was younger, my parents used to take Laura and me to Chicago once a year and we'd ride the subway down to the theater district to catch a musical."

"Well, I'm sure it's nothing like The Tube. You just have to come."

His sweet smile was adorable. Was he really asking me back to London to meet his family? The nerves had returned in full force.

As dinner finished, Adam graciously picked up the check before I could grab for it, and when I offered to pay for half, he refused.

Definitely a date.

I was surprised to see Adam getting out his car keys as we left the restaurant.

"Pioneer Park is only three or four blocks down the way. Why don't we leave the car here in the public lot and take the sidewalk following the riverfront down to the band shell?"

Adam smiled at my suggestion, but then said, "Are you sure? With the sun set it's pretty cold outside."

I estimated it was barely forty degrees as a chill ran down my back. "Yeah, it's nice out," I lied, as I put on my hat and mittens, shivering again.

The sidewalk was pretty empty this time of night, but I could see a crowd of people up ahead at the park. Old-fashioned black metal streetlights handsomely lit the way, and the sound of the river lapping up on the bank set a very familiar romantic mood. A warm yellow glow radiated from the stage in the distance and the sounds of instruments warming up was quite inviting.

Fallen leaves crunched under our feet as an autumn wind blew off the river and past our faces. I shivered again and Adam moved in close to put his arm around my shoulders. "Here, borrow some of my heat," he said.

I rested my head in the crook of his shoulder. It was nice to feel attended to and our position was warm and very comfortable. I closed my eyes for a quick second and took a deep breath. He smelled like a scent I'd smelled before, but I just couldn't put a finger on what. I slowly turned my head into his shirt and discreetly took another deep breath.

Instantly, as if there was poison in the air, my brain felt like it was on fire. I stopped dead in my tracks and bent over in pain.

"My head!"

And then I saw him again, the man from my visions—the drop-dead gorgeous guy with dark hair and incredibly beautiful blue eyes.

"Ava. Ava, come back to the present." Adam had bent down near my face and was coaxing me away from my dream man. My vision was getting hazy, and the burning pain in my head was fading away.

I stood up rubbing my temples and breathing heavily. "God, I hate when that happens." As soon as I had stepped away from Adam and tried to focus on the present, my throbbing pain was almost diminished.

"Are you with me?" Adam had concern on his face, but he tried to hide it, smiling inauthentically. "You're going to be okay."

"I hope so. I've been having fewer of these painful visions lately." At least it seemed that way.

"Well, that's good. No. That's great!" He took a few steps closer to stand facing me, hands on my shoulders. He was studying my eyes, searching for any leftover pain. After a moment I moved my hands down from my head and stared deep into Adam's face. I really was thankful for his patience.

"Now," he said, "I think I can hear the band starting. Are you up for some jazz?"

"Of course. Let's go. That's why I came!"

"Aww, and here I thought you wanted to spend time with me."

"Well, that too, Prince Adam." We smiled at each other and then continued down the walkway. Before we could get a few paces in, I felt Adam's palm find mine and take hold. I was wearing mittens, so the whole thing felt a little muted, but I knew I was wanted and needed in that moment, and I realized that was a feeling I sorely missed.

Whatever happens, happens. Just go with the flow, Ava.

The band was in the middle of a song when we arrived at the park. Many couples had brought picnic blankets and lawn chairs, but suddenly I realized Adam was unprepared. Were we going to have to stand for the entire concert?

Adam held my hand and led me through the maze of blankets and chairs as if he knew exactly where he was going. Over to the right side of the crowd, somewhat near the back, I noticed a green fuzzy blanket laid out with a small picnic basket and another felt blanket neatly folded on top. There was a little sign that said, "Reserved for Royalty."

Adam stopped us right in front of the blanket. "Well, Princess Ava, here we are."

"You did this?"

Adam sat down on the blanket and I followed his lead, picking a spot right next to him. With our shoulders touching, he leaned over and grabbed the extra blanket, held the corners, and spread it out over our legs.

We sat and listened to the smooth jazz for a while. Adam was a perfect gentleman and asked if he could put his arm around me—to keep me warm, of course. I snuggled in and enjoyed the good music with a good friend.

He's becoming more than a friend, my heart yelled.

"What's in the basket?" I asked, trying to distract myself from the truth of my heart.

"Dessert," Adam said smiling. He leaned over and pulled out a small plastic container of various cheesecake samples. There was a thin slice of strawberry on each piece. "I hope you like cheesecake."

"My favorite! You didn't make those, did you?"

"I'm sorry, I cannot take credit. The best baked good I can make is a box mix of chocolate brownies." Adam took two forks out of the small basket and offered me the plate of dessert. "Dig in!"

I took my fork and dug a bite off a slice. "This is so delicious. Thank you for bringing it."

Adam nodded, his mouth full of his own delectable bite. The music played in the background as we sat and indulged. Beyond Adam's head I could see the sky full of beautiful sparkling silver stars.

"Here, try this one."

Adam's fork slowly approached my lips, a bite of chocolate cheesecake on the end. I opened my mouth and closed my eyes, slightly smiling as I waited for the fork's cold metal to touch my tongue. Finally I tasted chocolate and closed my mouth around the fork as he gently slid it out.

Pleasant tingles ran down my spine.

Uh-oh.

"Ava," he said quietly.

I opened my eyes.

"Did you ever mistakenly discover something wonderful, and then realize that was why you were put on this Earth?"

I looked at him nervously. "Are you talking about cheesecake?"

Adam chuckled. "No, Ava. I'm talking about you."

Uh-oh.

He moved his fingers over the blanket and grabbed my hand. We were in our own world, unaware of the fifty people around us. His eyes were locked on mine, obviously searching for some kind of affirmation of my feelings.

My cheeks turned pink and my heart began to race, but I couldn't find a clear answer in my heart.

Suddenly the song ended and the audience began clapping, bringing us back to reality. The band started playing the first ballad of the night, and we noticed several couples standing up to dance in the grass.

"My lady, would you give me the pleasure of this dance?"

My heart felt like it was beating in my ears. "Sure," I replied quietly. I swallowed loudly. This meant we were going to get closer to each other.

Adam stood up and held his hand out to help me up, and then led me off the blanket to a free patch of grass nearby. Keeping perfect eye contact, Adam slowly took the hand he was holding, placed it around his neck, and then carefully ran his palm down my arm, ending at my shoulder. I eased my other hand up to his shoulder as he gracefully inched his fingers around my waist.

He pulled me in close as we swayed to the music, our eyes comfortably locked. His face was perfectly handsome in the moonlight, and I began to feel my heart drop its wall of protection. Maybe I could let myself fall for him. It felt pretty wonderful being wanted again. I suddenly realized how lonely I'd been.

As we danced, he hummed the tune in my ear and whispered, "You are so beautiful."

I could not stop the smile from my lips.

Adam carefully brushed a piece of hair from my face with his thumb and tucked it behind my ear. Then, still holding my head in his hand, he slowly moved his face closer and closer to mine. My eyes instinctively closed, waiting for what I knew was coming next.

Uh-oh. Uh-oh.

I wanted to kiss Adam. It felt right. He let his nose touch mine and then I could feel his breath so close to my lips, hovering there with careful anticipation.

"Adam," I whispered, surrendering to my feelings.

BOOM!

I screamed as some invisible force blew our bodies back several feet. My head slammed into the ground, and I looked up to see pieces of glass and flaming plastic shoot through the crowd. I felt one whiz by my head seconds before I covered it with my hands. A bright, fiery blaze and thick, black smoke poured out of the place where a car had been in the lot behind the bandshell.

"For the love of the Queen," I heard Adam say. "They know we're here."

There was mass chaos. People were screaming and running everywhere. Others were injured on the ground, some even on fire. My head started to throb and panic filled every part of my body.

Adam pulled me up from the ground. "We've gotta get out of here, now!" he yelled in my ear.

He grabbed my hand and I ran right alongside of him, confused, horrified, and scared.

"Adam, what's going on?" I hollered, my head aching.

"I don't know. But we've got to get back to the car as fast as we can!"

I knew it was true. If there was some kind of psycho car bomber on the loose, I was in no mood to stick around to see him. We finally arrived back at the parking lot and quickly jumped in the car. It was pretty quiet this far away from the park, but we could hear the fire trucks approaching and I could smell the smoke in the air.

Adam spent no time waiting to catch his breath or for me to buckle my seatbelt, but started the car instantly, squealing the tires and almost running over the stop sign at the exit. My body slammed into the passenger side window as Adam took the first corner out of the parking lot rather sharply. I quickly clicked in the seatbelt, and then braced myself with both hands on the dashboard in front of me.

"How's your head?" he asked as he drove like a maniac through the back roads of Point.

I ran my hand over the back of my hair. "Hurts like hell. I think I whacked it pretty hard when I fell down from the blast."

"I'll take a look when we get out of this neighborhood. Put some ice on it when you get home and take two acetaminophen." He cranked on the wheel, turning unexpectedly into an alley and I slammed into the door again.

"Please! Slow down!" I begged. Tears began to form behind my eyes. My head ached and I felt incredibly shaken. I moved my hand over the console and placed it firmly on the middle of his thigh.

Adam slowed down and looked over at me. "You're right. I'm sorry to scare you, Ava. I just need to make sure you are safe."

"I'm fine, Adam. I just think I'd like to go home now. I'd like to be safe in my bed."

"Right. I bet you are as anxious as I am." Adam drove the rest of the way home in silence. I could hear his phone vibrating several times in his pocket, but he ignored each call. When we got to my house he didn't say anything. Was he simply feeling uneasy because we almost got bombed out of the park? I stared at him for a few seconds, but he just looked out the windshield.

This was the second time he acted weird when he was dropping me off at home. Not that much about tonight was actually normal, but I expected him to act differently somehow.

"Here," he said finally, "let me look at the back of your head."

I turned and looked out of the passenger side window. Adam carefully moved my hair, inspecting my head. He ran his gentle fingers over the base of my skull and felt down my jawline and then around my neck. "How do you feel?"

"My head aches horribly."

I turned back toward him and he suddenly had a tiny flashlight out, shining it into my eyes and then peering strangely into them for what felt like a little too long.

"You're not bleeding and you don't have a concussion. But I'm sure you'll have a headache for a while. Go inside and place a cold washcloth on your head. A good night's sleep should help."

"Okay. Thanks for dinner and everything." I opened the door to leave, but just as I was about to get out, he grabbed my left hand, holding it with both of his. His warm touch and soft skin took me by surprise. I felt my heart accelerating.

I turned my shoulders around and he looked me right in the eyes. "Ava. I had a wonderful time with you tonight." Then he

88

smiled an odd, inauthentic smile. "And I'm sorry about your head." He released my arm and I said good-bye.

I shut the car door and walked across the lawn, confused over my cracked-up life. Good thing what just happened would be covered in the news. Otherwise my friends would never believe what happened to me on my non-date.

Chapter Nine

The news was calling it "Disaster at the Riverfront." Several people were critically injured from flying debris and fire, and the whole south side of the band shell was ruined. A police investigation confirmed it was a car bomb, but could not find conclusive evidence as to whom was responsible.

Adam called the next morning to make sure my head was feeling okay and to let me know he had to work at the radio station a few nights and had some fraternity event he was chairperson for on another night, so he probably wouldn't see me for most of the week. Although I knew I'd miss hanging out with him, I welcomed the chance to focus on my schoolwork and be alone with my thoughts. There was something magical about Adam, but I still had some strong feeling inside me telling me not to give my heart to him.

The beginning of the week flew by as I kept busy with classes and homework. I studied hard and got an A on my Math Methods quiz, and my Children's Lit professor told me I had the best project for the unit. I felt like calling Adam immediately to celebrate, but resisted the urge, considering he said he'd be busy all week.

I continued tutoring Mrs. Stewart's second grade students almost every afternoon to get some more experience in the classroom. The kids were so amazing, and the whole experience reminded me that teaching came naturally to me. I would work as hard as I could to become a teacher and someday have a class of my own.

On Wednesday I had an appointment with my advisor again. I climbed the stairs to the second floor of the College of Professional Studies building, wondering why my advisor requested to see me only a few weeks after our last meeting. I knew I hadn't failed any recent tests or quizzes, in fact I thought I had been doing well in all my classes.

It was quiet in the lobby. I sat down and read a chapter of my history textbook while waiting to be called into Mr. Weigel's office.

The phone on the receptionist's desk rang out into the silence, and then she sent me back into the office.

"Well, Miss Gardner," Mr. Weigel greeted me. "Do you have any idea why I made this appointment with you today?"

I wiped the palms of my hands on my pants, and then interlaced my fingers and placed them on my lap.

"Not exactly, sir."

Mr. Weigel clicked the keys on his laptop computer for a few seconds. "I have your current grades here in front of me."

I wiped my hands again and took a deep breath. He did not look happy.

My advisor took his reading glasses off and glanced away from his computer screen to me. "I am here to report to you, Miss Gardner, that your current GPA has risen considerably."

"It has?" The corners of my mouth started to turn up.

"There are several weeks left in the semester, Miss Gardner, but you should be proud of yourself. You've made some drastic improvements in only a few weeks."

I couldn't hide my smile, now. "Thank you so much, Mr Weigel. I've been working really hard."

"I can tell. Keep up the good work." He shuffled some papers on his desk, placing them in a neat pile in the middle. "But don't get too excited, yet. Getting into the School of Education will still take an incredible amount of dedication."

My smile faded slightly. This battle had not been won yet. "I understand. I will try my hardest."

Mr. Weigel looked over at me with his kind eyes. "I'm pulling for you, Miss Gardner. There's something special about you, I can tell."

I smiled again, straight from the heart. "Thanks, Mr. Weigel. I appreciate it."

Riding high on the compliments I'd received, I stopped by the cafeteria to pick up a sandwich for lunch and read a little for my Children's Lit class. I picked a small round table by itself off in the corner so I wouldn't be bothered by anyone. I had barely eaten any breakfast that morning and was so hungry I couldn't get the wrapper off the sandwich fast enough. Trying to juggle holding the paperback novel open with one hand and taking a bite of the overstuffed sandwich with the other hand proved to be difficult, as mayo and vegetables spilled out of the sandwich and all over the table. I would have been embarrassed if there was someone dining with me, but there wasn't, so I picked the vegetables off the wrapper and shoved them back in the ol' hatch.

An unattractive glob of mayo was dripping out of my mouth when I happened to look up and see a very skinny and extraordinarily beautiful blond storming my way. I quickly wiped my mouth. Was she going to sit at a table near me?

The lady stranger wore a tight-fitting orange sweater and trendy jeans with high-heeled leather boots going all the way up to her knees. Miss Stylish was headed straight for me, but I was the only person at the table and I was sure I had no idea who she was.

She must think I'm someone else.

I tried to ignore her and read my book, expecting her to turn around when she realized I wasn't who she thought I was. But she kept barreling toward me.

Just when I thought she was going to crash through the table, she stopped right at the edge and stared at me.

"Ava, is it?" She had an annoying voice that was just a bit too nasally and high pitched. She tossed her beautiful blond curls off her shoulder as her right hand found a resting place on her popped hip.

"Um, yeah?" I checked over her pretty face again, but was sure I'd never seen her before.

"You stay away from my boyfriend!" Her bitchy voice was so loud it about blew me right into the wall.

Huh?

"Excuse me?"

She stared at me. "You know exactly what I'm talking about."

I had no idea what she was talking about.

She shifted her weight to the other hip and snapped her gum. It was like something out of a bad teen movie.

"Sorry. I think you have me mistaken for someone else." I turned back to try to read a few words, but she smacked the book right out of my hand and it hit my sandwich, throwing them both off the table and onto the floor.

What. The. Hell.

I stood up from my chair, the back of my legs pushing it backward, causing a loud scraping noise on the floor. I had never been in a fight before, but you just don't throw someone's sandwich on the damn floor!

"I can't believe this is happening," she whined like she was the victim. All of the sudden her pointer finger was flying through the air, getting dangerously close to my face. "I don't know exactly *who* you are or *what* you think you are doing, but you better stay the *hell* away from Adam. That boy is mine."

Did she say "Adam"? Adam had a girlfriend? No. Couldn't be.

Suddenly all I could hear was my heartbeat in my ears. Crazy Blond was still ranting in my face, but it was like I had pressed mute on the movie—I couldn't hear a word she was saying. My mind was running through all the time I had spent with Adam.

Was he running off to her after spending time with me?

I suddenly started to feel furious. *What a jackass!* I knew I should have never trusted a frat boy. I had been played. How could I have been so stupid?

Tears welled up in my eyes, but I squeezed them back because I knew I had to save face while Crazy Blond was still peering over me.

"Bitch!" she yelled and then gave me one last evil look, turned on her heel, and stomped out of the cafeteria. I hoped she went right over to Adam's house and slapped him firmly right in the face. He deserved it.

Now that she had left, the tears came uninvited, so I quickly packed up my things and stormed out the other way, feeling like I could throw up the half sandwich I ate right there on the stairs.

I wandered around campus, my body full of anger and my eyes on fire. I tried not to be a blubbering idiot in case someone was alarmed and called campus police on me, but I couldn't hold back several tears.

Why was I reacting this way?

I had spent so much time trying to decide if I even liked Adam romantically, and now that I found out he was being unfaithful, I was upset over not having him anymore.

This was ridiculous!

Although I was still incredibly hurt, after about ten minutes of walking aimlessly around campus, I turned around. If I kept walking this way I'd be out wandering down the side of the interstate before I knew it. I needed some good friends who loved me and would never treat me like Adam had, so I headed for home and decided to not waste another tear on Adam.

My phone rang as I rounded the corner by the Student Catholics building and cut through the parking lot over to

College Avenue. I took it out of my backpack and looked at the screen. It was Adam. Did he know what just happened with Crazy Blond or was he calling just to say hi? Either way, he was the last person I wanted to talk to. Actually I wasn't sure I ever wanted to talk to him again.

He called twice more before I made it back to my apartment, but I couldn't get myself to answer. I stared at the phone in my hands.

No. You're done with him. He only means heartache.

Then my phone sang out its text message ring—*New Text Message from Adam.* With shaking fingers I swiped the screen: *Ava, please answer my calls. I need to speak with you straight away.*

I wasn't ready to face him. If I saw him right now this hurt would be ten times worse. The rest of the walk home was filled with four more text message alerts. I took my phone out, turned it off, and shoved it back into my backpack.

I finally arrived home and collapsed on the couch between Elaina and Kasie. I allowed my friends to comfort me as I gushed about what a jerk Adam was.

"Oh, honey. You don't need him," Elaina said. "Just erase that man from your mind."

"If only it were that easy," I whined. "I think I just need to take a nap. My head is pounding." I shuffled down the hall to my bedroom and slithered in between the sheets. It felt so good to rest my head on the pillow and cuddle up under the blankets. But quiet rest time made me think too much, and I was suddenly faced with the mess I called life. Feelings of frustration and confusion filled my mind, bringing forth the realization that I still couldn't remember anything about last summer and the weird visions and headaches were still present. My life felt like everything was in the wrong place, or like something was missing, but no matter how hard I tried, I couldn't figure out what it was. Normally I would lean on my parents to help me solve problems like this that felt insurmountably large, but they weren't around to hear my concern, and I was left feeling alone and miserable.

I must have fallen asleep momentarily because I was jerked awake when I heard a loud pounding on the front door. My heart rate sped up.

Was it him?

I could hear faint talking in the living room, so I sat up and strained my ears to hear. There was definitely a male voice mixed in with my roommates'. I couldn't quite make out what they were saying, though. Then the talking got louder, like they were walking down the hallway.

"She doesn't want to see you," Sharon claimed.

"Adam, get your cheating ass outta here!" Elaina was yelling right outside my door now.

Way to go, Elaina! Give him hell!

"I already told you, I didn't cheat. It was all a setup."

My aching heart climbed up my throat. A setup? What did that mean?

It was Kasie who spoke in a much calmer, but still forceful voice. "Listen, that may be true, but I am not about to let you walk in there and hurt my friend anymore. She's cried enough tears for you today."

There was a long pause when no one said anything, and then a gentle knock broke the silence.

"Ava. I really need to talk to you." Adam's voice had a tiny hint of terror hiding behind his voice box. His head was right up against the door, his voice flowing through the wood and into my heart like the ghost of any relationship we were developing. "Please…. Ava, please."

I wanted to let him in. I wanted him to climb into bed with me and snuggle up close to my body. To passionately confirm his feelings and to fervently apologize for hurting me. But when I opened up my mouth to allow him in, my voice was gone. I was afraid let him through my door or into my heart.

A single tear rolled out of my eye and down my cheek.

He spoke again, his voice soft and full of sorrow. "Ava Gardner. You are the last person in this entire world that I'd want to hurt. You are the only person in my heart." He was desperate now, that much was obvious in his voice. "You have to believe me."

I still couldn't say a word. I needed more time to think about it.

He was basically whining, clawing at my door. "Please. Don't push me out of your heart."

I knew opening the door would be a very bad idea, so as the unwanted tears flowed out of my eyes and down my cheeks, I stayed put and prayed he would just leave.

"Ava. I…I…" but he never finished. I heard the back door suddenly open and loudly bang shut, and then an empty silence filled my ears. A few more tears slid down my cheeks and then I drifted off to sleep, dreaming of a place where waves of beautiful brown river water soothed my soul and healed the emptiness in my heart.

Chapter Ten

I spent a good portion of the next few days moping around my room when I wasn't studying or dragging my butt to class. I carefully avoided my normal pathways to lectures so that I would have less chance of running into Adam on campus. He never came by the house again, and I left my phone turned off.

My friends tried to talk me into going here or there with them, but I always declined. I was overcome with feelings of depression differently than I had ever felt in my life before. All I wanted to do was leave this town, head back to the Dells, and live with my parents until I figured my life out. I still had gaping holes in my memory, and there was some incredibly beautiful man haunting my brain almost daily.

Friday was Halloween. I've never had a good Halloween experience. When I was growing up, my parents did not believe in fancy, store-bought Halloween costumes. Instead, my mother spent the weeks before that special night crafting, sewing, and hot-gluing costumes for my sister and me.

Usually they turned out okay, but one year, when I was eight, my sister Laura got to be a very cool and scary witch, and I was forced to be a Kleenex box. My mother found a large cardboard box sitting around, so she painted it white with the word "Puffs" stenciled perfectly across the front. Then she cut holes in the sides and top so I could wear the box with my arms and head sticking out. To finish off the look, she added large pieces of tissue paper around my head. It was hideous.

One year, Laura ate too much candy along the way and puked right on my carefully bedazzled sparkly red Dorothy shoes. Another year, I tripped in the dark on an uneven sidewalk and knocked my front tooth out. My face was covered in blood, and I cried all the way back to the house.

On the first year my parents decided Laura and I were old enough to go out on our own, we got lost. Crying and freezing cold, we sat on a curb for what felt like many hours hoping our parents would notice we had been gone too long. I really thought we were going to die right there on the street. Almost two hours later, my parents drove by in our yellow minivan and scooped us up. Right then and there I vowed that was my last Halloween trick or treating.

From then on, I stayed home to hand out the candy and that was fine enough for me. But for some reason in high school, my three best guy friends (Ted, Aaron, and Joel) talked me into dressing as one of the four Spice Girls with them. Why they all wanted to cross-dress and walk around town begging for candy was beyond me, but I reluctantly joined them anyway.

That was a mistake.

Out in the Oak Lawn neighborhood we ran into the biggest bully in high school, Anthony Vargas. Apparently high on drugs, he started stalking us through the neighborhood yelling obscenities at us. My guy friends oozed confidence and they had a talent for brushing off hurtful words. I, on the other hand, was freaked out, sure Vargas was going to hurt us. Aaron swore he would kick Anthony's ass if he tried anything, and I believed him. He was the quarterback of the football team, after all, and he had a good thirty pounds on Vargas.

After a while we seemed to have lost Vargas, until we turned a corner down a deserted and very dark dead-end street, and he jumped out of some bushes right in front of a small, crummy looking house. He scared the crap out of me, and I screamed wildly. But right in the middle of my panic, he grabbed me from behind and wrapped his right arm across my chest. Suddenly the blade of a pocketknife was half an inch from my face. He was much stronger than he looked, and I dared not struggle with that sharp point so close to my neck.

"Vargas. Let her go." Aaron's voice held steady and determined.

"Screw you, Aaron. Why should you always get the best-looking girls in school? It's my turn, now." He moved his face close to my cheek, and I could smell his disgusting breath. I whimpered with terror and prayed that Aaron would help me as silent tears streamed down my face.

"Vargas. Put the knife down…now." Aaron was inching closer to us, Ted and Joel right behind him. "We can be your friends. Just let Ava go."

Anthony's breathing quickened in my ear. "No! NO!" he screamed through clenched teeth. "Don't move!" I felt the tip of the knife dig a little into my skin, and I let out a terrified moan.

My friends stopped in their tracks, hands up. "Okay… okay…we're not moving. Now put the knife down, Anthony." I couldn't stop the tears from coming, and suddenly I was full-on sobbing. Aaron stared deep into my eyes. "You're gonna be fine, Ava." I tried to believe him but somehow I couldn't.

"Back off!" Anthony yelled. "I'll do it! I'll cut her throat so neither of us can have her!"

That was the last straw. Aaron suddenly lunged at Anthony's hips and we both fell to the ground. I heard the knife clink down on the street near the curb. Ted quickly grabbed my hand and pulled me up to my feet. Out of the corner of my eye I saw Aaron and Anthony rolling around on the ground. Ted and I ran as fast as we could around the corner and down the next street a bit. This area was much more populated, with several costumed kids strolling around us. I hugged him tightly, still hysterically crying, but so happy to be out of immediate danger.

"You're okay, you're okay," Ted said, trying to calm me down.

We could faintly hear grunts and yelling from around the corner. "Should you go back and help them?" I asked Ted through tear-streaked eyes.

"No. My job is to keep you safe." He held on tight and I was thankful for that.

A few seconds later we released our hug and looked down the street. Joel and Aaron came flying around the corner. When they met up with us Aaron yelled, "Let's get the hell out of here!" So we ran down a few more blocks to where our car was parked on the outskirts of the Oak Lawn neighborhood.

It was there that Aaron finally pulled me into his arms and kissed my head and face what seemed like a hundred times. "Ava. Are you okay? I love you so much." He pulled back and locked his eyes on mine. His right eye looked bruised and puffy, and I touched it gingerly.

"I'm fine." He pulled me in for another tight hug, and I said, "Are you sure you're alright? Your eye looks horrible."

"I'll have a black eye for sure. Don't worry. It'll make me look tough out on the football field."

I felt so safe and comfortable in his arms.

"God, I can't believe that asshole!" Then he pulled away and inspected my neck. "Are you sure you're fine? Should we go to the hospital?"

I was so glad he was my boyfriend. Someone who would defend my life and fight for me. "No. I'll be alright." Then I caught sight of Ted and Joel standing off to our left. "Thanks, you guys."

"Yes, Joel. Thanks for having my back," Aaron added.

"You bet," Joel replied. "With your tackle power and my wrestling holds, he never had a chance."

"Ava, you're like a sister to us! You know we'd do anything to keep you safe." Ted gave me a little pat on the back.

Suddenly a thought popped into my head and I laughed out loud.

"What's so funny?" Ted asked.

"It just occurred to me. I wonder what it looked like seeing Vargas get beat up by two spice girls!"

The boys joined in the laugh. It felt good to break the tension of the scariest night of my life.

Aaron grabbed my hand and kissed me gently. "Vargas won't be a problem anymore."

Now that I was in college, I didn't have to worry about Halloween, considering it was a children's holiday. At least that's what I thought until my freshman year when everyone kept asking me what I was going to be for Halloween. It was then that I realized that for the entire weekend, every house party, bar, or dorm mixer is a costume party—an excuse for the ladies to put on lingerie and headbands with little animal ears attached and strut around. Sexy Kitten or Dirty Puppy were the most popular costumes at the kegger I was dragged to last year. I'd seen enough leg and cleavage by eleven o'clock to last me until the next Halloween.

This year my friends were pumped to attend the Freakin' Scary Costume Party held at the Student Center. Considering my recent mood, it wasn't very surprising to my friends when I told them I'd much rather stay at home sitting on the couch in my pajamas eating popcorn balls and watching slasher movies.

First prize at the party was two hundred dollars cash, and Elaina was sure she was going to win this year. She had decided to go dressed as Katherine Hepburn and actually looked pretty spot on. Kasie went as a Flirty Fairy and Sharon borrowed her brother's camouflage jumpsuit so she could go as GI Jane.

"I'm not going," I flat-out told them when my roommates asked why I wasn't ready to leave.

"Yes you are," Sharon insisted. "It's time you get out of your funky mood. Come on."

She grabbed me by the elbow and pulled me down the hall and into my bedroom. Sharon scanned my closet and took out a blue strapless dress that fitted my curves just right and hit a few inches above my knee.

"Put that on. I'll be right back." She left my room quickly as I grunted unhappily at the dress in my hands.

My stomach twisted as I thought about what my friends were pressuring me into. "You'll be fine," I tried to tell myself. "What could happen, really?" But even as I tried to reassure my nervous stomach, my brain suggested several scenarios where I wouldn't be fine. Sharon came back as I was zipping up the dress.

"Here." She placed a red headband with devil ears on my head.

I looked at her. "What am I?"

"The devil with a blue dress on. Like the song!"

I heard Kasie yelling from the living room, "Come on you two! It's nine o'clock! We wanna go!"

"We'll be right there!" Sharon left the room as I pulled out a pair of red heels from my closet. If I was going to be forced to go, I was going to look good. My phone rang from the table by my bed. I hadn't remembered turning it back on. I swiped the screen—*unlisted*. Unlisted? Maybe it was my parents calling from Ireland. A smiled graced my lips as I accepted the call.

"Hello?" There was silence on the other end of the line. I tried again, "Hello? Mom?" All I heard was heavy breathing. "Adam?" Still more creepy breathing. "Is this some kind of sick Halloween joke? Who's there?" The breathing continued, but no voice. "Well, if you aren't going to talk, I'm hanging up now. Don't call me again." I shook my head as I ended the call.

That was weird.

"Ava! Are you coming or not?" Elaina called.

"Okay, okay. Here I come!" I grabbed my purse and ran out of the room.

The girls were waiting for me near the door and when they saw me, they all had strange looks on their faces.

"What are you?" Kasie finally said.

"Devil with a blue dress on." Their eyebrows were still crunched up, so Sharon and I sang them a little bit until they all said, "Ohhhhhh."

"That's good!" Elaina chimed.

The night was clear but brisk, so we walked quickly down the street to the back door of the Student Center. Next to the door there was a man wearing all black and leaning against the brick wall of the building, arms crossed across his muscular chest. I spied an earpiece hooked around the top of his ear. He looked very serious and stared straight ahead as we passed through. It seemed sort of odd to me—campus police were not dressed like that. Then I remembered it was Halloween, after all, and this misfit was most likely someone in costume.

We climbed the stairs to the second floor. Party music blasted through the fire doors separating the stairwell to the banquet room, but it couldn't drown out the dread pumping my heart deep inside me.

Elaina pushed open the door to reveal an elaborately decorated hall complete with spider webs, skeletons, black and orange streamers, and spooky smoke billowing off the dance floor. There were tables of snacks, freebies, and tons of costumed college students. The knots in my stomach had tied tighter and I had a bad feeling in my chest.

Ug. Halloween.

We showed our IDs at the door, and made our way through the crowd to the dance floor. I still felt weird. Not being able to see everyone's faces added to my uneasiness.

"Can we leave yet?" I yelled at Elaina.

"What? We just got here!"

I basically stood still on the dance floor while I constantly surveyed the crowd. I kept my guard up and tried to avoid all the guys rubbing up on me from behind, but the dance floor was packed and it was difficult. I usually liked dancing, but I was definitely not in the mood.

"I'm gonna get some food," I yelled over the loud music into Kasie's ear. She nodded in affirmation. Snaking my way through the crowd, I finally stepped off the dance floor and walked right past the table of food. I had no intentions of eating. Nothing would stay down until I was safe in my bed and this crazy night was over with. In the hallway I took a deep breath of fresh air. It was simply suffocating on the dance floor.

"Devil with a blue dress on. Brilliant."

I knew it was him the second I heard the British accent.

Of course he would be here—it's frat sponsored. Why hadn't I put that together? My heart somehow raced faster—there was no way of escaping. I reluctantly turned around to find a handsome man wearing black pants and a simple black T-shirt with the British flag covering the front.

Adam walked slowly towards to me, but I crossed my arms across my chest and retreated backwards a few steps.

"Ava, please give me a chance to explain what happened last week."

"I have never felt more like a fool in my entire life. Completely assaulted." Then I raised my voice, "My sandwich was on the floor!"

Oh, Ava, my brain complained, *why didn't you have this conversation planned out ahead of time?*

The people at the admissions table were staring at us. Adam swung his head around and quietly suggested, "Let's go in here." He pushed open the door that led from the hallway outside the ballroom to the student lounge. I followed, nervously wondering what I was going to say to him.

The lounge was empty, and the only light in the room came from the exit signs over each of the four doors and a soda machine in the far corner. I stopped a few feet in and stood with my arms still crossed over my chest. Adam moved in until he was only half a foot from me. I took a step back and realized this was the exact room where I met Adam.

"Ava, I am so monumentally sorry about what happened the other day. That girl, Thora, is the Theta Sig sweetheart. The boys in my frat paid her to pretend she was dating me and try to break us up."

"Ridiculous. Why would they do that?"

"Because that's what frat boys do. They mess with each other for entertainment." He took a step closer to me and carefully placed his hands on the outside of my arms, near my shoulders. Before I could think about protesting, his touch woke something up in my barely beating heart.

Adam stared deep into my eyes. "I've been worried sick about you this week." He rubbed my shoulders and let out a very heavy breath. "What they did was cruel and horrible and someone as sweet and caring as you never ever deserved such merciless behavior. You must believe I would never do anything to jeopardize our relationship. You are so important to me, Ava."

I wanted to believe him, but I didn't know if I should. He was, however, emanating calmness and sensibility and he conveyed no sign of panic or nervousness. He could be telling the truth.

My heart believed him. My brain wanted it to be the truth.

I allowed him to pull me in for a hug and I relished the safety I felt while wrapped up in his arms.

"I don't know, Adam," I said, still in his embrace. "What if your frat friends decide to screw with us again?"

"Don't worry. They've had their fun. They'll move on to another victim now. I promise."

I pulled back, but kept my hands on his waist. "Fine. I will allow myself to be in the same room as you again."

"Really? Woo!" His intense smile was simply adorable. His brown eyes lit up as he wrapped his arms around me, picked me up in a hug, and swung me around a few times in somewhat of an overreaction. "Oh, Ava! You will not regret this! You are an amazing woman!"

"Okay! Okay! Put me down! I've gotta get back into that party before my friends think I've been kidnapped."

"Right-o." He put me down promptly, opened the door for me, and then followed me out into the hallway. Adam grabbed my hand and began swinging it in his like little kids do out on the playground

"You look smashing, as always," Adam said.

"Thanks. You too. Not much of a costume guy?"

"Halloween is not one of my favorite festivals. My mates and I like to celebrate Mischief Night." His wide smile showed his perfect teeth.

"I have to ask—what's Mischief Night?"

"I'm glad you asked, Princess Ava." He stopped right in front of the door to the party. "The traditional British Mischief Night is on November 4th. It's basically a time when teenagers take the liberty of pulling outrageous pranks on their friends and families."

"I can imagine the mischief you must have gotten yourself into."

"Oh, Princess. You wouldn't believe me if I told you." He winked and I looked at him with imploring eyes. He sniggered a little laugh. "Maybe sometime. But right now, I wanna see you cut a rug!" He opened the door and pulled me in before I could protest.

Holding my hand, he led me all the way onto the dance floor. We passed my friends, clearly confused, as they gestured to ask if everything was okay. I nodded back at them and smiled as Adam continued to lead me until he found some space in the middle of the floor.

Some type of hyper pop song was on and we bounced around each other for a while, letting loose. It was like we were the only two in the place acting silly and not caring what we looked like. My nervousness had crept away, and I finally allowed myself to have a little fun. Several songs passed and we were starting to sweat.

But before I knew it, the music changed to a ballad. We stared at each other for a few seconds, wondering whether we should leave the dance floor or engage in a slow dance. I had told myself I would give him another chance, but was I was ready to jump back in right where we left off?

Before I could complicate the situation by overthinking it, Adam took charge and made the decision. Smiling sweetly, he placed his hands on my hips and pulled me into his body slowly and carefully.

"I missed you," he said.

Excitement rushed through my veins as he slowly and deliberately placed his hands on my bare shoulders and gently slid his palms over the skin on my arms. Then he lifted my hands up and laid them down on his shoulders and neck. He returned his hands to my hips and slid them around to my lower back.

His eyes stayed focused on mine, drilling deep into my soul and breaking down the wall I had placed around my heart. I moved in a bit closer, moving my arms from around his neck to around his waist. I laid the side of my face flat against his muscular chest. It felt so right and so perfect. I could hear his heart beating quickly and noticed mine was beating just as fast. My mind was racing.

Uh-oh. I've had this feeling before.

He rubbed my back as we danced there, swaying back and forth, and round and round for a few minutes until I heard him quietly call my name.

I pulled back from my position on his chest and looked up at Adam's kind face. His brown eyes were simply sparkling, peering out into mine. For the first time I saw a truly beautiful face looking back at me, and a smile crept onto the corners of my mouth.

"Ava," he looked so happy, "has anyone ever told you how wonderful you are?"

My heart was starting to melt. My face wouldn't stop smiling, but I couldn't say anything. Where was my voice?

He continued, "You are talented, fun to be around, intelligent." He took his time, letting each compliment sink in. "You're a superb dancer." That one made me laugh.

We were still swaying to the music. "Ava, I'm not supposed to feel this way about you. I'm in big trouble." We continued dancing as the song switched to another ballad.

"What do you mean?"

Adam slowly and deliberately brushed some hair from my face. "I think I love you, Ava. I think I need to spend every day of the rest of my life with you."

And as if those words were the soldiers needed to break through my wall, I suddenly felt as if I could love Adam, too. But how could this be? Just last week I had more hatred toward this man than anyone in my whole life. Could I simply be caught up in an unsuspecting romantic moment?

He was waiting for my answer; it was clear in his eyes.

"I...I..." I didn't know what to say, but he saved me before I said anything more, as he placed a hand on the back of my neck and moved his face closer to mine. He gently swiped his thumb over my lips and searched my eyes, contemplating whether he should kiss me. Last time we tried this a car blew up only a few hundred feet from us, and tonight I felt like my heart was about to explode out of my chest. I was unaware of the other hundred people in the room. I just wanted so badly to kiss him.

"Screw it," Adam muttered, and then his lips touched mine. We kissed slowly, drawing out the fullest length of the kiss each time our lips embraced. A rush of happiness flowed down my body, as our lips interlocked on the middle of the dance floor.

I moved in closer, my hands moving up the back of Adam's neck and my fingers running through the hair on his head. With each passing second I felt more and more like I wanted Adam to be by my side, like I wanted to call him my own, and to share all my life's experiences with him. I was falling hard for him—right there on Halloween night in the middle of an overcrowded dance floor.

"Ah!" I pulled away quickly and doubled over in pain. "My head!" No! It was happening again! Suddenly I saw myself in a cave filled with water up to my waist. That very handsome man from my other visions was kissing my neck and shoulder. It was incredibly romantic.

"Dammit, Ava! Ava! Not now!" Adam dragged me off the dance floor—people were starting to stare. For the first time I heard frustration in his voice. "Snap out of it! Come back to me!"

"No!" I pulled my arm free his grip. "Who is that man?" I desperately wanted him back. He was fading away quickly, taking his beauty and my heart with him. I closed my eyes tight, willing that sweet face to return to my mind.

"Forget about him! Ava, we have to leave straight away!" Adam took my hand and I allowed him to lead me out the back door into a dimly lit hallway.

I stopped walking as I noticed the pain was subsiding. "No, I'm okay. I'm better now."

I need to see a doctor tomorrow. Enough is enough. Something is seriously not right with me.

Adam's voice was urgent, filled with pressure and annoyance. "Listen to me, Ava. You don't understand. We need to leave right now."

Still holding my hand, he expertly led me along a back hallway, down several stairs, and into the kitchen behind the banquet hall. How did he know this was back here, and what were we running from?

"Wait! Let me tell my friends I'm leaving. Where are we going by the way?" I tried to stop walking and turn the other way, but Adam's hand had a tight hold and was still pulling me after him.

Suddenly a strange sound came from the darkness behind me, and then ZOOM!—something whizzed by, knocking the red devil-horn headband right off my head.

My hand instinctively went up to touch the place where the headband had been, and I quickly glanced behind me to see what the cause was.

"Get down!" Adam screamed.

When I turned back around to look at him, he was standing in a rigid position, pointing a gun into the darkness.

Where the hell did that come from?

I hit the floor as he fired several shots into the back of the kitchen. It was so incredibly loud; I screamed but couldn't even hear myself. I fearfully covered my head and neck with my arms as kitchen appliances broke and shattered all around me.

The shots stopped momentarily, and I felt Adam grab my arm. "Run!"

I followed him out of the kitchen and into a hallway through a door on the other side. My ears were ringing so loudly, I could barely hear the music from the party still blasting, everyone apparently unaware of the shooting in the kitchen. At the door Adam held me back with his arm while he took a quick survey of the scene and then told me to run down the hallway to our left. I did as I was told and ran as fast as I could, but while I rushed I heard two more gunshots from the hallway behind us. As he ran after me, Adam turned and shot a few shots in response.

I came to a service door and slammed my hands into it, trying to emerge as quickly as possible into the alleyway behind the Student Center. We ran down the length of the brick wall until we came to a loading dock area. It was freezing outside and I wished I was wearing something over my strapless dress.

"Hide behind this corner and don't speak."

I nervously nodded my head. Although I was afraid, Adam seemed to be calm and steady. I trusted him. I knew he'd keep me safe.

Footsteps sounded from the right. Someone was quickly approaching. Adam stood in front of me as I tucked in around the corner. I half expected Adam to take a bullet for me right then and there, dropping dead to the ground at my feet, but the approaching stranger didn't shoot.

"God, Adam! What the hell were you thinking? You were supposed to get her out of here hours ago!" I couldn't see the person but his voice sounded familiar. He was getting closer.

"I know, I know, sorry. Where are they now?" Adam stayed in front of me, blocking my view from the business at hand.

"We took out a bunch inside but the rest have retreated through a side door. We have a chance if we move quickly." There was a silence for a few long seconds and then the stranger said, "Wait, is she back there?"

Adam shook his head, but the stranger didn't believe him. "Get out of the way, Greene. I've waited long enough."

"No." Adam held his ground.

"What do you mean, 'no'? Let me see her!" The stranger was annoyed and forceful.

"She's not ready. Give me more time."

I pulled back a little further into the loading dock. Adam moved his hand and found mine. He held on tight. A few more seconds of silence preceded one strong word: "Move."

The stranger's arm pushed Adam aside, but he continued to hold my hand and stood off to my left.

I gasped. It was the gorgeous man from my visions. He was a real person, not just some made-up character my brain imagined! He was a million times more handsome in person than he was in my mind. My heart sped up, my breathing was shallow, and my jaw dropped open in shock.

"Ava. My sweet, sweet, Ava. I never thought I could, but I had forgotten how very beautiful you are. My dreams don't do you justice."

I couldn't believe what I was hearing. He knew me?

"I've missed you so horribly." He made a move to hug me.

Did he have a gun? I drew a sharp breath and moved into Adam like a shy child.

Adam grabbed me around the waist and shoved me behind his back. "She's not ready, Nolan."

I peeked my head around his torso and repeated the word, "Nolan?" Saying his name aloud sent a shiver up my spine and sharp knife into my brain. "Ow!" I screamed, grabbing my head.

"Ava? Are you okay?" Nolan took a step forward, but Adam stayed between us, blocking my view. I couldn't see anyway, my eyes were flooded with stars, and I felt dizzy.

"Ava, come back to the present." Adam's soothing voice coaxed my brain to drop the stars and release the pain. He kissed my forehead and his smooth lips sent a blanket of calm through my head. He slowly stepped aside, ready to pull me off in a different direction, but I stood my ground.

"Do you remember me?" Nolan meekly asked, looking concerned and hopeful at the same time.

Risking another episode, I carefully studied his face, his eyes, his lips. They all seemed vaguely familiar, but I just couldn't put it all together. I wrinkled my forehead in confusion, and instinctively raised a hand to rub my temple. I said nothing. Nolan was disappointed.

"Come on, Nolan. You said it yourself; we need to get out of here."

"You're right. Ava, go with Adam. I'll catch up with you two at the rendezvous point." Then he took a slow step toward me with his hands defensively up in the air. "I'm not going to hurt you."

He inched in a little closer and placed his mouth close to my ear, sending me out of my mind. Nolan whispered, "You smell like coconuts and it's wonderful."

His smell was absolutely intoxicating. I instantly felt drunk with dizziness.

Then he backed up, smiled the most beautiful smile I'd ever seen in my entire life, and ran off into the darkness.

The second he left I wanted him back.

Chapter Eleven

"That cocky, son of a—Who does he think he is?" Adam left me at the wall and began walking in the opposite direction of my apartment, obviously pissed off. "Come on, Ava. We've got to keep moving."

"Who is he?" I said, following Adam into the street. "Why are you shooting people in the service kitchen, and for God's sake, where are we going?"

Adam said nothing but kept walking. I caught up to his side and grabbed his elbow.

"Adam! Stop! I deserve answers right now! What is going on?"

He finally halted, turned around, and took a nice long look at my face. He let out a loud sigh and changed his demeanor. "I'm sorry, Ava. I'm sorry it has all come to this. I will explain everything, I promise, but for now, my job is to keep you safe. We need to get back to your house, immediately."

He stared deep into my eyes, waiting for me to accept his plea.

"Fine. But I live the other way," I said, pointing toward College Avenue.

"Yes, but we might be tracked. It'll be safer to enter through the backyard behind the garage." He grabbed my hand and walked off into the darkness of someone's yard.

"Who might be tracking us? Can you at least tell me that?"

"Ethan Myers's men." We snuck through a backyard and turned into an alley.

Who the hell is Ethan Myers?

"Is my life in danger?" Silly question considering bullets were flying by my head only a few minutes before.

"Possibly. But not if I have anything to do with it." We had arrived in the backyard directly behind my house.

"And who is—" Why was it so hard to say? "—Nolan?"

Adam ignored my question as he led me around the back of the unattached four-car garage behind our house. He stopped and pinned me up against the wall. He leaned in close, brushing his face only inches from my cheek.

He whispered in my ear. "Ava, it's time for me to defend for you. Time for me to prove my loyalty and show you how much you mean to me. But for me to do those things, you have to listen very carefully and do as I say." He paused for a moment and I nodded yes, even though I had no idea what he was talking about. "I have to look for something inside your apartment, and while I do that, you need to pack a few days' clothes, and then we need to get out of there as fast as we can. No leaving notes for your friends, no stopping to pack your makeup."

"Adam, I'm scared," I confessed.

He replied with a kiss laced with sweet intentions and strong emotions. My knees went weak and my head spun. After half a minute he rested his forehead on mine, eyes closed, breathing heavy.

"Trust me Ava. Just trust me," he whispered.

I let out a breathy moan and opened my eyes. "I do. I trust you."

That was it. I was crazy. Officially insane. I shouldn't trust Adam. I barely knew him, but something inside me told me to believe in him.

Adam smiled, took the gun out of his belt and held it with the barrel facing up. "Let's go."

He looked both ways and then we carefully snuck to the back door. I stuck my head in and listened intently. There was absolutely no noise coming from any of the floors inside the house—everyone was out.

I quietly led Adam past the shared laundry area and down the stairs to the rear, inside entrance of our apartment. I took the key from the hiding place above the door jam and slowly slid the door open, my heart pounding uncontrollably.

Were we going to open the door to bullets flying at our heads again?

Nothing happened as I turned the knob, so Adam and I walked through the door and took the first right into my bedroom. I moved my hand for the light switch, but Adam whispered for me to keep it off. He turned on the flashlight app on his cell, and I quickly got to work.

I took a backpack out of the closet and threw in a handful of panties and bras, four pairs of socks, a few long-sleeved T-shirts, a pair of jeans, and a pair of pajama pants. My hands were shaking so much I could barely zip up the bag. What if this was my last time in this bedroom? What if I never went to class at UWSP ever again? I started to feel sick to my stomach.

Adam had woken up my computer and typed something into it. The screen was black with some type of green code running across the screen.

How did he know how to do that?

"When's the last time you were on your computer?" Adam said while typing.

"Um...this morning I think. Don't turn around, I'm going to change."

"Okay, but hurry. We probably have only ninety more seconds." He was typing wildly again.

I unzipped my dress and let it drop to the floor. Then I grabbed a pair of jeans and threw on a T-shirt and my favorite UWSP grey hoodie. I pulled on some white socks and slid my feet into my tennies.

I loudly released a nervous deep breath. "I'm ready," I said, anxiously waiting for my next instruction.

Adam turned off the computer, took one look at me, and said, "You're doing great. We're almost in the clear now. Come on."

He led me by the hand out the bedroom, up the stairs, and to the back door of the house. He carefully slid the door open and glanced around the driveway and garage. Then he leaned back toward me and whispered, "We're going to run like bloody hell through the driveway and back behind the garage the same way we came in. Ready?"

I nodded, although I felt like my feet were going to fail me and I was going to throw up on the gravel.

He kissed my forehead and whispered, "Now!"

I ran as fast as I could down the same path we had come, past the garage and through the neighbor's backyard. We raced all the way through that yard and onto the next street over. Adam took a right and led us running down the street.

We hadn't made it all the way to the next block before I heard a loud BOOM and saw an explosion rise above the trees behind us. I screamed loudly, stopped in my tracks and turned around toward my house. I was in complete shock watching the flames and smoke rising from what remained of my house.

"We just...we could...we could have been..." I couldn't say it. I couldn't believe what was happening to me. "My house!"

Adam grabbed me by the shoulders and turned me to face him. "You're fine. You're fine." He kissed my head but I didn't respond. He shook my shoulders to try to snap me out of my shocked state.

"Ava. Come on, sweetheart, my house is just around the corner. We have to keep going." He pulled my hand and my feet finally moved, joining his sprint down to the end of the street and around the corner. "Two more blocks," he reassured me.

I could hear sirens approaching my house. My mind raced, picturing my room up in flames, my things burnt to a crisp, and my roommates out front, homeless. That was the second time a bomb went off while I was within blocks of it.

Adam turned us around the corner and I saw the large, white, two-story house with two big, black Greek letters nailed to the siding come into view.

He slowed down to a walk. "Act normal."

The Theta Sigs were hosting a house party and a steady stream of costumed collegiate were pouring in and out of the back door. A handful of guys were sitting on the porch, probably on cop watch. Adam's car was parked in front and he hit the unlock button as we approached.

The guys on the porch were obviously drunk and were loudly yelling Adam's name.

"Did you guys see the fireworks?" one of them slurred.

"Hi guys," Adam yelled back, barely making eye contact. Crazy Blond was straddling the porch railing clearly intoxicated. I stilled burned with rage for these people and wanted desperately to run the other way.

"Hey, Ava!" She let out a loud hiccup. "You forgave him! Sorry about my little joke." She loudly belched and waved a beer bottle toward me, spilling little bits on her slutty nurse costume without noticing. "Hope you didn't take it personally—you're kinda cute." Then she tipped herself right over the railing and landed with a light thud in the bushes, legs spread-eagled up in the air. The whole porch erupted with laughter and I couldn't help but join in. She popped up quickly, yelling, "I'm okay! I'm okay!" before she stumbled onto the lawn.

Adam quickly opened the passenger side door for me and I got in. As he walked around the back of the car I could hear the guys on the porch yelling something to Adam. He opened the driver's side door laughing and said, "Okay guys, I will." Then he pushed the ignition button on the dash and loudly peeled out away from the house.

Before I had the chance to ask anything, Adam pulled his phone and dialed a number. "This is Agent Greene, identification number 670121."

What?

He was driving crazy fast and I slammed into the passenger side window as he took a corner.

"Yes. I barely extracted the Carrier. Awaiting an emergency transport order.... No, we cannot meet Agent Hill at the rendezvous point.... We need...absolutely... Yes, thank you." Then he hung up.

My jaw hung open in shock, eyes wide. Suddenly I felt overcome with panic. I had trouble taking a full breath and found myself gasping for air.

"Take a deep breath, Ava."

Who is this guy? I thought as I forced myself to breathe in and out.

"Adam...?" My lips quivered, my eyes threatening tears.

"It's still me." He reached his hand across the console and placed it on my thigh, but I slapped it away quickly and retracted towards the window.

"'Still you'? Who the hell are you?" Rage was quickly creeping up from my stomach and into my heart. How could he have deceived me?

"Trust me," he began, but I cut him off.

"Trust you?" I yelled, anger now overriding any other lingering feelings. "Pull over, I'm getting out."

"Don't overreact, Princess Ava."

"Don't call me that!" I clawed for the door handle, but it was locked. "You don't get to call me that!"

"Wait, Ava. Just wait!" He pulled onto the interstate and accelerated. There was no way I could jump from the car.

"I can't tell you everything right now." He looked over at me. "But please know I am essentially the same guy you've been getting to know this past month."

"How dare you!" I said, tears streaming down my face. "I have no idea who you are, or if I can trust you." The angry fire continued to burn deep within my heart, but fear came to the front of the flames.

"Sweetheart. I know you're freaked out, but please believe me, I'm here to keep you safe."

His sincere words twisted my heart in confusion. "You have to give me something. If you want me to trust you, you have to tell me what's going on."

Adam exhaled loudly and kept his eyes on the road. "My name is Adam Greene. I am from Britain. I'm in love with you." His eyes pleaded with mine.

"Not enough. Let me out."

"Where? Right here in the middle of the interstate?"

"Yes." I knew I was being stubborn, but I was riding on my raw emotions. I blew my nose loudly into a Kleenex from a box Adam kept on the floor.

"Do you really want to be out there alone? Need I remind you someone was shooting at you in the Student Center kitchen and then blew up your house?"

Crap. He was right.

"I hate Halloween. Always have." Still crying, I cynically laughed between an agonizing whimper, and looked out the window at the passing Wisconsin pines zooming by. This whole thing was too unbelievable.

"At least tell me where we are going. Will my friends be okay?"

Adam said nothing.

"They have to be worried sick about what happened to me. They're probably assuming I was inside the house when—" And then an uncontrollable sob took over my voice and I couldn't finish my sentence.

"Shhhhh....Oh, Ava, honey. I know you have a million questions for me. But I'm also sure you're exhausted." Adam tried again to put his hand on my leg, but I brushed it off, less violently this time. "Why don't you close your eyes and take a nap before we get to where we're going. I promise you you're safe now. And I'll be able to explain more tomorrow. Just sleep now."

I was exhausted—emotionally and physically. The sounds of the road beneath us and the motion of the car lulled me to sleep like a baby. There would be time for tons of questions tomorrow, if I was still alive. So I closed my eyes and tried to let myself drift off to sleep.

*   *   *   *

I woke up what seemed like hours later to the sound of Adam talking quietly on the phone. He was still driving, and I was slumped up against the passenger side door. I kept my eyes closed so I could eavesdrop on what he was saying.

"Yes, I've extracted the Carrier and am transporting her south to headquarters... No, I didn't have to administer the Methohexital." He paused. "Of course I will, if necessary....Not sure....I searched her computer before the house was destroyed but was unable to find the Schematics. Perhaps he passed it to Agent Hill." He paused again. "Thank you, Agent Harper. I will report when we arrive." He hung up the phone and set it down on the console, letting out a lungful of air.

I slowly opened my eyes and sat up, rubbing them. The clock in the dash read 1:45 a.m. We must have been on the road for hours. Adam looked over at me, but said nothing. I didn't know who he was, or if I could trust him, but right now I needed

122

some comfort and when I looked at Adam, I could still see the sweet guy I was falling in love with. The man who helped me escape my impending death twice tonight. I reached over the console and grabbed his hand, holding tight.

"Go back to sleep." There was a sense of urgency behind his voice that was somewhat alarming to me.

"No. I'm feeling better. I can stay awake and keep you company." There was no way I could go to sleep, pretend or not, at this point.

"Ava. Please…" Something was terribly wrong—his voice was strange. Several seconds passed, like he was giving me a minute to reconsider his plea. Then it all happened quickly. I saw his hand inconspicuously digging in the little compartment built into the driver's side door.

"Ava, I'm so sorry it has to be this way. I truly do love you."

There was something very familiar about this. And then I saw his left hand swing around toward me, holding some type of needle. Shaking, I tried to push his hand away, but he was able to plunge it deep into my neck. I let out a grunt and then suddenly it was like someone was slowly turning off the soundtrack to my world. The music on the radio gradually lowered in pitch and slowed down in tempo. And then it was like someone was pushing on my brain, forcing me to fall asleep.

Worst. Halloween. Ever.

Part Two

Chapter One

Saturday, October 10th

I hadn't seen Ava in six weeks, and we decided to meet in the Dells to reconnect. There had been no activity from Ethan Myers or the CBB for those six weeks, and I desperately wanted to be with Ava in the very place we had fallen in love. I had figured it would be safe, but now I knew I had been a fool believe so.

He just blew up Make Out Rock. While we were standing right on top of it.

I could kill Myers.

It had only been four and a half short months since I had met Ava, and about three weeks since I realized I wanted to spend the rest of my life with her. Last week I nervously walked into that jewelry store in Virginia and bought the one-and-a-half-karat diamond ring that was currently burning a hole in my pocket. I had wanted to revisit Make Out Rock to help Ava overcome the horror of that night, but I also wanted to replace the memory of the worst night of her life with a new memory of the best day of her life.

But Myers had intervened, attempting to blast us from the cliffs of the Wisconsin River. I could hear sirens approaching and was positive it was Myers's men posing as local authorities, on the lookout for our remains. It was crucial to hide Ava and then call the agency. But she was stunned and confused, and not willing to run with me into the forest for cover.

And that's when I my brain told me I had jumped the gun: *If you had pulled out that diamond ring right there on that rock, she would have declined.*

No, you'll fall apart without her in your life, my heart contended.

But she was in a different place than I was. Our relationship was somewhat new to her since she learned I was an FBI agent, but she was exactly the same person I knew her to be since the day I met her last June.

After the FBI released me from their hospital in August, I spent several magical days glued to Ava's side, telling her the truth of my life, pledging my love, and soaking up every single second with her before she had to go back to college. When I found out the CBB was not what I thought it was and Ethan Myers was an enemy of the United States, I knew there was no way he would let me get away with what I pulled in August, and I wasn't ready to sit back and allow him find Ava. I knew the best way to protect her was to enlist myself in the actual FBI and learn the best ways to out-scheme Ethan Myers. Ava struggled with my decision, knowing I would have to go away for training. In all honesty I wasn't entirely excited at the prospect of being away from Ava either, but I trusted our relationship could survive five weeks without each other.

After Ava and I were released from the hospital, I applied to, and was immediately accepted into, the real FBI. I insisted Ava go back to college in Stevens Point, and after a long conversation, we agreed that for precautionary measures Ava should not mention me to any of her friends at school. I didn't know what Myers was up to, and I wasn't about to risk any kind of leak.

For all of September, plus a week in October, I trained in Virginia. My previous training at the CBB enabled me to quickly pass the preliminary tests and accelerate through the training program at Quantico. I had finally finished and was ready to be field rated.

While I trained I had lots of time to think about my relationship with Ava. I was still in awe of the strong feelings I had developed for her—how quickly I fell in love and then the horror of the night when I was forced to stab her and leave her to possibly die. I still suffered nightmares of that moment, as I was sure she had, too.

And now Ava would have a new nightmare of seeing her favorite place being blown to pieces. I finally convinced her to run with me into the forest and climb a tree. Although Ava was aware of my training and alliance with the agency, I had a certain obligation to be discrete with all matters FBI, so I walked several paces out from the tree to make my call to the agency.

An automated voice answered, "Classification and identification, please."

"This is Outlier 90913. Agent Hill calling for Agent Murphy, please."

"Passage granted. Please hold."

A few seconds later a new voice came on the line. "Agent Hill, this is Agent Moreno. Agent Murphy is tied up at the moment. What can I do for you?" I heard typing and wondered what Agent Murphy was doing—he always took my calls. Agent Moreno continued, "Records indicate you aren't due to check in for another twenty-four hours. Do you have impending intel to report?"

"Yes! Myers attempted to bomb Ava and me off the damn cliff just now!"

Stay calm, Nolan.

I took a deep breath.

"Ethan Myers?" Moreno sounded surprised. "Are you sure it was him? Intel indicates he's been inactive for several weeks."

"Of course I'm sure! Who else would attack us?" *Okay, this was ridiculous.* "I need Murphy. Put Murphy on the damn phone!" I heard silence. "Cripes! Get somebody who knows something!"

He could most certainly hear the frustration and anger behind my voice, but Moreno stayed cool, despite my emotionally charged accusation. "Agent Hill, at this point in time

Mr. Myers is number nine on the FBI's most wanted list. Unless you actually saw the man in the vicinity, there isn't much we can do at the moment. Come back to the office, we'll take your narrative of the situation at hand, and then I'll send it straight up to Agent Richardson who will—"

I cut him off, "No, dammit! I need a reconnaissance team in here now!" My pulse was quickening and I could feel my blood beginning to boil.

"Agent Hill, I regret to inform you that your field rating is unsatisfactory."

I clenched my teeth in anger and then repeated slowly, "What do you mean my field rating is unsatisfactory?"

"After the fiasco at the CBB headquarters last week, Agent Murphy downgraded your rating to first level."

Oh, this is complete bullshit—I was never told that. Nothing that happened at the CBB was really my fault!

"A civilian's life is at risk!" I was screaming now, and quickly realized I had given away our position. I slammed my finger in frustration on the phone to end the call and looked up at the tree line. The faint sound of helicopter blades cut through the air above us. It would only be a matter of seconds now before—CRACK! The sound of a gunshot flew through the air and I felt a sting in my left shoulder. I crumbled to the ground, my body beginning to fill with waves of numbness.

Ava. My sweet Ava. Stay hidden.

I could barely talk, but rolled over to my back and stared up at her in the tree. She looked absolutely horrified. I tried to move my tongue, but it felt like it wasn't there. Even so, I was able to slur out the words, "Greeeeeeeeene. Trust Greene."

I had met Adam Greene during training last month, and soon discovered that he was the neurogeneticist the agency called in to oversee the treatment Ava and her family underwent at the end of the summer. I knew Ava wasn't literally or figuratively

129

out-of-the-woods yet, and she'd most likely need Greene's expertise again.

Ava's mouth opened to say something but my world suddenly lost sound, became grey and white, and then shut down.

*   *   *   *

I woke tied to a hospital bed in a stark white room. A clock on the wall read 10:44 p.m. Two older men dressed in doctor's coats were standing under the clock, arguing quietly. My eyes went up to the ceiling above me, filled with surgical lights and mirrors. Monitors beeped at the bedside and tables of medical tools and stainless steel receptacles were placed on tables to my right. I turned my head slowly to the left. Ava was lying unconscious a few feet from me on another table.

Panic and feelings of helplessness crept into my heart. Myers had found Ava. What had they done to her? My heart rate skyrocketed.

Calm down, Nolan. Don't blow this.

If I could lure the doctors over, then perhaps I could knock them out and drag Ava out of here.

With my eyes closed, I began to slowly work the leather straps holding my wrists to the bed.

"Noooolaaaan…. Myers…" Ava moaned.

Through the slits in my eyes, I noticed Ava's noises caught the doctors' attention and they began to walk her way.

My left hand was barely out of the straps—I wasn't ready yet! The men checked her vitals and consulted the monitors. I continued to fake sleep while inconspicuously wiggling my right wrist.

"Her vitals are stable," one of the doctors announced.

"Yes, but what was she saying just now? We don't want her waking yet." He checked a roll of paper flowing out of a small machine near the foot of her bed. "Should we administer more Methohexital?"

"Yes."

If I wanted to get Ava out of here, then I needed to break free soon. I yanked my hands the rest of the way out of the leather straps, and ripped off the monitors connected to my chest. The machines blared loud warnings, but as the first doctor turned around, I jumped up, punching him in the side of the head. He hit the ground, taking a tray of medical tools down with him. The second doctor skirted around Ava's bed as I grabbed a scalpel from the table in front of me and jabbed it toward the man.

"Agent Hill. Stop! You are in FBI headquarters!" The guy had his hands up in a defensive position. "You're safe here." I slowly encroached on the distance between us, still brandishing the scalpel. I searched his eyes for the truth while Ava lay before me, breathing unevenly, my heart beating wildly.

Then the door to the room burst open and a man with wild, out of control blond hair and an older, graying gentleman stepped into the room. They both displayed their FBI badges as they swiftly closed in on me.

"Nolan, believe him. You're safe." I recognized one of the men immediately as Adam Greene. The agent was from British Intelligence, recruited by the agency for his extensive research and expertise on the topic of neuro-genetic engineering.

I let my weapon fall to the floor, and I felt my shoulders relax the tension. "Adam? I'm in US guardianship? But how? I tried to request help but some Agent Moreno denied my request."

The older man stepped in with the answers. "Intel indicated Myers was possibly planning to capture you and Miss Gardner, so we watched you carefully all weekend."

"Well, that would have been nice to know," I said under my breath as I thought back to a few intimate moments I wouldn't have wanted intelligence to be following. I grabbed Ava's limp hand as it rested on the table in front of me and noticed a small bandage on her forearm.

"What's this?"

One of the doctors answered. "Miss Gardner fractured her radius falling out of the tree she was hiding in. We've used a state of the art laser technique to repair the bone so she should only feel mild pain not unlike a bruise for a few weeks."

"But I still don't understand. Myers's men took me from the forest."

"Myers's Intel ran a trace on your cell and was able to use his personal satellite network to intercept and redirect your call for help to his tech department. They kept you on the line by faking Agent Moreno's voice to successfully track your location. They tranquilized you both and dragged you out of the forest, but we intercepted them a mile outside of your location and brought you back here for observation."

I suddenly felt special. All that for Ava and me?

Agent Greene came around the table and stood next to Ava's monitor, checking her stats. He took a syringe off the table and injected something into Ava's IV. Apparently he was her doctor. It suddenly occurred to me that maybe something was not right with her. I was up walking around and yet she required some sort of treatment.

"What's wrong with Ava?" A wave of concern washed over my heart. "Did the gene therapy from last summer fail?"

Adam gave a look of solicitude to the other man. "Nolan, why don't you have a seat?"

Oh no.

My knees gave way and I lowered myself onto the hospital bed behind me.

"Ava has undergone an experimental preventative procedure." Adam was carefully choosing his words.

What the hell was he talking about?

The older man stepped in to explain. "The agency believes the DNA in Ava's brain cells is key to Myers advancing his game. Agent Hill, we believe he could use her as a weapon to carry out his final event. We're not sure he's discovered this yet, but we are certain Myers needs to be stopped."

I suddenly felt thankful they had made me sit down. A nasty concoction of anger and nausea was setting in, and the room was beginning to spin.

"In order to protect Ava and prevent Myers from accomplishing his agenda, Agent Bowman, the head of the case against Myers, ordered that we retrieve these valued cells and preserve them in our secure lab. Ava underwent the procedure an hour ago."

Adam cut in to continue the brief. "Nolan, a problem occurred while we were trying to protect her. Ava's brain underwent a partial memory wipe."

Suddenly my breath was absent. *No.... This wasn't happening.* I put my head in my hands, trying to hold it together. But my momentary sorrow for Ava quickly turned to anger as I stood up.

"You son of a—" but I bit my bottom lip, trying to control myself. I lowered my voice but kept the intensity. "Protect her?" I stepped closer to Adam until I was inches from his face. "You just ruined her entire life. No, now she doesn't have a life! She has no idea who she is, where she lives, who she loves!" And then it hit me—they had ruined my life, too. I slammed my fist down on the table making the tools jump, some clattering loudly to the floor. I let out a loud emotion-filled roar.

133

"Calm down, Agent Hill. We didn't wipe her entire memory. Tests indicate she won't remember only the months since she's learned about herself being the Carrier, about Ethan Myers, and unfortunately about—" he paused, not wanting to finish his sentence— "you." The old man looked down at the floor, and backed up a few steps as if he was afraid what I might do next.

I began to lunge forward just as Greene came over to restrain me. I took several heavy breaths before Adam attempted to console me. "Nolan, we did consider Ava's overall welfare." He dropped the arm that was across my chest when I relaxed a tiny bit. "She'll be out of recovery in the next hour and then we'll fly her back up to university and place her back in her own bed. When she wakes up, she may be disoriented for a short while, but we have full confidence her flatmates will support her. She'll be none-the-wiser."

I didn't know what to say. I simply stared at Agent Greene.

"Listen, once this is all over and they bring down Myers and the CBB, it's possible we may be able to reverse the process."

He raised a hand to place on my shoulder, but I hit it away with my hand. I was not in the mood to be comforted by the man who ruined my girlfriend's life.

"May be able to?" My thoughts shifted quickly. "Why wait until it's all over?"

"There's little research on partial wiping, so naturally, we're unsure of the outcome. And as for the wait, we can't be exactly sure how her brain will react to the recent trauma it's been under. Attempting another surgery so quickly is a massive risk."

"This is all crap." I walked to the foot of Ava's bed. "How do you expect her friends at school to help her recover from this trauma when they don't even know what she's suffering from?"

One of the other men spoke up, "Gentlemen, might I suggest we send Agent Greene to Stevens Point to oversee Ava while she recovers? After all, he is very familiar with Miss Gardner's medical file."

I shot the man a look of disgust. "What do you mean, 'very familiar'?"

"Nolan, I was in the operating room last summer when Ava underwent gene therapy. I know everything about her medical history." Then he turned toward the old man. "Great idea. I could pose as a college student for a while, befriend Ava, and keep an eye on her recuperation. And, of course, if Myers tries anything, I will be within arm's reach and pull her out of town if needed."

"It might just work," the older doctor said. "I know you're almost twenty-nine—"

"I'm twenty-seven, sir," Adam corrected him.

"Right. Twenty-seven. I think you could pass for a college student, not a problem."

"No, no," I interrupted. "Absolutely not. I'll do that myself. I can watch over her." No way was I letting some fancy-haired Brit hover over my girlfriend for a few weeks.

"Agent Hill," said Adam, "if Ava sees you, it may trigger partially wiped memories and sacrifice the effects of the whole procedure. Her brain will get confused and she may undergo prolonged blackouts. It's too risky."

I came back around the bed and into Adam's space. "Dammit, Adam! I can't just sit here while the woman I love is suffering and disoriented, not to mention being hunted by one of the FBI's most wanted criminals!"

The first old man spoke up again. "You won't be sitting idle, Agent Hill. I've been told the agency has an important mission for you. The swifter you achieve this assignment, the faster we can take down the CBB and the quicker you can return to Miss Gardner."

I knew it was too late. The procedure was done, and there was nothing I could do about it. The old man was right. I needed to focus on the task at hand so that I could find my way back to Ava. I walked over to her side, took her soft hand in mine, and stared at her peacefully slumbering face.

Adam quietly offered, "Nolan. I may have altered her brain, but I cannot change her heart."

I raised Ava's hand and kissed it gently, taking in the scent of her skin and placing that smell deep within my brain. I knew it could be weeks before I'd be given the pleasure of being so close to her again. I gently placed her hand back on the bed and leaned over to whisper in her ear, "We'll find our way back to each other, I promise." Then I kissed her forehead and slowly backed away from the table. The old man escorted me out of the room as the vision of Adam tending to my girl was etched into my brain.

"You take care of her, Adam. Take care—" and then my voice trailed off as I got choked up.

"You've got it, mate."

Chapter Two

Late that night I was led to the housing wing of the Milwaukee FBI building. Despite my exhaustion, I barely slept a wink, agonizing over Ava's new life without any memories of the past three months. I didn't believe in the plan presented, but on the other hand, I lacked a better scenario to offer. My hands were tied.

In the morning I was to meet with my new handler, Agent Bowman, to be briefed on the mission I was assigned to. My plan was to complete whatever it was as quickly as possible so that I could return to Ava and hopefully reverse the surgery. One thing was for sure; I'd be going through hell, waiting and wondering what she was up to and how she was doing.

My phone rang out from the bedside table, calling for me to wake up. When I swiped the screen, I discovered a text message from Agent Bowman: *Good morning Agent Hill. Please meet me in room 596 at 8:00 am.*

Next to my phone under the lamp was a black fuzzy box sitting exactly where I had left it right before I fell asleep.

Ava, my heart ached as I carefully opened the box. A beautiful princess-cut diamond ring sparkled in the ray of sunlight peeking through the curtains.

Her memory's been wiped, my brain yelled. *She doesn't even know you!*

A deep sigh accompanied the snapped shut box lid. I had to defeat Myers no matter what it took. I replaced the box back on the bedside table and climbed out of bed, head pounding from lack of sleep.

The room was small but adequate enough for my needs. I sauntered over to the closet and opened the sliding door. There were a few two-piece suits, in my size, waiting for me on the hangers—the official uniform of the FBI while we were in the office.

I quickly showered, changed into the suit, and then grabbed my wallet, cell phone, and the ring box as I headed out of the room. I found my way down the hall and over to the elevators.

Agent Bowman's name was displayed on the nameplate next to his office door. I drew a deep breath and knocked. I wondered if Ava had woken up in her bed in her apartment at school yet or if she was still sleeping.

"Come in," a voice called from inside the room.

I turned the handle and walked into a very cushy office. One wall had a fish tank about the size of a mattress built into a large bookshelf that covered the entire length of the wall. There were two brown leather couches to either side of an oversized mahogany desk that was placed in front of floor-to-ceiling windows.

"Ah, Agent Hill. Right on time." Agent Bowman stood up from the desk and walked around it to shake my hand. "You probably didn't sleep a wink last night. Would you like a cup of coffee?"

"Yes, thank you." First impression, my new boss was down to earth, but I wasn't ready to completely trust the guy yet. After I had been duped by Myers, I've noticed I look at people I meet for the first time with a little caution.

"Superb." He walked over to the console behind his desk and poured two mugs of coffee. "Agent Hill, please have a seat."

I sat down on one of the couches as Agent Bowman took his place behind the desk. Bowman had short, black hair with specks of grey here and there and looked like he was probably in his late forties. His dark-rimmed glasses rested on his sharp nose, his intense green eyes glaring through the lenses. A tidy goatee polished off his square jaw.

"Well, let's get right down to it. I've been assigned this case for a specific reason, Agent Hill. For the twenty-six years I've worked for the agency, I have been attracted to cases involving genetics and futuristic advancements in genetic medicine. This study has led me to follow and track the activity of Ethan Myers. Mr. Myers is one the FBI's most wanted for a multitude of reasons, most of which you are oblivious to." He paused to take a deep drink of coffee.

"The FBI had reason to believe that Myers was relatively benign until last August when we discovered he had tracked down a specific blue meteor the Gardner family had in their possession, and was planning on using it for some unknown reason.

"What we are most concerned with these days is the safety of several Americans that Myers is covertly targeting. At this point, our researchers have their theories, but we have not entirely concluded what exactly Myers is soliciting from these particular Americans, and we can't be sure who his next prospect is. The most unsettling part is that we've found three young women murdered, most likely at his deliberate hand."

I didn't thoroughly understand everything Agent Bowman was telling me, but I nodded in agreement anyway.

"Agent Hill, there is a reason Myers had Miss Gardner tranquilized and not killed. We believe he needs her alive."

"Any idea why, sir?" My mind flashed back to that horrible medical room in the CBB.

"Not entirely, but we do have reason to believe that Myers is acting in accordance with a certain conception he was brought up believing. The motivation supporting the details behind this mysterious theory is still somewhat unknown, but we speculate the key to defeating Myers is to study his past."

"With all due respect, sir, I've seen a map of the spider web containing all the CBB offices in the US. It's expansive, to say the least." Taking down Myers was going to take a lot more than a little digging through his past. "Shouldn't we be focusing on taking down each office one by one?"

"Unfortunately, cutting off the limbs of this monster may not prevent his brain from thriving." Agent Bowman stood from his desk and took a few steps over to the windows. He spoke to me as he stared down at the city below us. "The FBI is not a small operation, Agent Hill. We have been following Myers for many years and know a lot more about him than perhaps you do." He turned back toward me. "Ethan Myers is up to something monumental. I can feel it."

"Sir, I don't know if you read my report, but when I discovered the whiteboard in Ethan's lab, there was a date written at the bottom—November first. Do you think this is a deadline or sorts?"

"Yes, I'm sure of it. We have twenty-one days to determine what Myers is planning and cut him off before he can accomplish his agenda." He stared at the ground, thinking. "So soon," he muttered to himself. Agent Bowman returned to his seat at the desk. "I better get you started on your mission. Sorting through Myers's past is a necessary piece to our advancing forward. If we don't stay one step ahead of Myers, we're going to uncover more innocent Americans dead, and that is unacceptable." He turned over a piece of paper on his desk. "I'm sending you overseas to Dublin."

"Dublin? You're sending me to Ireland?" I always wanted to see Ireland, and a little flutter of excitement filled my heart.

"Yes." The corners of Bowman's mouth turned up for a second as if he was happy to bring me joy, but knew he needed to fulfill the role of a serious FBI handler. "Ethan Myers's bloodline runs through Ireland. There is valuable information over there. You'll have two days to prepare for your mission overseas."

I knew deep down in my heart I needed to see Ava one more time before I headed out of the country. Since I was dealing with Myers there was, of course, a slight chance I wouldn't be returning alive, and I needed to see for myself that Ava was going to be alright.

"Sir, I was wondering if I would be lucky enough to be granted one personal favor." Bowman said nothing so I continued. "I'd like to see Ava before I leave."

For a few moments Agent Bowman looked down at the ring encircling the finger on his left hand. "Many years ago I lost the only woman I have ever loved. That morning I was running late for work and didn't take the time to say goodbye to my wife." He took another moment to pause. "If I could do it all over again, I wouldn't waste one single second I had with her." He looked up into my eyes. "You are in a precarious situation, Agent Hill. I can't pretend to imagine what you are feeling, but you should consider the fact that you are still deep within her heart."

"Thank you, sir." The sentiment meant a lot, especially from a boss I just met.

"I will allow you to go as long as you don't interact at all with Miss Gardner."

"Yes, sir. I will look from afar."

"Good. Oh, and you should know I'm not sending you to Ireland alone. I'd like you to work as a team with Agent Smith. I'll contract the express chopper to transport you and Agent Smith up to the Central Wisconsin airport in Wausau later today. There you will find an agency vehicle you may use to take down to Stevens Point Monday morning. This short excursion will not only have a personal objective for you, Mr. Hill. You and Agent Smith will spend your time discussing the overseas task, reading the research documents, and you will be advised by tactics through email and video chat. It is imperative you spend your time preparing, or you could risk failing this mission."

"I understand, sir. I will stay focused." I stood up from my chair and headed toward the door. I knew I couldn't truly focus until I saw Ava's sweet face—until I knew she was recovering alright from the trauma of the surgery.

When I pushed open the door, Agent Smith was waiting for me in the hallway, leaning up against the wall, one foot crossed over the other.

"What's up, Nolan? I just heard the good news about our overseas adventure together! This is going to be epic!"

I was happy Bowman was sending me with Drew, an agent whom I became friends with during training and had enjoyed working with. Although he was twenty-eight, Drew had been with the agency for several years and was already training new agents. He was somewhat of a mentor figure to me. I trusted him and knew we got along nicely.

"Yeah. We need to get this psycho quickly so I can get back to Ava."

"I heard what Greene did to her. I'm sorry, my man." He and I began to walk down the hallway together. "But don't worry, I have no doubt we shall be successful." Drew had a lot of energy and had a way of making everything he said sound like a line from a movie.

We were briefed by Mission Tech all afternoon and then spent some time studying the mission manual. There was a lot to know before we went on our first overseas operation, and I found myself having trouble focusing when all I could think about was Ava's safety.

By late evening we boarded the agency's express helicopter and buzzed up to Wausau Airport where a black Tahoe waited for us outside the terminal. Drew took the driver's seat and we followed the GPS south to Stevens Point.

Agent Smith's specialty was all things computers, so at the hotel that night he hacked into UWSP's computer network and found Ava's address and class schedule. Then he engineered a program to piggyback off the system so he could check if anyone was seeking her information.

Genius.

We planned to search out Ava after her morning biology lecture and observe her for a while until I was satisfied she'd be fine. I called Adam to tell him we were in town and to see how Ava was doing, but he didn't answer my call. I'd try again tomorrow.

Later that night I lay in bed staring at the ceiling. It wasn't fair. I had just gotten Ava back in my arms when Myers separated us again. A small fire started to burn deep within me. I had a feeling it wouldn't be put out for quite some time.

Chapter Three

A knock at the door woke me up and I opened my eyes quickly. Where was I?

"Hill, you up?" Drew was knocking at the hotel room door. "We've gotta get going!" he sang loudly in a girly opera voice.

Right—hotel room in Stevens Point. I crawled out of bed and peered through the peephole. Drew was standing in the hallway dressed in his work suit, checking out a painting in the hallway and holding two disposable cups of coffee. He was a little over six feet tall with a ruggedly handsome face. A goatee and sideburns stood proudly beneath his stylish light brown hair. Drew's slim, yet muscular figure, white smile, and tanned skin had to be a magnet for women everywhere.

Drew turned around and saw me standing in the doorway in my pajamas. "Cripes, kid! You're not up yet? You better drop trou and hop in that shower if we're going to go find your girl." He plowed through the door and walked right into the bathroom, turning on the water in the shower. He stood by the door holding out a towel for me. "Hustle up, buddy. I'll watch Sports Center while you scrub down."

"Yeah, thanks." I took the towel, walked into the bathroom, shut the door, and quickly undressed. Drew was right: I needed to hurry if I wanted to see Ava after her biology lecture.

I let my mind wander as I showered. There were so many sweet memories of this summer with Ava I couldn't bear to forget anytime soon. My heart ached when I thought about the fact that the agency had wiped those same memories right out of Ava's mind, possibly never to be restored. What would my life be like if I had never met Ava? I didn't even want to consider it.

When I emerged from the bathroom, Drew stood up from the bed and turned the TV off with the remote. He took one look at me and said, "You ready for this, buddy?"

I let out a deep breath. "Let's go." The truth was I was extremely nervous about seeing Ava again. It was hard for me to consider a version of Ava without a thought of me in her memory. We left the hotel room and headed down to the car waiting for us at the front door. I called Adam again on the way to campus.

"Good morning, Agent Hill, how are you?" His voice sounded annoyingly light and bubbly. What was he so happy about?

"Fine," I said, disgruntled. "Be advised Agent Smith and I are on campus this morning."

His tone changed suddenly. "Which campus? UWSP? Why are you in Steven's Point?"

"Bowman is sending us to Ireland and I need to see Ava once before I leave. I just need to know she's okay."

There was a few seconds of silence before he answered. "Agent Hill, you are not to let her see you." He was bothered. "Seeing a vision of you even from across a room could seriously undermine her brain's prospects of healing correctly."

"Cut the psychobabble. I just need to see her once."

"It's out of the question. You've got to trust me, Agent Hill. I will take good care of her without her ever knowing my true intentions."

What did that mean?

"That may be, but I'm not changing my plans. I need to see her once more." I inhaled loudly. "But I'll try my best to stay out of her view." I hit *end* and shoved my phone back into my pocket.

Drew had calmed me down by the time he parked the car in the lot adjacent to the Student Center. We got out and walked

145

around to some benches outside of the library. This spot was directly on the path from the science building to Ava's house on College Avenue, and we were sure she'd have to cross through any minute.

"She really must be special." Drew tapped his fingernails on the top of his coffee cup while staring out over the sidewalk.

I looked at him, "You have no idea." I scanned the sidewalks as several twenty-somethings strolled by wearing backpacks. "She's the most amazing woman I've ever met. I think the phrase *head over heels* would cover it."

"You're a lucky man, Nolan. We don't all get to meet the woman of our dreams."

"What? No lovely lady in your life?"

Drew half-smiled out of the corner of his mouth. "No, I couldn't say there was. Not today anyway." He drummed on his cup again and started singing, "You shift my heart into four-wheel drive."

"Excuse me?"

"Sorry, song lyrics. They just roll around my noggin all day long."

"You write songs?" A trait I completely didn't see coming.

"Absolutely, and not just any songs, country songs. Oh, and I write the music, too. I'll play my guitar for you sometime. I'm waiting for the right words to spin together and I'll have a number one hit. You'll see."

Confidence was not something Drew lacked.

I looked over the scene before me as Drew hummed a melody and then I saw her. I sat up from my slouched position and watched Ava walk toward the Student Center. "There she is," I whispered to Drew. My heart stopped for several seconds as I observed her beautiful brown hair bounce with each step she took.

Drew let out a down falling whistle. "That's her?" he asked, hushed.

I nodded but he didn't see me because his eyes were stuck on Ava.

"Like I said, you are a lucky man, Agent Hill. A lucky man." Drew got up off the bench. "Come on, Nolan."

We crossed the street, carefully following Ava into the Student Center.

From a corner by the front doors she took the stairs to the second floor and wandered into the student lounge. Drew's phone rang just as we were about to climb the stairs, so he turned and took the call in the lobby. He motioned for me to go on, so I continued to the lounge and took a seat on a leather bench butted up to the wall near the exit. I had to watch her a few moments to convince myself she was fine.

From my perch in the corner she looked like normal Ava in every way I could tell. She had found a seat on a couch, people watched for a while and then before I could duck out of the way, she looked directly at me.

Crap!

In that split second I couldn't help but smile as I felt myself connect with her gorgeous brown eyes. But she wasn't smiling— she cocked her head and wrinkled up her nose.

It was true then. She had no idea who I was. My heart sunk with a thud.

Ava bent down to get something out of her backpack, and I dodged for the exit. Once out of the room I peered back in through the long window next to the closed door. Adam was there sitting on the couch next to her. Where did he come from? He was smiling and talking with her and then she put her head on his shoulder!

What the hell was going on here?

That rat.

I turned away quickly—suddenly my head was spinning and my stomach started to turn sour.

"Nolan!" Drew called from the bottom of the steps. I turned around. "Come here," he called.

I took one last look into the room. She was standing now, Adam still on the couch. At least they weren't touching anymore. I reluctantly walked down a few steps toward Drew. I'd much rather be monitoring what Adam was doing with my girl.

I reminded myself Adam was an expert on what Ava had been through and, as hard as it was to admit, she needed him right now, not me.

"Did you get a gander at your lovely lady? 'Cause we have a schedule to follow. Gotta get a move on."

"Hold on a sec." I quickly hopped back up the stairs and looked into the window one more time. Adam was gone, and Ava was standing up in the middle of the room looking puzzled. I wanted desperately to go in there and wrap my arms around her and kiss her before I had to fly off to Ireland.

My heart ached horribly for her. I had a long journey ahead of me.

With sorrow in my voice I turned back toward Drew. "Let's go." I started walking down the stairs when I heard my name again, this time from behind me.

Adam emerged from the door at the top of the stairs and quickly descended. "Nolan! What in the hell were you doing in there?" He came to stop only a foot from where I was standing. He was pissed.

"It's fine," I said, backing up a little. "Ava only saw me for a split second."

"That's because I plowed into her to distract her!" He was inching closer to my face and I started to feel a little territorial. "You're lucky I was here or she could have gone into serious shock! I told you—"

But Drew cut him off before he could finish. "Hey, hey there ol' pal!" he said, stepping in between Adam and me, trying to prevent a fight. "Listen, buddy. No harm done. She's fine. We need to jet, anyway."

Adam was acting a little too protective for my comfort and I knew exactly where this was going. I angrily stared at Adam for a few seconds.

"Don't you dare fall for her."

"You're being completely ridiculous, mate." He held my gaze for a few more moments, and then I turned and walked right out the front door of the building.

Once outside, I turned to Drew, "Why do I get the feeling that guy's a complete jerk?"

"Oh, I don't know. He seems okay to me. A little high strung, but okay." He clicked the car locks open, we hopped in, and headed out of town toward the airport.

It killed me to leave her behind with that guy. There was no way I could be there with her, but something about Greene rubbed me the wrong way. I felt completely trapped. I guess I'd have to believe that Agent Greene was the best person to watch over Ava for these few weeks until we could get enough info to truly take down Myers.

Chapter Four

Tuesday, October 14th

The FBI used a private wing of O'Hare International Airport in Chicago. It was early evening once we arrived from north central Wisconsin, got our bags checked through security, and boarded the plane. The eight-hour flight to Dublin did not feel that lengthy probably due to the fact that they flew us out of the Midwest in one of the agency private jets. Drew and I took advantage of the space, spreading our files out and discussing the mission at hand in comfort and peace.

An hour into the flight Drew was staring into his tablet looking confused. "I'm having trouble uploading the data packet to my computer. Bowman filled me in briefly, but I'll need some more information." Then he looked up at me, "I guess you'll have to give me the skinny, kid. Why exactly are we off to the magical country of leprechauns and whisky?"

"We have been sent to Ireland to track down the family history of Mr. Ethan Myers."

"YES!"

Drew looked up from his tablet. "I got the downlink," he said matter-of-factly. I watched him scroll down through the document. "Alrighty, we are looking for any and all info on Mr. evil Myers."

Drew leaned forward, picked up his coffee cup, and took a long drink, thinking. "Not that I want to complain, because I'm pretty stoked we are heading to Ireland, but why don't we just get the geniuses over in Info Tech to scour the Internet or something? You can Google anything these days, you know."

"Of course Info Tech has been digging deep on this one, but somehow Myers has either blocked or pulled all records of his family from all public and private archives."

"Ah yes. Nowadays it's possible to wipe yourself from the inter-workings of the web. Sounds like Myers is hiding something, Mr. Hill." Drew scrolled through a few more pages on his tablet, smiling widely, as if this was very exciting for him. "Although I have to admit it sort of sounds like finding a needle in a pineapple field."

"Pineapple field? It's haystack."

"Needle in a haystack? Maybe where you come from."

"And where do you come from?"

"I hale from the beautiful white-sand beaches of Hawaii."

"Really?"

"Born and raised Honoluluan! You should come back with me sometime. You'll never see more gorgeous half-naked women on the beach anywhere else in the world."

I smiled at him, letting my mind wander to a tropical scene enhanced with bikini-clad babes.

"You'll also see ridiculously overweight half-naked women on the beach, but I usually try to avert the ol' peepers."

Laughing, I let my daydream go and scrolled through my tablet until I found the document I remembered Bowman showing me a few days ago. I ran my finger down the page. "Here's what we know—Myers's grandparents were living in Ireland between 1899 and 1950 and his grandfather, Alec, was a local physician."

"I assume the agency wants to get into Myers's head. I've seen it before." Then Drew put on a deep and official voice, as if he was reciting something he'd heard a million times. "If we ascertain his past we are well on our way to deeply understanding what makes Myers tick, in turn we can deduce what he's planning next." Then his voice returned to normal. "At least that's the plan." There was something condescending about the way Drew said that last part.

"Bowman is confident the solution is in Ireland," I offered. Was I a fool to believe what Bowman had said? I started to feel anxious, and Ava's beautiful face popped into my mind.

My heart interrupted, *You need to find a way to ensure Myers will never hurt Ava again.*

"We've got to figure this out, Drew," I said out loud.

Drew noticed the agony on my face. "Hey, Nol, don't stress." Then he put on his best superhero voice and raised one hand into the air. "We shall succeed!"

No matter how goofy he was, I knew I was happy to have Drew on this assignment with me. "Thanks buddy, I hope we will."

"So where does Agent Bowman suggest we start?"

"Bowman thinks we should begin by physically looking through the historical records at St. Patrick's Cathedral, one of the oldest and largest churches in Dublin."

"Sounds like a great place to start." We had a rather large job in front of us.

I spent the rest of the plane ride reading the documents, surfing the web, napping, and listening to Drew play the guitar. He wasn't half bad at playing and singing, but his lyrics definitely needed some help.

We arrived at Dublin airport at three a.m. Wisconsin time, nine a.m. local Dublin time. We deboarded the plane, and were taken to a bare and cold room to wait to meet our foreign agency contact. I checked my email and Drew played on his tablet while we waited.

"Who is the contact? Do you know the guy?" I asked Drew.

"Nope." Drew replied, not looking up from his tablet.

A second later the door opened and a rather tall, attractive woman walked in. She had a slender nose centered between two sharp, yet kind blue eyes, and long, silky-smooth, strawberry-blond hair. She wore a low-cut navy blazer, a short navy skirt, and matching high heels. She somehow managed to appear very professional and very sexy at the same time. Drew, was just about drooling onto the table.

"Hello, agents. I'm Agent Darcy McCombe." She flashed a badge and then continued in her local Irish accent. "I am a liaison with the Irish Intelligence Agency. My job will be to provide any local intelligence you may need while on assignment here in Ireland."

"Wonderful. Thank you very much, Agent McCombe. I am FBI Agent Drew Smith and this is FBI Agent Nolan Hill."

I almost busted out laughing as Drew introduced us so seriously. An obvious departure from his typical jocularity.

I jumped in with some additional information. "Our mission is to retrieve records belonging to the ancestors of a US citizen who is wanted by the FBI."

"Thank you, Agent Hill. I've been briefed. I have collected a list of places you may want to begin your search. But first, you must be exhausted from your travels. Let me take you to your hotel which will be your home away from home during the duration of your stay here in Dublin."

Agent McCombe stood up from the table and clicked her heels out the door.

I could barely stand up before Drew leaned across the table and whispered in my ear. "Damn! Did you see the ass on that one?"

"Yeah. Pretty nice." I hadn't actually noticed, there were other things on my mind.

Agent McCombe expertly walked us through a series of deserted hallways in the airport until we emerged into what seemed like a back alley. A car with dark windows was waiting patiently for our arrival. We all climbed in, Drew eagerly taking the seat next to Agent McCombe. I shook my head, hoping that Drew's libido wouldn't get in the way of our finding Myers's info fast and getting back home to Ava.

The car drove us down the M1 highway from the airport into downtown Dublin. Drew could barely keep his eyes off Agent McCombe, but my interests laid in the scenery passing by my window. The morning sun was well over the horizon as we entered the city's center, casting glorious rays of light onto the beautiful cream and red brick buildings that oozed the flavor of an era long ago. Intricate designs had been applied to several of the structures, and the blue street signs were posted not on poles like in the US, but at the top of each corner building.

We had been assigned two rooms at the Arlington Hotel right on the River Liffey. The car drove around the front of the cream building, past beautiful white window boxes overflowing with pink and orange flowers on each windowsill. A dark brick facade separated the front entrance from The Knightsbridge Bar, which occupied part of the lobby. A small convenience store held the rest of the space.

The car stopped near the alley entrance and Agent McCombe got out. "Stay here while I check you in," she said.

As soon as she got out, Drew leaned right into my personal bubble and whispered, "Dibs!"

I laughed—he knew darn well that I had no interest in Agent McCombe. "Fine, but no hanky-panky until we get some info on Myers."

Drew smiled widely. "I can't promise that, my friend." Still in my space, he held up his phone with a newly added contact—Agent McCombe.

"Dude! How did you do that?"

"Have you no faith?"

"Come on! We have a job to do! Besides, she's all business, I can tell. I doubt she has any time for an American intelligence agent."

Drew scoffed. "You'll be eating your words, young man. You just wait and see."

The door to the car opened quickly and Agent McCombe stuck her head in. "Agents, follow me. The doorman will bring your bags up." She took us up the elevator and escorted us to our fourth floor rooms. She kept a solemn demeanor the whole way, and I felt certain Drew would not be successful in his personal mission.

Agent McCombe stopped right in front of Drew's door. "I recommend you take a short nap and then try to stay awake until tonight. The quicker you adjust to the time change the quicker you can achieve your mission. There is a card on the table inside your room with my agency's contact information. I will check in with you in twenty-four hours if I don't hear from you before then."

"Thank you, Agent McCombe. We appreciate your hospitality." Drew stuck out his hand and she shook it. He smiled deeply, and I swore I saw a hint of a smile behind her sober face.

Maybe I was wrong. Could he crack this girl?

"Yes, thank you." They were still holding each other's hands and gaze.

I cleared my throat after a few seconds. "We'll be in touch, right, Drew?"

"Ah, right...yes. We will certainly be in touch, Agent McCombe."

"Farewell, agents." Agent McCombe walked down the hall and into the elevator, and Drew turned toward me with lights in his eyes.

"Try to get some sleep, Drew." I patted him firmly on the back as I opened the door to my room. Drew laughed and shook his head.

*   *   *   *

The next morning Drew and I took a cab over to St. Patrick's Cathedral. We paid the tourist's fee and entered the historic church. I was immediately overwhelmed by the size of the enormous building. Immense arches of stone supported a vast ceiling that must have been at least a hundred feet tall. Handsome, polished wooden pews proudly stood atop colorful mosaic tile floors. The grey block walls boasted bright flags and placards displaying the bios of past church leaders.

I wandered away from Drew and read a sign indicating that the original part of the present-day Cathedral was first built as early as 1259.

Incredible! The year 1259!

Our country is so young—only a few hundred years. There is no standing structure in America even close to as old as this beautiful cathedral. This place was dripping Irish history from its seams, and I suddenly felt privileged to be standing in it.

Drew startled me when he snuck up and said my name. "Nolan, this is Mrs. Quinn, head of the ancestry department at the cathedral." There was a little old lady at his side. "She's graciously agreed to lead us to the record room in the basement."

"Thank you, Mrs. Quinn," I said, noticing an annoyed look on her face.

"I'm very busy, young lads." Using a cane, Mrs. Quinn slowly lead us down a broad staircase underneath the cathedral. "I've only a few minutes."

Drew buzzed in my ear. "At this rate we'll have to leave as soon as we get to the basement."

I snickered as we followed the elderly-pace of Mrs. Quinn. At the foot of the stairs stood a row of life-size stone statues depicting Catholic saints. Each was up-lit by a dim spotlight, and they were downright creepy gatekeepers to the crypt. The old woman said nothing as she expertly led us through a hallway framed with four-foot columns supporting ancient brick arches every six feet. We continued past poorly lit graves built into the walls and massive stone tombs tucked into corners. An eerie feeling crept across my skin as we walked by the catacombs—a very different feeling from that of upstairs. The long hallway descended deeper and deeper underneath the cathedral.

At the very end of the dark hallway, Mrs. Quinn stopped at a small wooden door bearing a sign that read, *Record Room*. She pulled a thin blue rope out of the neckline of her shirt revealing an old key on the end. Mrs. Quinn unlocked the door and pushed it open with a creek. A cold and uninviting room complete with stone walls and a dirt floor lay in front of us. A dehumidifier hummed in the corner of the room, and an ancient rectangular wooden table sat in the middle.

"You have been granted thirty minutes. The records are to be kept in perfect order. Use the gloves." Mrs. Quinn pointed to a box in the corner of the room. "I'm very sorry to leave you, but I'm just so busy." Then she turned and slowly retreated back down the hallway, leaving us alone with hundreds of years of information. It was slightly odd that we were allowed to peruse these priceless records without a chaperone. My heart leapt slightly—somewhere in this room was very important morsels of information. Something perhaps Myers didn't want us to discover.

I turned toward Drew, not knowing where to start. He had already opened his tablet and was trying to access our notes. "These walls are thick, and it feels like we're halfway to hell. I

157

can't get much of a signal down here." Drew typed frantically onto the screen.

"I don't have any reception down here, either."

I studied the walls of books and had trouble discovering how they were organized. Counting quickly in my head I found there were thirty-two shelves, each with a colorful wooden coat of arms nailed to the top. There were no words or labels on any of the shelves, only numbers on the spines of each book.

"You don't suppose Mrs. Quinn would scuffle back down here to give us a quick orientation?"

Drew rolled his eyes. "You should have the graveling I had to do to get her to allow us down here in the first place." He dug a small grey device out of his jacket and lined it up on the table next to his tablet.

"What's that?"

"This little baby will piggyback off an Internet signal from miles away—even through these stone walls. I should be connected in seconds."

"Nice."

Drew took a picture of one of the crests with his phone and then sent it to his tablet. I pulled a random book, set it on the table, and started to page through it. I couldn't read a word; most of it was in Gaelic. I put it back and grabbed another book from the shelf on the adjacent wall. Nothing but Gaelic. My heart dropped as I realized this was a dead end. I snapped the book shut in frustration.

"How the hell are we supposed to figure this out, Drew?"

Without looking up from his computer he said, "These are the coats of arms of the thirty-two traditional shires of Ireland."

"Shires?"

"Counties, my friend." His eyes met mine. "Do you know which county Myers's ancestors were from?"

"I have no idea." I tried to hide it, but I was sure he could hear the disappointment in my voice.

"Can we look up Myers's county of origin in these books somehow?" Drew suggested.

"They're in Gaelic! Do you read Gaelic?" It came out laced with a little more sass than I had intended, but Drew didn't seem to notice.

"Not the slightest." He let out a few chuckles and then realized how serious I was. "Listen, this is just one setback. We've got the Internet and our arsenal of agency apps. I'm sure I can find a translator." He went back to his tablet. "Grab a book off the shelf and turn to the back. Is there an index?"

I did as he said, but couldn't find anything that looked like an index. I turned to a random page in the middle and picked a word. Drew translated it on his computer, and it turned out to be the word "farm." We thought we could tell which words were names and translated for a few more minutes, but in the end we knew our search would simply take too long this way.

I let out another frustrated sigh.

"We'll figure this out another way, I promise." Drew's eyes looked sincere, but still they didn't encourage me much.

"Fine. Let's get out of here."

Drew packed up his things, and hurried through the creepy cathedral basement. Mrs. Quinn was standing guard at the top of the steps. "Done so quickly, my dears?"

"I'm afraid the records weren't as helpful as we had hoped," Drew replied.

"Too bad," she said, not too sadly. Mrs. Quinn bid us good day as we passed a children's school group waiting near the front door.

On the cab ride back to the hotel I texted Agent Bowman to let him know about our dead end, and within a minute he had sent a reply—*Contact Agent McCombe for further suggestions. Don't give up too easily.*

After I showed Drew the text, he said with a smile, "Orders are orders. I better call her right away."

*　*　*　*

Agent McCombe agreed to meet us the next day for a pub lunch at some place called Buskers. Drew and I got up early and went for a jog through the Temple Bar neighborhood around our hotel before our meeting. It felt nice to burn off some steam and clear my head. I didn't know if it was because of the time change, but I hadn't slept well at all the night before, alternating between dreams of Ava and nightmares of Myers. As we ran I tried not to, but I wondered what Ava was doing that very second. I decided to call Adam later to check in.

Shortly after noon, Drew and I waited on the bumpy cobblestone sidewalk outside the bar. "Hello, boys," Agent McCombe greeted us as she approached from behind. Drew swung around, smiling a charming grin.

"Good morning, Agent McCombe." He spoke long drawn-out words and reached for her hand to shake.

"Please, call me Darcy." She smiled, looked him straight in the eyes, and pulsed her eyebrows quickly with a hint of flirt.

That little bugger. He broke her.

"Agent Hill, how are you?"

"Fine, thanks, Darcy."

Drew took the first step toward the door and opened it. He motioned for Darcy to head in. "Shall we go get a table? I've got a hankering for a pub lunch."

160

Darcy smiled at him as she entered, and then stood by the long mahogany bar for a few moments. She met eyes with the bartender, a redheaded local man.

"Darcy! How are you this lovely day, my dear?" The old man stopped wiping a glass with the bar rag and looked up at her.

"Wonderful, Liam. And you?"

"Not a care in my heart. I see you're here with company today. Will it be the usual table?"

"Please."

"It's all yours, dear."

"Many thanks. Could you bring us three Smithwick's and bowls of your pot roast Guinness stew please?"

"At your service." His head did a little bow.

"Best stew in Ireland," Darcy said as she led us past several patrons and to a quiet table at the back of the pub. Liam arrived with three tall glasses of beer before we could even settle into our places at the table.

When Liam walked away Darcy got right to business. "So, what have you discovered about Myers so far?"

"Unfortunately we don't have much to report. Our trip to the cathedral left us with nothing."

"Really? Absolutely nothing?"

"It seems our Gaelic isn't up to par, and without knowing his county of origin, we weren't able to narrow down any of the information." Drew took a long pull from his beer. "Ooh, that's good."

Darcy suggested we inquire at Eneclann, a well-respected genealogy and history research firm associated with nearby Trinity College. She asked Drew to call to set up an appointment, and although they were reluctant at first, they agreed, but requested a day for research. We were to meet on Sunday afternoon. It was killing me how long this was taking. I had been hoping we'd uncover all we needed in a matter of days and be back in Wisconsin by the end of the week.

Before Liam brought our stew, Darcy and Drew engaged in small talk while I shuffled through the pictures I had of Ava on my phone. My heart was flooded with memories of the way she looked and how sweetly she spoke. I missed her a great deal and would give anything to have her back in my life, to be the way we were last summer. My agony turned quickly to anger as I thought about the state of our relationship now.

Myers. Who was he to ruin what we had?

Drew poured on the charm, inducing laughter from Darcy and showing interest in her by asking personal questions. I was very quickly beginning to feel like the third wheel, and my heartache was about to explode, so I excused myself to the bar and sat in front of a pint for a while, watching people pass by the window.

Liam was wiping again, but stopped the old wet rag right in front of my beer. "If I've seen it once, I've seen it a thousand times before—heartache. It isn't young Darcy you're after, is it boy?"

"No, no. I've got a girl back home—or at least I used to."

That was depressing to say out loud.

"Ah, yes. Is she beautiful?" He looked at me with a gentle smile on his face.

"Incredibly."

He smile grew larger. "Is she funny—does she keep good company?"

"Without a doubt."

Liam leaned forward, placing his elbow on the bar and his chin on his upturned palm. His soulful eyes lit up to full power. "Is she good in the sack?"

I just about spit my mouthful of beer in Liam's face, but was able to recover and swallowed it. "Well…I…I…um…we…" I coughed, trying to cover the fact that the old man's question took me off guard and I was flustered.

"Just remember this, my son—The man who is worthwhile is the one who can smile when everything is dead wrong." He stared me deep in the eyes for several long seconds. "You're a good man. I can feel it in me bones. She'll find her way back to you."

"Thanks, Liam." But I wasn't so sure that could be true.

Liam got back to work, whistling an Irish tune and leaving me with my thoughts. After five more minutes I swiveled on my stool to check if Drew and Darcy were still flirting, and suddenly it felt like my heart stopped beating for a full three seconds. I grabbed my chest with my hand and stared at the sight in front of me, eyes wide in awe. It couldn't be. I was stuck frozen on my stool, ears flooded with the sound of my heartbeat.

Ava Gardner was in Ireland.

Panic added to my overly astonished state. Had Myers captured her and brought her here?

She was sitting with her back to me at a table with three other women about her age. I could see her familiar body type and her straight, brown hair. One girl said something funny and as soon as I heard the laugh I knew it was definitely her. I slowly slid off my chair, and with my jaw inevitably hanging to the floor, I willed my feet to move one in front of the other. A hummingbird was drumming inside my chest cavity as I cautiously approached the table.

You're not supposed to let her see you, my brain reminded me.

Shut up, my heart replied.

My feet continued to carry me forward as I wondered if she would even know who I was? Did she still have no memories of us?

I barely heard Drew call from a few tables over, "Nolan? What are you doing?"

163

I stopped right in front of the table, but Ava's back was still facing me. I swallowed a big lump of nerves hiding in my throat. One of Ava's friends noticed me. " 'Lo, boy. Can I help you with something?"

I couldn't find a voice inside me.

And then she turned around and stared right at me.

"Nolan? What the hell?"

I should have known.

"Hey, Laura," I tried to sound enthusiastic but I felt like a deflated balloon. It was Ava's sister. My heart was so desperate to have Ava's sweet face in front of mine at that moment, I felt like I might lose it right there in the bar.

I was still in a stupor when Laura stood up from the table and gave me a big hug. "What are you doing here?" She threw her hands up in the air and swung her head around looking for her sister. "Is Ava here?"

"Ava's not here. I'm sure she's in Stevens Point." As far as I knew, Laura had no idea what had happened with Ava's memory wipe. I didn't have a backstory ready so I answered with another question, "What are you doing here?"

"I'm studying abroad at Trinity College. It's just down the way!" She pointed out the window and then slid a hand through her hair. "I just can't believe I ran into you halfway around the world!"

"Yeah. Incredulous," It really was amazing that we would happen to meet in the same pub at the same time on the other side of the world, but I was still so disappointed I didn't have much enthusiasm behind my voice.

"Do you have a few minutes? We should share a pint!"

I accepted her invitation and returned to the bar to pick up my beer. Drew quickly got up from his table and slid into me like a giddy teenager. He half-whispered rapidly about an inch from my face. "Did you just pick up that hottie?"

I wiped Drew's spit from my forehead. "That hottie is Ava's sister, Laura," I whispered back.

"Shut. Up. Ava's sister?" He blatantly looked over at Laura and checked her out. She was chatting with her friends and not paying attention to us. "What the hell is she doing in Ireland?" He rubbed his hands together like an excited chipmunk.

"She's studying at Trinity. I thought I'd sit and chat with her awhile, so calm down."

"Take your time, Darcy and I are having a nice little conversation." He winked and I rolled my eyes.

"Oh, don't forget. You can't say anything about Ava's memory wipe. Remember, it's all classified."

"Yeah, I know." I glanced back at Laura. Her friends were getting up to leave the table. "I'll be careful."

"Good luck, buddy." Drew threw me a slap on the back and then quickly returned to Darcy. I took a long drag from my beer. Liquid courage.

Stop feeling so nervous, my heart instructed as I sat down at the table.

Laura spent the first several minutes rambling on about school in Ireland.

Say something about Ava, my heart shouted, *Is she doing alright?* But I played along, trying to be interested. As she spoke I studied her face. She had many of the same features that Ava did, but looked completely different at the same time. Visions of Ava floated above her head as she spoke. I kept in the conversation with my words, but in my head I was picturing myself sitting with Ava at the table.

"So Nolan, have you talked with my sister lately? I've been so busy since I moved over here that I haven't had time to call her and she isn't returning any of my emails."

She's not returning any emails to her sister?

"I figured she was busy studying to get into the School of Ed, anyway."

I lowered my voice since I didn't know who could be listening. "No. I haven't talked to her much since I've been training for the agency." I took a drink from my beer and swallowed a bit too loudly. "But I do know she's been busy with school."

Laura followed suit, lowering her voice almost to a whisper, too. "Oh right, the real FBI. I know Ava is happy for you being able to go through training, but I know she misses you terribly while you're gone."

"I miss her too, more than she will ever know." I stared out the window for a moment while I waited for my heart to stop aching.

"Oh, you are such a sweetheart. I'm so happy my sister found you. Don't you go messing it up with her now, you hear?" Then she laughed the same sweet laugh I heard Ava laugh many times.

Soon I realized it was torture and bliss at the same moment. Hearing Ava's voice and seeing her face through Laura's was both filling my heart with joy and ripping it apart with hopelessness.

"Since Ava is so busy with school and I don't want to be a distraction to her, my cousin Drew and I took a short vacation to Ireland before we have to return to work." I turned back toward Drew and Darcy and gave a wave. They were staring at us and waved awkwardly in return.

"Oh that's cool! Hey, how long will you be in town? My parents are flying out to visit in a few days. Apparently my dad's bank needs him to set up some new branches in Great Britain, and so my mom took some time off of school to come with. They thought they'd sneak in a visit with me while they are overseas. That would be cool if we could all go out to dinner or something."

Before I knew what I was saying, I agreed to dinner with Laura and her parents.

My brain loudly retorted, *What are you thinking? You don't have time to be social!*

Don't piss off your potential in-laws, my heart argued.

Laura's phone rang on the table so she checked the screen. "Oh, sorry Nolan but I've got to run." Then she looked at me the same way Ava did when she wanted me to know she was sincere. "It really was great running into you."

She dug a pen out of her purse and wrote her number on a napkin from the table. "Here, give me a call if you want to get together again while you're still in town."

Then she stood up from the table and I did the same. "Since Ava can't be here to give you a kiss, I guess you'll have to settle for one from another Gardner girl." For a quick second I thought she was about to lay one right on my lips, but she leaned forward and kissed me on both cheeks, true European style.

I took in a whiff of her hair and just about fell over. It smelled of coconuts—she must use the same shampoo as Ava.

I wished she were Ava. I wanted so badly to have Ava in my arms. I wanted to be the one to keep her safe from Myers. How could I be so defenseless in Ireland while she was back in the US unknowingly dodging Myers and recovering from brain surgery without me?

"Thanks, Laura. I appreciate it."

Then she turned and left, ringing the little bell above the wooden door. I stood there, staring out the door's window, wondering what had just happened to my heart.

Chapter Five

Drew and I had a day to waste while Eneclann did their research. He attempted to talk me into touring the best attractions in Dublin, but my heart wasn't in it. I felt obligated to be back at the hotel continuing my research, so I faked a headache and sat in the room sipping hot black coffee and Googling everything I could on the name Myers.

After almost an hour with no avail, I frustratingly shut the laptop and grunted, throwing my pen and blank pad of paper across the room. I had found absolutely nothing helpful. Bowman's suspicion that Myers's tech crew blocked content on the web must have been true. I stood up from my chair.

Come on, Nolan. There had to be a way to beat this evil villain.

I began to pace the room.

How's Ava doing? My heart wondered. *You should call her.*

I took my phone and found her name in the contacts. I stared at the screen, my finger hovering over the send button. I could pretend I was some survey company just to hear her voice.

Don't do it. Focus on Myers.

It took everything in me not to press that damn button, but I set the phone back down on the dresser and walked to the window. Would I ever be able to hold her close to me again, or would Myers be able to carry out his agenda?

"No!" I said aloud to no one. "I will defend her life even if I die trying."

The little black fuzzy box sitting on the desk caught my eye. I packed it in my luggage when I left Milwaukee a few days ago. Not that I intended to use it, but I couldn't leave it there. I took the diamond ring and held it up to the light streaming through the window. The prism sent beautiful sparkles of color all over the wall.

My heart ached. *Just like the sparkle in her eyes when the sun hit them just right.*

Stop! What are you thinking? Ava doesn't even know you're alive at this point. You could possibly never see her again, let alone be able to propose marriage to her.

I put the ring back in the box and threw it in my open suitcase on the floor.

I sat down on the chair again, opened my laptop, and took out a new document. I labeled it "Ethan Myers." The cursor sat at the end of the line blinking at me, waiting for me to write something. But we didn't have any more information, and at this point I wasn't sure we'd ever find any more. I wanted more than anything to search out whatever I needed to take down Myers, but how could I advance the next piece in the game when I didn't even know what game we were playing?

I snapped the laptop shut again and threw it on the bed. Then I let out a loud grunt filled with disappointment and defeat, and I kicked the bed, knocking down the contents of the bedside table. A glass lamp fell to the floor and broke. I let out another groan, more subdued, and sank to my knees, head in my hands.

Suddenly a knock on the door broke me from my desperate sense of failure. I jumped to my feet and went over to the door. Drew and Darcy were visible from the peephole. Why was she here so early in the morning? Drew moved in close, placing his hand on her hip and whispering something into her ear, his cheek intentionally brushing hers. She giggled and hit him playfully on the shoulder, whispering something in return that I couldn't make out.

Drew's attention went back to the door before him. "Nolan? You okay?" He called from outside my door, knocking again.

I slowly unlocked the door and opened it. "I'm fine, why?"

"We heard a crash." He plowed past me and surveyed the scene. "Have you got a girl in here playing naked pillow fight with ya?" His joking face quickly turned sour when he found the broken lamp. He turned toward me for an explanation.

"I knocked it off accidentally."

Darcy cut in before Drew could shame me. "No problem Nolan. Don't worry." She crossed the room and began to throw pieces into the garbage can near the desk. Why she was coming to my defense, I had no idea.

"It looks like you really need to get out of here. Darcy suggested we go take the Guinness factory tour. Why don't you call up Laura and have her meet us there?"

A factory tour? "I don't know, isn't there a better way to spend our time? I don't want to waste the day knowing I could be researching somehow."

"As much as you don't like it, Nolan, it seems you are somewhat at a standstill." Darcy had finished cleaning up the glass from the carpet. "Come take the tour. If you're in a better mood, you'll be able to think more clearly when we get some relevant information."

I took a deep breath. "Fine." Maybe being with Laura would help my mindset. If not her, then a few pints might do the trick.

Drew and Darcy headed toward the door. "Get yourself together and meet us in the lobby in twenty minutes." Then Drew stopped, just before he left the room, and turned toward me, looking me right in the eye. "We're gonna get him, Nolan. No doubt about that."

"Thanks, Drew." It was a good thing he had confidence because mine was as broken as the lamp that had smashed to the floor.

I let the door swing shut, and then entered the bathroom. My cell vibrated on the bedside table, buzzing the wood. I picked it up—Adam was calling.

"Adam. How's my girl?"

"She's doing well. I've been watching her from afar, and she seems to be able to go about her normal life."

"Are you confident in that? She just underwent major brain surgery. Perhaps you're not watching her closely enough."

"I'm working on it, Nolan. I can't just force myself into her life. I have to ease my way into it. You know, form a friendship with her so she feels comfortable letting me into her life a little."

"And how do you plan on forming this friendship with her?" I picked up some dirty clothes lying around the room and threw them into my open suitcase.

"Bowman's nephew is a Theta Sig and he was able to get me into the fraternity undercover as an exchange student. No one in the frat knows I'm not really a student except for Bowman's nephew."

"Nice cover." I took a pee and then flushed as I walked out of the bathroom.

"He made me cut my hair, though. He said I looked too old the other way."

"Darn! Those big blond curls looked good on you!" It was a bold-faced lie. Those curls were nasty.

"Yeah, sure, Hill," he laughed. "Oh, blimey, I almost forgot, you're a computer tech, right?"

"Not really, Drew's more—"

"I think we'll have to run a trace on Ava's cell. I'm concerned her mother might mention you in casual conversation and trigger a dangerous flashback within her brain."

I sat down on the bed. He was right. "When you hang up, call Bowman right away. We'll want the agency listening into all of her calls. If someone she talks to mentions me or anything about last summer, they'll have to terminate the call right away." A tiny stress headache was beginning to form behind my left eye and I rubbed my skull trying to invite relief. "They'll have to scan her emails, too."

"Right, right. I'll make sure the agency takes care of that. Thanks, Nolan."

Silence followed for a few seconds as I considered what Laura had said. Maybe the agency was already screening Ava's emails.

"So, how are things going with you two over in Ireland? Making any progress?"

"So far it's been pretty dry."

"Hang in there. You'll uncover something soon, I'm quite sure of it. Well, I better call Agent Bowman. Bye, Nolan."

I hung up and stared at my reflection in the mirror for a while. My mind placed a very beautiful brown-haired woman kneeling on the bed behind me. She ran her arms down the front of my chest and sensually kissed my neck. It was so real I could smell her scent lingering under my nose. I closed my eyes, taking in a deep breath, and then raised my hands to grab the ones resting on my chest, but nothing was there. My daydream quickly ended as reality set in around me.

I opened my eyes and picked up my phone, letting out a loud sigh. I found Laura's number in my contacts and stared at the phone for a while, grabbing some courage deep within me.

One hour later, Drew, Darcy, Laura, and I stood at the bottom of an escalator in the atrium of the Guinness storehouse. The world's largest pint glass rose up through the floors to the top of the building. Our tour guide, a local gal named Bridget, met us at the bottom and spouted out facts about one of the world's most favorite stout beers.

"Let's take the escalator to the second floor to begin your journey through the history of Guinness. Follow me, please."

"Thanks for texting, Nolan," Laura said as we rode up the escalator. "I'm glad I had my afternoon free. This is awesome!"

She craned her neck to see through the space in the middle of the building. Laura looked pretty with her hair pulled back in a loose ponytail and a dark green scarf nesting around her neck. She was wearing a tan jacket and jeans with tastefully furry brown boots.

"I don't think I've asked you, what are you studying while you are here in Ireland?"

"Russian Literature."

"Russian Lit? Why would—?" She cut me off, laughing.

"No, of course not!" Her laugh was identical to Ava's. "I'm studying stage management and technical theater."

"Really?" I liked how she teased me, just like Ava used to.

"Yes, really!" She furrowed her brow at me. "Does it not sound like something I would do?"

"No, no. It's just a career I don't hear too much about. I'm guessing you're interested in working backstage on a Broadway production?"

"Yeah, something like that." We were almost to the top of the escalator. "I love theater, but I don't have the talent or the guts to get up in front of a crowd. I find the inner workings of the backstage just as satisfying."

Ava would have no problem singing in front of a crowd. Her confidence in that category was unwavering.

"There is a tremendous amount of work that goes into a musical production—the audience usually has no idea."

We stepped off the escalator and assembled into a small group by a sign titled *Arthur Guinness, 1759, St. James Gate, Dublin.* A handsome old-time photograph of Mr. Guinness himself hung underneath.

After a quick explanation of who Mr. Guinness was and how he bought his brewery, the tour guide sent us through the four floors of exhibits, and we learned many facts about the history of this two-hundred-year-old stout beer.

The tour ended on the top floor of the factory at The Gravity Bar, a three-hundred-sixty-degree room high above Dublin with floor to ceiling windows facing a gorgeous view of the city. A handsome, circular wooden bar occupied the center of the room complete with a Guinness tap every few feet. We learned how to pour a perfect Guinness from a master barman, and then sat down at a table on the south side of the building.

"To life!" Laura raised her glass in the air.

"To life!" the rest of us echoed as we clinked our glasses.

Laura took a good chug of her beer and almost spit it out in Drew's face. "Oh my God! That is disgusting!"

The rest of us laughed as she took a napkin and tried to vigorously rub the beer residue from her tongue.

"Oh, come on, it's delicious!" Drew replied and I agreed.

Darcy took another sip, "I guess it's an acquired taste." She closed her eyes and made a quiet mmm sound. "Reminds me of Mama and Papa."

"Maybe you need another taste. Send it down the hatch one more time!" Drew pushed the glass closer to Laura's fingers, and we all laughed.

"Oh, jeez." Laura picked up the pint and drank the whole glass, pounding her fist down on the table, eyes shut tight. Then she slammed the glass onto the tabletop, let out a loud belch, and groaned.

I patted her on the back. "You're a good sport, Laura." She looked like she might vomit on the table. "Perhaps you need a more mature tongue. Mine adores Guinness completely."

"Then bring me another!" she called. "Maybe I need a few to really form my opinion."

Drew smiled and went to the bar to buy Laura another. Darcy and Laura chatted a little about Dublin, Laura asking the local for some advice on the best places to eat, shop, and visit.

When Drew returned, Laura chugged half the beer, scrunched up her faced a moaned.

She pushed her glass toward me, "Here, you drink the rest. I can't do it." I pulled her glass over to stand next to mine. "I'm going to hit the ladies room. Do you have to go, Darcy?"

"Sure," Darcy replied.

As the women got up I excused myself too, and headed past the bar over to a secluded section on the other side of the room. I wanted to look out the windows and be alone with my thoughts.

The view of the city's skyline went clear out to the Dublin Mountains bordering the town. I could see Phoenix Park to the west, one of Dublin's largest public park areas, and the rolling Irish Sea to the east. Printed on the glass window every few feet was a list of points of interest visible from that vantage point. Poking up throughout the red and grey brick rooftops were spires of cathedrals and castle bell towers.

This is magnificent, my heart expressed. *Ava would love the view.*

I missed her with every inch of my heart.

"I'm sure she misses you, too." A familiar and soothing voice rang in my ear. Laura was standing only a few inches behind me.

"I'm sure she does," I said quietly.

My brain retorted the painful truth: *Ava doesn't miss you at all.*

"Ava has never said a bad word about you. Even after what happened last summer." Laura moved over to my right side and stared out the window with me, shoulder touching mine. "She knows what a perfect catch you are."

"She's pretty wonderful, herself." My heart ached so intensely for Ava to be right in the moment with me. I longed to wrap my arms around her and stare out the windows over the beautiful foreign city together. I released a ragged breath as a lump collected in my throat.

No. No crying. My brain warned. *Especially not here.*

I swallowed hard.

"Nolan," she said sweetly.

A gentle hand turned my shoulder until I was facing Laura, only inches from her face. I looked into her eyes. I wanted so desperately to find a piece of Ava inside those eyes.

Then she lightly touched my cheek gently. My knees went weak and I closed my eyes, leaning into the palm of her hand. She let my face rest, cradled there while I pictured Ava's sweet skin next to mine. And then beyond all of our control, we both leaned in slowly at the same time, heads tilted. My heart beat madly as I felt her breath so close to my lips. We held our position for a few quiet seconds while I instinctively moved my hand onto her waist, pulling her hips a little closer. I involuntarily let out a breathy sound followed by the word, Ava, the second our lips touched.

"Oh! Oh, oh…Nolan! I'm so sorry." She backed away from me quickly. "I just…I'm so lonely here, and the beer…. Oh God! Please don't tell Ava!"

What the hell are you doing? My brain asked.

"No no no. I'm so sorry, Laura. It's just as much my fault." I took a few steps back. How could I have let this happen?

"Let's swear right here and now that no one will ever know about this." Laura's face was flush with embarrassment.

"Absolutely. I promise." My stomach felt tied up in knots.

"You know, I should probably find my way back to campus now." Laura reached into her purse and grabbed her cell, checking the screen. Her eyebrows scrunched up in confusion for several seconds and then she shook her head as she replaced her phone back into her purse. "Well, thanks for…well, I mean…I'll see you around, Nolan." Then she turned and left before I could apologize again.

I let out a huge sigh.

You idiot! my brain scolded.

You miss Ava, my heart explained. *You just want her here with you.*

Chapter Six

Right after a quick pub lunch, Drew and I walked the few blocks to Trinity College. We entered through an old wrought iron gate off of College Green. A tall building of smooth grey stone stood before us. The sidewalk led to two oversized, wooden doors offering entrance to the university. There was very little activity on campus this early; the college kids were inevitably still sleeping.

We walked through an ancient stone tunnel and emerged in a colorful courtyard. Signs led us across grey cobblestone walkways, through beautiful gardens, and over Fellows' Square until we came to The Old Library. The Old Library was home to the lavishly decorated Book of Kells, a ninth-century gospel manuscript on display for tourists and locals alike. Housed in the building were also the offices of Eneclann.

We were greeted by a woman sitting at an oversized mahogany desk. The burnt orange wall behind her was softly up-lit from the floor and displayed a large, antique-looking map.

"May I help you lads?" Glasses hung from a green string and rested on her low hanging bosoms. Her stark white hair was pulled up into a bun, stray pieces escaping around her wrinkled face.

"Yes. I'm Drew Smith. I believe you are expecting us?" There was no one else in the lobby; in fact it was oddly quiet.

"Yes. Brynn is waiting for you in meeting room 10B. Just follow the hall."

The building had obviously been remodeled—the inside was very modern looking with sleek lighting and smooth, long lines. We walked down the quiet hallway past several doors and windows looking into a series of meeting rooms, all with no lights on. I had an eerie feeling; it seemed like there should be more people around. One room had its light on farther down— room 10B.

Upon entering we were greeted by a middle-aged, mousy woman. She had pale white skin and wildly wavy hair. Brynn got right to business. "Hello, gentlemen. Welcome to Eneclann, please have a seat. Agent McCombe has alerted me to your inquiry. In preparation for our meeting I have made a few guesses at the origin of the name you are researching."

We took a seat at the oval table in the middle of the room. Brynn put on gloves and opened a timeworn book. A silver laptop lay beside the book and a small cup of tea on a flower-patterned saucer was off to the side.

"We are looking for the place of origin of the surname Myers." I spelled it out for her. "We also have interest in identifying where two specific Myers could have lived in the time period of the late 1800s to about 1950."

"Yes. I was able to find record in our archives of several Mayers families in County Kerry in the mid 19th century, but haven't found the spelling M-y-e-r-s anywhere in my research. Is it possible Mayers is the name you are looking for?"

She slid the book over for us to see the page with dates and addresses of several Mayers families. "This man goes by the name Myers now."

I noticed a strange handwritten insignia in the margin near the names.

"Is it possible the family changed their name upon coming to America in the early 1900s?" Drew questioned her.

"Entirely possible," Brynn checked her computer. "I also found some other possible spellings of Myers—Meyers and Myars." I put the spellings into my phone for the time being.

Brynn pulled over another old book that was sitting on the table and opened to a marked page near the middle. "I decided to dig a little deeper and found an old Celtic spelling of Myers in this manuscript. It is spelled Ó Meidhir, which seems to come from a Scottish or English origin, probably deriving from a word meaning 'physician.'"

"That's it!" I knew deep in my heart—Ethan Myers's ancestors had to have been Ó Meidhirs.

Brynn shot me a strange look, but continued on. "Unfortunately I wasn't able to find much more about the family Ó Meidhir through my research. You'd have to go to a local primary source to dig up any more information."

"County Kerry you say?" Drew was taking notes on his tablet.

"Yes. I'd be happy to email you a report of my research findings if you'd like."

"That'd be perfect, thank you." Drew exchanged email addresses with Brynn and then she hastily stood up. We stood and shook her hand, thanking her for her research, and then Brynn left the room quickly, taking the books with her.

"There is something very odd about that broad." He stuck his head out the door and glanced down the hallway.

"We're off to County Kerry!" I was so excited to uncover some useful information and finally move forward in our search. I took my cell phone off the table and checked the screen—*no new messages*—and then took a few steps toward the wall, turning the lights off.

"Hold your roll, kid. We'll have to disclose this information to Agent Bowman first and see what he recommends as our next move. He may want us to go back to St. Patrick's now that we've discovered the Gaelic spelling and shire of origin."

I knew he was right; I just didn't want to hear it. But before I could protest, a faint electronic spit from behind Drew sent my world moving in slow motion. The glass wall behind the table shattered as shots came whizzing by my head. Drew and I hit the floor instinctively. I immediately pulled the Glock from my belt and crawled to the wall. I stood up and shot into the direction of the shooter, with the doorjamb as a shield. Drew crawled past me and hung slightly out the door where he had a better vantage point. He shot twice from the floor and then retreated and waited.

I paused, trying to listen past the heartbeat in my ears. Who the hell was shooting at us? Could Myers know we were here?

The shooting stopped suddenly and a strange alarm sounded. Then over an intercom, a friendly female Irish voice rang out over campus: "Attention all students, employees, and visitors of Trinity College. There is a dangerous intruder on campus. Please follow Emergency Code Ten procedures immediately."

We stood frozen for a few seconds and then carefully ran down the hallway in the direction of the shooter. We jumped over damaged furniture and broken glass, but no more shots were fired. At the end of the hallway we found Brynn lying on the floor, a single bullet hole between her shocked, open eyes. The books she had shown us lay next to her, pages ripped out. We walked over her body and into the lobby only to find the secretary awkwardly slumped over onto the desk.

Drew checked her pulse. "This was no accident. Someone was trying to prevent us from getting this information." He craned his head around, checking for signs of the intruder.

"It's gotta be Myers." I spotted a red exit sign leading the way out the backdoor. "Come on, we need to get out of here before the police arrive. I don't want to stand here and answer questions when we could be getting closer to stopping Myers."

We stealthily ran through the seemingly deserted campus, staying close to the buildings and not running through the open areas. We didn't want to be mistaken for the "possibly dangerous intruder." I thought about Laura and if she was in danger, but I had no idea where she was staying and didn't have time to find out. We jumped a fence and made it out to the street just in time to catch a cab right outside of campus. We paid the driver an extra twenty Euros to get us out of there as quick as he could.

On the cab ride to The Arlington, Drew texted Agent McCombe—*We've been sabotaged. Meet us at The Arlington ASAP.* A second later I heard Drew's text message alert respond. "She'll be there when we arrive," he said. "I'm calling Bowman."

"I've got a bad feeling about this. If Myers knows we're actively researching, he'll likely retaliate and go after Ava." I calculated it was about nine in the morning in Wisconsin, so I dialed Adam's number.

"Good day, Nolan!"

"When's the last time you've seen Ava?" I snapped. No time for niceties.

"Late yesterday. She's just fine, Nolan, relax a bit."

My blood began to boil. Why did he have to be so condescending?

"Shut up, and listen to me, Adam. We've just been shot at and I'm fairly confident Myers may be in pursuit of Ava now that he knows we are digging through his past. Get to her now and do not let her out of your sight all day."

"Really? Okay, hold on. I installed a GPS program on her phone so I know where she is at all times." I could hear typing on a computer. "Looks like she's at Iverson Park. I'll find her and stay with her today."

The cab pulled up in front of The Arlington and Drew threw some money at the driver while still talking with Bowman. As I stepped out of the cab, I finished my conversation with Adam. "Check in with me later, even if it's the middle of the night here. I need to know she's safe."

"Fine. Bye."

As we walked through the front doors, Agent McCombe approached us from the lobby. We explained what happened as she swiftly led us around the lobby elevators and through a fire exit.

"Myers knows someone is burrowing into his family tree and he is not happy about it." She led us down a flight of stairs and along a stark basement hallway. "We're sure he sent someone to destroy the information you found in the Old Library." She pushed through a door labeled *Boiler Room* and charged between some chugging black metal machines that seemed older than Ireland itself.

Drew and he looked as surprised as I felt.

"We're pretty sure Myers had your tablets and phones scrambled while you were on campus." She took a sharp right at the back of the boiler room, and punched in a seven-digit code on a box to the right of a steel door around the corner. I took my cell phone out of my pocket and started poking around the menu.

No, no...no! All the pictures of Ava were wiped!

"What do you mean, 'we're pretty sure'?" I asked her as the box at the door spoke—"Access granted, Agent McCombe"—and it cracked open.

She turned toward me before opening the big, heavy door all the way. "Irish Intelligence, of course. We've been following your every move since you arrived."

Drew's eyebrows scrunched up and he mouthed, *Following us?*

My pocket vibrated. I was a text from an unknown number—*Found her running at the park. Will stay with her until I get word from you.* It was Adam. My contacts were empty, thanks to Myers, so I added his number in.

I followed Drew through the door Agent McCombe was holding open. We were submerged into an opulent, futuristic room filled with a dozen people in black suits. It was dim, only lit by blue lights around the perimeter of the ceiling. A curved grey desk faced a humongous, yet invisible computer screen that took up most of the south-facing wall. Computerized images floated above the desk and workers touched midair, manipulating maps and graphics. They typed into keyboards that lit up on the glass desk in front of them.

How many hundreds of unsuspecting tourists slept while this whole operation conducted business under their heads?

A tall man approached us, his eyebrows expressing his probably grumpy disposition. He held out his hand and greeted us glumly. "Agent Hill, Agent Smith, I am Agent Aeden Kane, commander of this office." His short brown hair and prominent freckles reminded me of a childhood friend I once knew. "Follow me." Agent Kane turned and led us into a conference room, Agent McCombe close behind.

"Please, take a seat." Agent Kane switched on an image that projected from the middle of the glass table onto the air above it. "Ethan Myers has recently become somewhat of a concern to the IIA." A picture of him flashed in front of us, and my stomach instantly twisted.

"Yesterday a young woman was found dead under, let's just say, odd circumstances." He flashed a picture from the morgue. The brown haired woman was missing the entire left side of her skull, exposing a mutilated brain. "Evidence has forced us to consider the proposition that her death is associated with Ethan Myers."

Why would Ethan be after a young Irish woman? Could she be in connection with Myers's family?

"Very recently we joined forces with the FBI as a result of our concern regarding what Myers's endgame might be." He pushed a button on a remote and a new image appeared showing several faces, all named. I took a deep breath when I noticed

Ava's picture among the others. I counted quickly in my head—ten.

"These are the faces of women who Myers has either killed or captured in the last year. They are all Americans except for this last woman, Emilee Brady. Our research scientists have desperately been trying to decipher the connection between them all, but so far have been unsuccessful."

Agent Kane switched the screen to a map of Ireland's counties. "Our explorative geneticists have discovered the alternate spellings of Myers and the connection with a family in County Kerry."

Drew looked at Darcy. "You already knew?" I could hear the anger behind Drew's voice as he pounded his fist down on the table. "Then why send us on this wild goose chase?"

I was thinking the same thing.

"You could say there's a little bad blood between Eneclann and IIA," Agent McCombe replied smugly. "Apparently they don't appreciate the federal government digging into their precious files."

I stood from my chair and leaned forward over the table. "My girlfriend is one of his victims! I don't have time to screw around, wasting time!"

"Calm yourself, Agent Hill. The IIA and the FBI have the same objectives. I believe we can work together here."

"Agent Kane is right. There is still much to do, and we could use your help." Darcy tried to catch Drew's eye, but he did not return her glance.

After several seconds of silence, Drew answered like a kid finally agreeing to his parents' terms. "Fine, as long as we are privy to the same intel, I suppose Agent Bowman would expect us to cooperate."

Drew finally peeked at Darcy, but his expression was not pleasant.

"Great," Agent Kane replied. Then he turned to the screen and continued his speech. "The IIA has been investigating a strange and rare phenomenon affecting Irish citizens for the past several decades, and we now have reason to believe it could have ties with Mr. Myers."

Suddenly, a young man in a suit poked his head into the conference room. "Excuse me, sir. We have Agent Bowman."

"Perfect. Thank you, Agent Flynn." The man left the room and Agent Kane pressed a few buttons on the computer built into the glass table. Agent Bowman's face showed on several screens around the room as an image projected above the middle of the table. I heard his voice over the speakers built into the walls and ceiling.

Bowman pushed up his glasses with one finger. "Good day, Agent Kane. Agent Hill, Agent Smith. Nice to see you all."

"Hello, Agent Bowman. Thank you for calling. May I introduce Agent Darcy McCombe. She's been acting as liaison for your agents while they have been in town."

"Nice to meet you, sir," Darcy said.

"You as well, Agent McCombe."

"Agent Bowman, what progress has the FBI made since we've spoke last?"

"We know Ethan Myers is interested in genetic mutations and diseases treated with gene-based medicine, but unfortunately his research and lab was destroyed when we blew up the CBB headquarters in Milwaukee."

"We blew it up?" I yelled at the computer screen. Agent McCombe shot me a rude look.

"Yes. Thirty minutes after you and Agent Smith exited that day, our team hit an invisible detonator and the building exploded, including all the records inside it."

"So we have nothing?"

"Not necessarily, Agent Hill. Myers would never risk ruining his invaluable collection of data. We simply need to locate his auxiliary cache. Meanwhile, our research team and genetic scientists have been studying types of induced gene mutation and their repercussions. We're making some good advances and we suspect our mole on the inside will be bringing us the information we need to proceed even further."

"You've got a man on the inside?" Drew asked.

"We have a double agent playing for both Myers and the FBI. So far the double has provided several important bits of intelligence, including the whereabouts of Myers's current refuge and research facility."

"What about Ava?" Drew asked. "Is she considered safe, or does Intel believe Myers will go after her?"

"All our intel indicates she is currently secure. We'd like Agent Greene to continue watching over her, of course, but we have reason to believe she is in no immediate danger."

I let out an audible sigh of relief. "I'll text Adam and let him know." *Bowman says no immediate danger. You can back off.* Was that too pushy? I didn't care. I put the phone back on the table in front of me and tried to listen, but my mind was filled with thoughts of Ava. They discussed something about a cure, the vulnerability of the blue meteor, and the November first deadline.

Darcy whispered into Drew's ear, her hand on his shoulder. He was smiling.

Agent Bowman addressed Drew and me. "Agents, it is imperative that you unearth the motives behind Myers's obsession with genetic engineering. Find out specifically what Myers's grandfather, Dr. Ó Meidhir, discovered through his medical practice."

"We're sending you to the quaint city of Killarney in County Kerry," Agent Kane added.

Finally, a little progress. "When do we leave?"

"In the morning. Now you two go up to your rooms and get some rest. It looks like your journey here in the Emerald Isle isn't over yet."

"We're happy to stay as long as you'll have us." Drew glanced over toward Darcy, and she smiled confidently.

"Good luck, agents. I will be in touch." Agent Bowman disappeared from above the table as the screens turned black.

Agent Kane opened the door to the conference room. He led us past the busy agents and to the door to the boiler room.

"It was nice meeting you, boys. I wish you the luck of the Irish on your next task. So long!"

"Thank you," Drew and I replied.

Darcy led us back through the basement boiler room and to the lobby elevators where we rode to the fourth floor. I thought for a short second that I caught them holding hands. We walked down the hallway and they paused near Drew's hotel room door.

"So…Darcy thought she should stick around here for dinner in case we need to consult her for anything. Did you want to join us?" Drew was giving me an eye message—it was obvious he didn't want me to join them for dinner, but felt obligated to ask.

"No thanks, I'll just order in. You two have fun. I'll see you in the morning."

"The Arlington has great room service, Nolan."

"Thanks, Darcy," I said, unlocking my room. I closed the door and peeked through the peephole. Drew kissed Darcy in the hallway, and then she opened the door to his hotel room and pulled him in by his shirt collar, giggling.

I sighed and slid my room key into the little white box on the wall so that the lights would turn on—a trick that took me almost thirty minutes to figure out my first night in Ireland. My cell buzzed. It was Adam.

"Nolan." There was anxiety in his voice.

"What's wrong, Adam?" My heart rate began to sputter. "Is Ava okay?" There was a long pause. "Adam!"

His voice was quiet and calm, but there was still something disturbing about it. "No, she's safe at home. I just dropped her off and am sitting in my car around the corner with an eye on her front door."

"So? What's the problem?" I sat down on the chair by the window and leaned back.

"I don't know how, Nolan, but I think...I think he saw me with Ava."

"Who? Myers? Impossible." I sat forward and put my elbows on my knees, my mind thinking. "Where do you think he is? Did you see him?"

"Well, not exactly, but a dark car pulled out right behind me today and followed us for several blocks until I was able to lose it."

I gave a little half laugh under my breath. That's what was so upsetting?

"That could have been anyone! Look, I'm sure Bowman has good reason to believe Ava is safe."

"I guess." Then he said something under his breath. "I just hope Myers doesn't know I'm here—I mean, Ava's here," There was a pause in which neither of us knew what to say until he said, "Oh, and there's something else."

I stood up from my chair and stared through the window out over glorious Dublin. Nervous butterflies were sneaking up on me again. "What's wrong?"

"I'm slightly concerned about Ava's health. She's experiencing environmentally induced blackouts coupled with severe pain and confusion."

"And what does that all mean?"

"Well, basically events from Ava's daily life trigger a vision within her brain from the time period which I thought had been erased."

"How could that be?" A tiny glimmer of hope swelled inside me—maybe they didn't erase all her memories of us!

"The brain houses carbon copy imprints of memories. Ava's visions are these imprints but her brain is confused because it has no actual memories to attach the visions to. I'm afraid these painful blackouts may begin to disintegrate parts of her brain and if not stopped, she could suffer from permanent brain damage."

The River Liffey sparkled with sunlight outside my window, and in contrast, my heart felt like it was blackened and dull. My poor Ava was suffering, and I couldn't be there to help her through it.

"What do we do? We have to discontinue these visions."

"I've been emailing one of my colleagues in London and searching all my medical journals."

"And?" I tapped the window with my finger.

"And I haven't found an answer yet, but I know I will. Have faith in me, Nolan."

Faith was something I had been lacking lately.

"Perhaps the reversal procedure may have to take place sooner than we had thought. You two better hurry up and catch Myers before he can decide he wants Ava in his lab immediately."

"Just take care of her. Keep her safe until I can come back to her."

"I will, Nolan. I promise."

Chapter Seven

Darcy came to see us off the next morning wearing her routine skirt suit and two-inch heels. She stood on the street curb leaning onto the passenger side door of a metallic blue BMW Z4 Roadster.

"Hot ride, Darcy," I called, wondering how she got her hands on such a fancy car.

"Woo!" Drew hooted as he dropped his suitcase on the sidewalk and scooped up Darcy, swinging her around. "Yes! This is it?"

"What?" I asked as I picked up Drew's bag and brought it closer to Darcy and him.

"The IIA has issued you this junker to drive across the country to County Kerry. I hope she'll do."

"Sweet," I said, eyes wide.

"There is a GPS unit installed into the dash and I've taken the liberty of programming a trip map for you. In the accommodations screen is the hotel information for when you get to Killarney."

"Thanks for your help, Darcy. It was a pleasure working with you." I shook her hand and then opened the passenger side door. Once inside I could see Darcy and Drew kissing outside the window. I wondered just how attached Drew had become in the short week we were here. A soft mumbling of their voices filled my ears, and I painfully remembered the last farewell I said to Ava.

Several minutes later the door opened and Drew slid in. He sat still for a moment, keys on his lap, and let out a loud sigh. Then he said with little enthusiasm, "Let's do this." He started the ignition, slid the shifter into drive, and pulled out into traffic, leaving Darcy waving on the sidewalk.

"You'll be back for her." Then the thought hit me that we'd both be suffering from a broken heart on our journey to County Kerry.

*   *   *   *

The trip across Ireland was absolutely amazing. We spent four hours driving on rolling roads through lush green mountains that towered over small crystal clear lakes with little colorful rowboats waiting at the rocky shorelines. We passed many beautiful country farms with white, fluffy sheep grazing on the grassy hillsides around ancient grey stone fences marking territories. I'd only once before seen scenery so spectacular and that was in Wisconsin Dells.

Right outside of Limerick we took the N21 southwest into Killarney. I noticed a beautiful mountain out in the distance, and put on my best Irish accent. "According to this website, that mountain is Carrauntoohill, Ireland's highest mountain." Drew laughed at my obviously murdered pronunciation of the mountain. I continued, speaking louder as a protest to his poking fun. "At the base of the mountain sits the majestic Lakes of Killarney: Lough Lea, Muckross Lough, and nearby Lough Guitane."

Drew's laughter had settled into a breathy giggle. "You are a wealth of knowledge, my friend, but you better stop there before you find your end." He smiled through the windshield, humming a tune.

"Another song rolling around your brain?"

"Roger Doger. There's always a tune floatin' around my noggin." He hummed a few more notes until the voice on the GPS interrupted, telling him to turn. Drew followed the N22 to

Port Road—a local hint from Darcy to avoid one-way streets. We followed along the Killarney National Forest and then drove into the quaint village of Killarney.

The FBI had booked us two rooms at the handsome Killarney Randles Court Hotel. We parked the car and then took our suitcases up the stairs to the front entrance. The white-walled lobby was very fancy. Two fireplaces sat on either side of the room and very expensive looking oversized artwork hung on the other walls. Red velvet chairs were clustered in fours around mahogany tables under crystal chandeliers. Exorbitant collections of fresh flowers filled the room with an air of high society.

We approached the pleasant-looking lady at the front desk and she directed us to our rooms on the second floor, wishing us a restful stay. Upstairs we stopped in the hallway between our rooms. Drew twisted his torso to crack his back before he stuck his key card in the door. "Man, I could use a visit to the ol' chiropractor." Then a thought hit him and his eyes lit up from the inside. "Oh my God. Did I ever tell you about my gorgeous chiropractor?"

I shook my head.

Drew opened his door and set his bag in the way to hold the door open. "She was smokin' hot so I faked some back pain so she could lay her sweet hands on my skin twice a week."

Drew jumped to a new level in my book. Faking back pain to get touched by a doctor?

"She was totally into me, too. I just knew the way she smiled her cute little pink lips at me. Anyway, our sessions were awesome. She mixed in a little massage with her chiro junk and God, she knew exactly how to put me right into a state of pure relaxation, right?"

"Seriously, Drew?"

"So this one time," he went on, ignoring me, "I was lying on the table half naked while Dr. Hottie was cracking my back and

193

everything was going just fine until she put the perfect amount of pressure directly between the T10 and T11 and...I farted."

I burst out laughing, and Drew continued his story, talking over me.

"Oh jeez, it smelled like week-old raunchy egg salad in that little room, but she went right on working! Dr. Hottie didn't even crack a smile! It's like there really is a genuine gas button right between the T10 and T11!"

"Oh my God, Drew."

Then he slapped his hand on my lower back and said, "Come here. Let me see if I can find the fart button!"

I pushed Drew back into the wall. "Knock it off! You are no Doctor Hottie!"

Drew laughed and then picked up his bag and let out an overly obnoxious yawn. "I need a nap from that long drive." He walked through the door and then stuck his head out for one more comment. "After a few winks let's hit the pub I saw down the street for supper."

"See you in a few hours." I opened the door to my room just as Drew's started to close.

The guest rooms were just as lavish as the lobby. When I used the bathroom I noticed heated marble floors, and when I slid under the bed sheets I felt the softest linens I had ever touched. What I wouldn't give to have Ava with me enjoying this beautiful country and comfortable hotel.

My sleep wasn't very restful—I dreamt of Ava kissing another man in a vast, dark room filled with masked people. I woke up feeling delusional, heartbroken, and tired, but more motivated to get started on our research than I had felt since the trip had started.

At the pub that night we read the mission documents Bowman had sent us and discussed our plan. We knew church archives, graveyards, and public records would be the first places to search. We needed to find Myers's relatives and figure out what prompted Myers to become the person he is.

Doubt was looming in the back of my mind. Our quest to find knowledge wouldn't be too easy.

*   *   *   *

Tuesday, October 21st

Drew checked online and found nine churches in town, but decided to take us to St. Mary's Church of Ireland since it looked the oldest and probably had the largest source of records. The clergy agreed to meet us late morning.

The church looked like it had been occupying that green patch of grass for several hundred years. The front doors were comprised of ancient wood with two circular iron door handles.

"Should we knock?" I asked as we approached.

"I don't think so. Let's just go on in." Drew lifted one of the metal rings and pulled open the heavy door. It creaked in protest as it swung open into a cozy nave which opened into a large sanctuary.

"Hello?" He called as we walked into the cold, open space. His voice echoed over the pews.

We wandered past a few rows, but there was still no sign of anyone. "Hello?" I repeated.

"Can I help you, gentleman?" A quiet and peaceful voice spoke behind us. We turned around to see an old greying man wearing a brown robe enter the sanctuary.

"Yes, hello there. My cousin and I are researching the history of certain Irish surnames and suspect your church may have some helpful information for us. We were wondering if you'd be kind enough to share some of your church records."

The old man agreed to take us to the record room. We found books after books on shelves lining walls much like the basement room at St. Patrick's.

"We are looking for information about a family with the last name Ó Meidhir." The old man gave me a perplexed look. Maybe my Gaelic wasn't up to snuff. I wrote the name down on a piece of paper and handed it over.

"Ah, Ó Meidhir. You wouldn't be speaking of Alec and Lara Ó Meidhir, would you?" The old man walked over to the shelf without waiting for my reply.

"Possibly. Do you know them?" My heartbeat began to speed up. Could this be the break we needed?

He set an old dusty book onto the table in front of us and began to page through it as he spoke. "My father was a parishioner at this church for many years before me. He became good friends with Alec and his family, who were active congregation members long ago. Alec was the local physician in town and was well known for his research medicine."

"What exactly do you mean, 'research medicine'?" I took out my tablet, ready to take notes.

"In the early twentieth century, several townsfolk were suffering from unusual and unexplained symptoms. Some even progressed to extremely violent behaviors. Word floated through town that Dr. Alec kept a medical study on his patients' digressions. He spent his life dedicated to solving the medical mystery surrounding these poor people."

If this man was a friend of Myers's ancestors, it's possible he was still in touch with Myers and we wouldn't want to say too much in front of him.

"That sounds interesting. Do you have any more information about these strange symptoms?"

"The answer is always in a book." The old man flipped through until he finally found the page he was looking for.

196

"Here." He pressed his finger to the page. "Our records indicate that Alec, Lara, and their only child, a boy named Clennan, lived on Pluckett Street in an apartment above Dr. Ó Meidhir's office." He looked up from the text. "I believe the office still stands and is property of family members." He looked down again. "This says Alec went to our Lord in 1933, only two years after little Clennan was born."

"Does it indicate his cause of death?" Drew tried to peek at the open page in the book but the old man noticed and pulled the book closer to himself, running his fingers down the page.

"This book does not list a cause of death, although if I remember correctly, he did not pass of natural causes."

Drew was onto the next question before I could ask the old man more about his last statement. "What about the strange symptoms the people of Killarney were suffering from? Do you perhaps have additional information about that?"

He looked nervous and paused for a second before answering. "There isn't anything written down about that, young man. Dr. Ó Meidhir wouldn't allow it." The old man started to get fidgety, like he was saying too much.

"He wouldn't allow anyone to keep track of their symptoms?" There was something fishy about this story. Perhaps the old man was going senile. Could we really trust anything he was saying?

Drew and I waited for the man to answer my question, but he stood staring at the wall, silent.

"Well, cousin," Drew slapped me on the back. "I guess we are at a dead end here. Poor Grandma will cry tears."

The old man jerked to life, "I suppose I would be dishonest if I said my knowledge of this topic ended there." He leaned forward and lowered his voice to a loud whisper. "My father told me the story many times. You see, all this took place ten years after the meteor shower of 1901. Some of the residents of

197

Killarney began experiencing strange and unexplainable symptoms."

"A meteor shower?" I whispered.

Why were we whispering?

"Yes. The gates of heaven itself opened up and dropped colorful rocks from the Promised Land onto the earth."

"Rocks from space?"

This couldn't be a coincidence. I remembered my visit to Hayward Kubas at the campsite in the Dells and how I thought he was crazy at the time.

The old man continued with careful caution. "These weren't any ordinary, run-of-the-mill rocks, boys. They were glowing blue with purple blaze and they fell from the sky with great abundance." His intensity turned up as he continued sharing his secret. "Cottage roofs were damaged and vegetation caught fire. Mass panic and confusion ensued as the people of Killarney thought the end of the earth was near." He stopped to take several deep breaths. Drew and I thought he was finished, but he started up again. "Once the storm settled, everyone in town picked up several meteors as curious keepsakes of that horrible night."

"Wow," Drew commented.

"For years after, Alec concocted very strange remedies to relieve the headaches and violent mood swings in his patients that he thought were associated with exposure to the space rocks. Soon some of the members of the community began to think Dr. Ó Meidhir was going insane and convinced local officials to revoke his medical license. Finally, Alec made a newspaper announcement indicating his office was closed to the public, and then began privately and secretly treating his patients."

"Wow," Drew said again.

"But what happened to him?" I inquired. "To his patients?"

"I haven't a clue. That's where my father's story always ended." He closed the book and placed it back on the shelf. "I do know that our Lord took Dr. Ó Meidhir when he was—" he calculated in his mind "—thirty four years of age, leaving behind a young child and a journal full of research."

I needed to get my hands on that book.

I carefully crafted my words. "What an important piece of medical history. Do you know what happened to that journal?"

"Last I knew it was lost in the family archives."

I hoped Myers held it secure in a secret safe in his temporary office and not in the CBB building that we had blown up. I decided not to press the issue with the old man on account of him acting so skittish.

"Thank you for this information. I know this will help us with our research." Drew and I turned to leave the book room when the old man grabbed my forearm forcefully with his weathered, wrinkled fingers. He looked me straight in the eye and his voice dropped into a frightening tone. "I'd be careful if I were you. Some people don't like the skeletons in their closet rattled."

I felt a chill down in my bones. "Uhh...thanks. That's good advice." But he didn't let go of my arm right away. I tried to gently shake it loose, but the bony fingers held tight. I looked at Drew for help.

"Right, well, we should be going. Thank you, sir." He grabbed my other arm and pulled me in the direction of the door. The old man finally loosened his grip, and I left the room perplexed.

Neither of us said anything until we reached the car, got in, and slammed the doors shut.

"What the hell was that?" we both said in tandem. Drew laughed, but I felt too weirded out by the old codger and couldn't join in. I knew Myers was nothing to mess around with, but could that elderly clergy actually be afraid of the ghosts of Myers's ancestors?

Drew and I decided to try to find Pluckett Street and search out the site of Dr. Alec's old office. The in-dash GPS took us right downtown and over to Pluckett easily. Several scummy, two-story stucco buildings with dark brown shingles stood in a row down the block. Each house looked exactly the same except for their worn-out colors: cream, canary yellow, hunter green, or light grey.

As if someone was looking over our shoulders guiding us, we came upon a building with a wooden carved sign hanging from two rusty chains above the front door. It was quite worn, but we could read it: *Dr. Alec Ó Meidhir, Medical Physician.* The place looked run down and possibly even abandoned.

Drew slowed the car and stopped just past the house. "Well hot damn, here we are. We should go knock."

"I was thinking the same thing."

Drew turned off the car and reached below his seat for his Glock. "You never know what we'll find in there." I knew he was right, so I reached into the glove compartment and retrieved two flashlights.

"Let's get the journal and get the hell outta there," Drew advised as he reached over and grabbed one of the flashlights from me.

"Deal," I agreed.

Drew knocked on the wooden door and we waited, but heard nothing.

"Hello?" he called. "Anyone home?"

I looked up and down the street. There was no sign of life anywhere, and not even a car had passed on the street since we parked in front of the house.

"Let's check the back," I quietly suggested.

There was a small patch of grass behind four rotted wooden stairs leading up to a back door. Drew climbed the stairs and knocked on the back door. It swung inward with the force of his knock, creaking the whole way. "Well, Agent Hill, I think the luck of the Irish is on our side today." Drew smiled as he pushed the door open further and called into the house. There was still no answer. "In we go!" he sang, and disappeared into the house before I could protest.

I anxiously followed into a very old and dirty kitchen with filthy wooden floorboards, dusty furniture, and a nasty smell that could only be described as stale death. I wrinkled up my nose and whispered to Drew, "Go toward the front of the house; look for something that could be an office." Apparently it was empty, but we held our guns at the ready position anyway and shone our flashlights straight ahead.

There were no lights on in the house, and the curtains had all been pulled closed. Our feet creaked as we shuffled across the floorboards through a dark living room, and into another at the front of the house. A long wooden table sat along one wall, and a desk and antique bookshelf were pushed into the corner. It had to be the office.

Drew approached the bookshelf and scanned the spines as I opened the drawers in the desk. There were pens, papers, and a blank prescription pad, but nothing that looked of importance. I found a picture of a young boy who looked suspiciously like Ethan Myers. I threw it back in the drawer and picked up a piece of paper with a handwritten symbol carefully drawn on it. My mind raced back to the book Brynn showed us at Eneclann. The same symbol was drawn in the margin of that book next to the name, Ó Meidhir.

I pocketed the paper just as Drew said, "There's nothing here." He had emptied all the books off the shelf onto the floor and was checking for a false back.

"It's gotta be here." I shone my flashlight around the room, and Drew got down on his hands and knees to examine the floor.

"What are you doing?"

"It is not absurd to hypothesize that the good doctor had a hidden room built into his office." Drew pulled a tiny, flat, black gadget out of his pocket and scanned the floorboards. "Panic rooms and secret chambers date back to ancient Egyptian times." The machine displayed a series of colored lights, but Drew kept scanning. "In the seventeenth century, cathedrals built priest holes to hide their leaders from the persecution of Catholics."

Drew stood and scanned the walls deliberately. "I suspect Dr. Alec knew he was discovering something monumentally important." Different colored lights began to flash, and he stopped scanning. Drew quietly knocked on the wall and listened carefully. Then he used his little device to scan higher up. "Especially if the public began to rise up against him." He let out a grunt as he pulled down on a stubborn light sconce apparently not screwed into the wall. "And protest his methods." The sconce shifted down, revealing a lever.

"Ta-da!" he announced proudly. "Would you like to do the honors, Agent Hill?"

I walked over to the lever, excited nerves rumbling in my stomach, and I forced it up, half expecting to set off some kind of intruder alarm. Instantly, a section of the wall in front of me slid sideways, unsettling a ton of dust and making a loud metallic squeaking noise.

A smile grew on my lips—a secret room.

"What are you waiting for? Let's go." Drew led the way through the doorway, shining his flashlight.

Inside, the room wasn't much bigger than the bathroom back at the hotel. There was a desk covered in untidy papers, another ancient medicine cabinet, and a small shelf of books.

202

Drew searched the bookshelf while I looked through the medicine cabinet. I rummaged through some antique medical supplies. Something under a piece of medical gauze caught my eye—a familiar blue rock about the size of a potato. I picked it up and turned it in my hands for a moment. Here I held the wretched reason for Ava's loss of memory. I tossed it to my other hand. It was also the reason I met Ava. This little blue rock was our beginning and could very well be our end.

"Harper told me these rocks blow up after exactly twenty years on earth," I said, partially to myself. "Apparently he was lying. This one has been here well over a hundred years."

"Found it. I found it!"

My heart picked up as I turned to look at Drew. He was holding a brown leather-bound journal. The cover had little gold foil letters spelling out the name Dr. Alec Ó Meidhir.

"Yes!" I jumped up and swiped the book out of his hands.

Suddenly something moved above our heads. It sounded like furniture being scraped across the second floor.

"Someone else is in the house!" Drew whispered urgently. "We gotta get outta here!"

I threw the blue rock down as we jumped through the secret room's entrance. Drew pulled on the lever and replaced the sconce.

Then we heard more footsteps, scraping, and a muffled female voice. She was walking slowly toward the stairs, no doubt. With hearts in our throats, we bolted out of the office, gracefully jumping over furniture and carefully running on our toes toward the back of the house. The stairs from the second floor came out in the kitchen near the back door. We had to beat the woman to the stairs, or she'd see us for sure.

"Who's there? You fluthered fools! Get out of my house!" Her screechy old voice sounded like it was at the top of the stairs. Drew reached the back door first and pushed it open just as I tripped on a wooden kitchen chair and stumbled to the ground right at the foot of the stairs, crashing into the wall with my shoulder.

"You knackered gouger…manky sleeveen!" I could see her ugly old face at the top of the long staircase, staring down at me sprawled out at the bottom. She was clearly drunk, speaking gibberish, and about to topple down the stairs on her own accord.

"Nolan!" Drew yelled from the backyard, "Come on!"

Shoot! The journal! It slipped out of my hands when I fell!

With my shoulder still throbbing from the fall, I groped around the dark kitchen floor while the old woman wailed at the top of the stairs.

"Get your banjaxed, minkin—" and then she let out a wail of surprise as her foot slipped off the top stair and she came tumbling down. Clouds of dust filled the air as her heavy body crashed into each wooden stair, cracking and breaking several in the process.

Drew yanked on my injured arm, pulling me out of the door just before the old woman hit the landing of the staircase. A sharp pain hit the back of my shoulder like a knife shoved into the muscle. I screamed as I got to my feet and ran like hell through the backyard, around to the front, and into the car waiting at the curb.

Drew had already gotten in and started the engine. I opened the door and stuck my head in. "No! We've gotta go back, I lost the journal!

"Get in the car, Nolan!" He screamed at me.

I reluctantly jumped into the front seat as Drew peeled out of there as fast as he could. I pulled the door shut, and then banged the fist of my good arm on the dash. "Dammit!"

"Calm down, Nol. The journal flew out the open back door when you fell. It practically smacked me in the face!" He pulled the leather book off his lap and passed it to me.

I took it, excited. I knew I'd be up all night reading but didn't care about lost sleep if it took me one step closer to solving this mystery. I kissed the cover. "Yes!"

I tried to catch my breath for a second, and then became cognizant of the hot pain radiating through my arm. "I think I dislocated my shoulder." I felt around with my hand. Something was not right.

"Don't worry, my friend. I'll pop that sucker back in when we get to the hotel." Drew honked the horn twice in celebration. "Wooo! That was so much fun! I thought the old goat had us for a moment!" Then he laughed a wonderful laugh and I had to smile—we had Dr. Alec's journal.

* * * *

Thursday, October 23rd
I felt a line of drool flowing down my cheek, and I woke with a snort. A crack of sunlight shone through the pulled drapes, revealing the fact that I still had my clothes on from the day before. I was awkwardly sprawled in an armchair in my hotel room, the small leather journal sitting open on my chest. It took me a second to figure out where I was.

I shifted to move out of the chair and soreness spread from my right shoulder and into my upper back.

You fell on your shoulder in Dr. Ó Meidhir's kitchen like an uncoordinated doofus, my brain reminded me.

A painful grunt escaped my mouth as I rubbed my muscles for relief, replaying the scene in my head.

My phone buzzed on the dresser, interrupting my thoughts. I carefully stood up and checked the display: *Drew calling.*

"Hey there, buddy." I wiped some sleep from my eyes and let out a loud yawn.

"Morning, sleepy. So are you coming down here or what?"

"Down where?"

"You said you'd meet me down at The Court Restaurant for breakfast! Did you just wake up?"

"Yeah. What time is it?" I looked around the room for a clock.

"8:30. Hurry up! The eggs are getting cold and soon all the blood sausage will be gone!"

"Oh, what a tragedy," I said facetiously. "Just make sure there is a cup of coffee left for me." I hung up, changed clothes, and brushed my teeth. Then I grabbed the leather journal and my tablet on the way out.

There weren't many people in the restaurant. Drew was sitting at a table by the window eating from a full plate. "Morning," he greeted me with his mouthful.

I sat down and took out my tablet to check over my notes from the night before. It took me a second to notice the other plate and steaming coffee cup next to Drew. "Who's sitting there?" I pointed to the mysterious guest's chair.

"Well—" Drew smiled as I heard a female voice behind me.

"Agent Hill. Good morning." Darcy walked around the table and took her place next to Drew.

Drew. That sneak.

"Agent McCombe? What are you doing here?"

"I talked Kane into letting me chaperone you two fools." She picked up her fork and popped a piece of sausage in her mouth.

"What? Look, we don't need—"

But Drew interrupted, his eyes wide, eyebrows high. "Ah ah ah, Nolan! Of course we could use the IIA's help." He gave a pleading look.

Of course Drew wanted Darcy with us. Something told me perhaps we shouldn't allow her on this quest, but Drew was practically begging. "Fine," I allowed, pointing an empty fork at her, "but you better be helpful."

"Nolan!" Drew shamed me.

Darcy put a hand on Drew's arm to calm him. "I'll be nothing but helpful. Now, fill me in on what's new. Drew tells me you were able to find an important journal?"

I placed the leather-bound book on the table. Darcy picked it up and flipped quickly through the pages, unable to hide her excitement.

"The journal belonged to Dr. Alec Ó Meidhir, Myers's grandfather," I said. "He was a doctor in Killarney from 1923-1933."

Drew continued the story where I left off. "During this time he began to see bizarre symptoms in his patients—momentarily painful, intense headaches that only lasted a minute, wild mood changes, severe pain behind the eyes, memory loss, and abnormal lethargy."

"Interesting. Does the journal mention what he suspects are the causes of these symptoms?" Darcy set the book back down on the table. She apparently would rather hear the abridged version from us.

I began to recount what I had read the night before. "The entries at the beginning of the journal seem to have no hypotheses, but rather a list of symptoms for each patient he saw. In the middle of his writing, Dr. Alec began expressing his theories on DNA, genetics, and mutations, often referring to some type of family symbol passed down through the years."

"Family symbol?"

Drew continued our findings. "He calls it a replicator, but there's not much of an explanation. What we found the most interesting were the pages near the end of the journal where he mentions that he, himself, was suffering from the same symptoms as his patients."

"I see," Darcy commented. "Do we know how he died?"

"We can only guess his death had something to do with these strange symptoms. Dr. Ó Meidhir noted that several of his patients died while he was treating them." I looked around the room. It suddenly dawned on me that perhaps this wasn't the best place to discuss our findings.

Drew must have read my mind because he lowered his voice and leaned into the table a little. "Near the end of the doctor's journal, he begins to refer to the patient's disease as *Caducuspetra Morbus*. It sounds like Latin to me." He looked at Darcy, "Do you have any idea what that might be translated to?"

"It sounds—" she thought for a moment. "—something like—"

"Fallen rock disease," she and I said in tandem.

Drew looked at me quizzically. "I know Latin, too," I reminded him.

Darcy scrunched up her eyebrows and took a sip from her coffee cup. "Fallen rock disease. Would that make sense?"

"Actually that makes perfect sense." I typed into my tablet, feeling satisfied.

"The meteor shower of 1901." Drew thought outloud. "Those suffering from *Caducuspetra Morbus* must have been keeping meteors in their homes."

Darcy put her two cents in. "I'd be willing to make a bet that Dr. Ó Meidhir had one of those rocks in his possession. He must have been suffering from *Caducuspetra* himself."

"He did! I found one in his secret office yesterday." Something didn't make sense to me. "But if the doctor knew what was causing the disease, why would he keep the rock in his house?"

"That is a good question." Darcy picked up her coffee cup and let the sides warm her fingers as she searched for a reason. "Maybe he was already infected and didn't care." Drew pointed a finger at me. "Didn't you say Ava's symptoms didn't start showing until she had been exposed to the rock almost twenty years, anyway?"

"Ava?" Darcy asked.

Drew looked at Darcy, "Nolan's girlfriend. The one I was telling you about last night."

Last night? Drew had stayed up with me reading the journal for a while, but then retired to his room where I had thought he was going to get some sleep.

"Oh, right," Darcy replied.

"Would it be possible that Dr. Ó Meidhir's family kept a rock in their house when he was growing up? What do we know about Alec's parents?"

Darcy took out her tablet from her purse. "The IIA knows that Dr. Ó Meidhir grew up in Cornwall, England. He moved to Ireland in 1916 when his father, Declan, died at age thirty-eight."

"Okay! Now we're getting somewhere!" Drew commented.

We all sat back with satisfaction on our faces. But my smile faded as it dawned on me—what actually had we discovered? Were we at all closer to figuring out Myers's agenda?

"Wait. How does this all help us?" I questioned.

Drew stared into his coffee cup and Darcy looked out the window, both apparently deep in thought.

Their silence is bad news, my brain explained.

"Myers sent someone to block us from getting information from Eneclann. If he knew we were here I bet he'd have someone shooting bullets at our heads to keep us away from this journal. There has to be a reason Myers doesn't want us to find this information." Drew joined Darcy's gaze out the window.

"There has to be something in here that is linked to what he is doing now."

"Or maybe he wanted you to find the journal," Darcy suggested. "Perhaps he couldn't get to it himself."

I let out a loud sigh and picked the book up off the middle of the table. If that was the truth, then I couldn't let it out of my sight. I thumbed through it quickly and landed on a random page near the back. I read the entry. The doctor was writing on his theory of gene mutation caused by *Caducuspetra Morbus*. Darcy and Drew had begun conversing quietly but I ignored them, reading the journal page.

"Hey guys. Listen to this." They stopped talking as I read quietly from the page.

Nearly twenty percent of Killarney now suffer from Caducuspetra Morbus. Several members have become violent threats to the community and two more were arrested this week. They will all find death unless I discover a treatment for this malignant disease. Through my research I have come to the hypothesis that the cure lies within the DNA of the affected.

Drew cut me off. "That's it, Nolan! The cure lies within the DNA of the affected. Myers needs the DNA of the people who suffer from fallen rock disease."

I excitedly turned the page to continue reading, but the next page was blank.

"Are there no more entries?" Darcy asked as I flipped through the rest of the journal.

"None. The rest of the book is blank," I said, disappointed.

Drew took a sip of coffee. "I wonder if he died right after he wrote that last entry."

Feeling like we had hit another dead end, we all let out a slow breath and continued picking at our breakfast.

Drew offered to continue the investigation. "What do we know about Myers's parents? Are they still alive? If his grandfather was onto something, don't you think his father might have continued his research?"

"It's worth a try. I'm going up to my room to call Agent Bowman. Maybe it's about time we head back to the US." With the joyful prospects of returning home in my heart, I stood up, holding tight to the journal.

Drew held his hand up to caution me. "That sounds great, buckaroo, except it's the middle of the night back home right now. You better sit your butt back down and finish your breakfast before you call the big boss."

He was right. As much as I wanted to move forward with what we had discovered, I knew Agent Bowman would not appreciate a call at 3:30 a.m. So I lowered myself back into the chair, and wondered what Ava would be doing today.

*   *   *   *

At noon it was seven in the morning in Wisconsin. I dialed the agency's number, went through the proper protocol, and finally got Agent Bowman on the phone.

"Greetings, Agent Hill. I assume you have a good reason for calling so early?"

"Yes, sir. We've made a wonderful finding." I explained the journal and our discovery of *Caducuspetra Morbus*.

"This sounds like an encouraging advance in this mission. I congratulate you and Agent Smith."

"Thank you, sir. Please advise our next step." I paced across the hotel room.

"Intel suggests Myers is still hiding somewhere out of reach of our surveillance. However, we have reason to believe he is not an immediate threat to Ava at this time. I must warn you,

211

however, that Miss Gardner wouldn't be too hard to find when he wants to. We are watching her carefully, of course, but our office is sure Myers needs her alive at this point."

My stomach felt uneasy. *Was she really safe at school?*

"What else can we do to discover Myers's agenda?"

There was a short pause, and I thought I had heard a pencil tapping on the desk. "I've been debating. Yes, I'd like you and Agent Smith to head over to St. Ives, Cornwall."

I wasn't going home? A wave of disappointment and then confusion washed over me.

"Cornwall, sir?"

"Yes, Cornwall. The westernmost part of the southwest peninsula of England. Just across the channel from your location right now. Myers's great-grandparents lived in Cornwall, and I believe it might be worth a trip abroad. Discover everything you can about Charlotte and Declan Mayers—who they were, where they lived, and what they did. Any miniscule factoid could help."

It sounded like the FBI had little idea how to put a stop to Myers. Any little factoid about Myers's great grandparents could help? To me that was code for, "We have no idea where to go from here. We're screwed."

Chapter Eight

Agent Kane tasked Darcy back to Dublin for another assignment, so Drew and I flew alone in a tiny private plane the FBI had chartered for us. After the two hour flight over the Celtic Sea, we landed on an airstrip in Land's End that was usually reserved for scenic day trips and aerial photography.

A man driving a black Mercedes Benz, most likely rented by the agency, picked us up from the airport and took us along a tiny two-lane road called the B3306 north toward St. Ives. The GPS on Drew's tablet said the trip was only sixteen miles but would take thirty-one minutes.

The rural, winding roads led us through tiny Cornish villages, around scenic English farms, and alongside the enormous, blue Celtic Sea. The view was just as breathtaking as the Irish countryside, and I felt myself longing for Ava again.

"Only a few more days," Drew said, watching me stare out the window.

"I know. I just hope she—" But I couldn't bring myself to finish my sentence. I wanted to say that I hoped she hadn't forgotten about me, but the truth was she had already forgotten about me. She had no idea who I was. Would I ever be able to slip that diamond ring on her finger and keep her by my side forever? I exhaled loudly, trying to force some of the discomfort of my heart.

Drew slapped a hand on my knee and squeezed for a quick second. "Board up, surfer. Let's focus on the info Bowman needs, and get the heck out of this place as soon as we can." He let that settle for a moment, and then it was Drew's turn to stare out the window, eyes far away, dreaming of a girl just out of reach.

The driver drove us into the coastal city of St. Ives, and Drew and I quickly realized we were in English paradise. Colorful fishing boats stood waiting in the harbor, the bright blue sea standing as a backdrop. I was surprised to see beautiful white sand beaches, bordered by cobblestone walkways.

Later that afternoon, I made a call to Adam as I sat on the patio of our suite at the Blue Hayes Hotel.

"She seems to be adjusting adequately, Nolan. Ava's brain is able to memorize new information and her blackouts are not increasing in number. She's coping incredibly well for someone who has is oblivious to the trauma she's been through."

"That's good to hear. I am worried about her, you know." I stood looking at the view from the balcony. It was incredible. "Do you truly think you may be able to reverse the operation?"

He paused a little longer than I'd wanted to hear. "Nolan, let's just be thankful Ava is progressing unbelievably well at this point. Oh, and her academics are outstanding!"

"Great," I replied with little enthusiasm. I disliked the joy I heard in Adam's voice. Why did he get to celebrate with my girl while I was stuck here searching for something that seemed impossible? But on the other hand, I was truly proud of Ava if she was focusing on her grades and working towards getting off academic probation.

"Bowman suggested I upload a program his techs developed onto Ava's computer." Then his voice changed like he was thinking out loud. "It'll allow us to search her files remotely."

"What are you searching for?" I asked.

Adam ignored me and kept talking as if he was talking to himself. "Problem is I have to transmit the program from my cell phone to her computer, and can't be more than half a foot away. I'll have to get her to take me into her bedroom tonight."

"Excuse me?"

"Nothing, nothing. I'm just working out the details. Anyway, I gotta go. Have a nice afternoon." Then he hung up before I could return the salutation.

Drew closed the door to the hotel room and walked through the living room. "And you said snooping my nose around was rude. I just hooked us up, my friend!"

"What are you talking about?"

Drew walked out onto the patio and continued. "The concierge downstairs has incredibly gorgeous legs, and she was stupendously helpful as well." That sly dog took a seat on the lounge chair on the balcony next to me, stretched out his legs, and placed his hands behind his head. "She's a local, and her father is the president of the Cornish National Historical Society, St. Ives District." Then he put on a British accent. "I somehow got us invited over for tea and crumpets in a few hours!"

"Get out! How do you do it?"

"A little charm, my friend, a little charm." Drew leaned back in the chair, closed his eyes, and laughed.

"But over to their house! Seriously?"

"The Cornish are incredibly hospitable, Nolan! Don't you know anything?" I might have been offended had it not been for the smile on Drew's face. "I gave the Mayers name and the little lady's father is going to dig into his collection of books at his office to share with us."

"Unbelievable." I smiled as I shook my head.

Drew grabbed his guitar from behind the chair and worked for a while on a lyric about a girl with legs a mile high. I closed my eyes and listened, soaking up the sunshine on my face.

* * * *

215

A few hours later our driver took us up Bedford Road, which, like all the other streets we had traveled through, was merely feet from the row houses on either side. The farther from the beach we moved out, the more claustrophobic I felt. The roads went every which way, darting around storefronts and houses. The driver took no caution as he sped around the corners and I thought we might be in trouble a few times.

Corinne Jolliffe and her family lived in a quaint little two-story, whitewashed stone house only inches from the one next to it on Bedford. We knocked on the door and waited as we heard footsteps approaching the door.

A tall, very cute young lady opened the door. "Drew! You made it." She let out what could only be described as a hyper cheerleader's scream of excitement, and then gave him a hug, her brown hair bouncing on her shoulders. She turned her sparkling green eyes to me. "You must be Drew's friend, Nolan?"

"Yes, hello. Thanks for inviting us over," I said as she hugged me, too.

"Not a problem. Come on in. My parents are waiting in the dining room."

The inside of the house felt just as crowded as it did out on the street. A freestanding coat rack brimming with jackets overflowed into the path of the doorway. Drew and I brushed through and waited at the base of a wooden staircase leading up to the second floor. The living room was stuffed with furniture, books, and knickknacks. There was barely room for Corinne to lead us through the long, skinny row house.

We arrived in a tiny dining room covered in blue floral wallpaper. Two middle-aged people sat at a clothed round table chatting with each other. Several light blue teacups and a dark blue pot sat waiting on the table.

"Hello, gentlemen. Welcome to our home!" Mrs. Jolliffe stood and held out her hand for us to shake. "Would you like some tea?"

Mr. Jolliffe pointed to the empty chairs at the tables. "Please. Have a seat. We understand you are seeking some information on the Mayers family."

"Yes." I noticed a collection of old books sitting on the table near Mr. Jolliffe. "Would you happen to know any information about a Mayers family that lived here in the late 1800s?" I took a sip from the blue cup in front of me.

"I do recall reading about a couple, Charlotte and Declan Mayers, that lived in town until probably 1915 or so." He took a drink from his teacup and his wife immediately refilled it.

"That sounds about the right time period," Drew commented.

"Mr. Mayers was actually the town physician." Mrs. Jolliffe poured more tea for Drew.

"Yes, yes. That has to be it," I said.

"According to the records I found, Declan was a well liked and respected man in town. He and his wife raised one small boy, Alec. Declan died young, and I believe—" he paused while he turned the page of the book, "—Mrs. Mayers moved out of the country at that point."

"Mr. Jolliffe, have you ever heard the name Ó Meidhir?"

"Actually, that sounds like a rough Gaelic translation of the name Mayers."

"Yes, we believe that might be right," I acknowledged.

Drew stepped in with a great question. "I know this sounds weird, but through your research, have you ever come across evidence of a significant meteor shower that may have hit St. Ives early in the century?"

Mr. Jolliffe raised his eyebrows. "Yes, actually. I do believe there was some type of meteor shower in 1900." He paged through a different book he had laying on the table.

"No, honey, wasn't it 1901?" Mrs. Jolliffe refilled all the teacups even though Drew gave a hand gesture suggesting he did not want any more.

"Oh, you're right dear. It was 1901." He turned to another book and found an old newspaper article pasted in. "Ah, here." He ran his finger down the page as he skimmed the text. "Oh yes, this storm was a doozy! There were hundreds of rocks that fell from the sky that night. Many citizens thought it was the end of the earth; that heaven was crumbling before their very eyes. Once the panic settled, people took rocks into their homes as souvenirs."

"That's right," I said under my breath.

"Years later, the local doctor, Declan Mayers, began to report strange symptoms in his patients, and attempted to treat them with local remedies—you know, berry salves, plant balms, and flower petal cocktails. Nothing he tried worked, of course, and more modern medicine wouldn't come around for another half a century."

I felt my excitement begin to fade. None of this was any new information, or even helpful at all. "Is there anything else you can tell us about this mysterious disease, or how Dr. Mayers treated his patients?"

Mr. Jolliffe took a few seconds before he replied. "No, I don't think there was anything else recorded."

"I hope we were of help to you boys," Mrs. Jolliffe said as she refilled our teacups again.

Drew answered since I was too upset to say anything. "Oh yes, thank you, Mr. and Mrs. Jolliffe. We appreciate your hospitality." He stood up from the table and I did the same.

Another dead end. Why did Agent Bowman send us to St. Ives? I hate wasting time.

Corinne led us back through the cluttered house and to the front door, where she bid us a friendly farewell and good luck.

We turned around on the stoop to see that the car was not waiting where we left it. "Didn't we tell the driver to wait out front?"

"Yes, I thought so." Drew looked up and down the street. "Maybe he went for petrol."

"Petrol, Drew?"

"Gas. It's what they call gas over here."

"I know, I just...nevermind. Do you have his cell number, or should we just wait here on the front steps?"

"I don't have his number." We both sat down on the curb as two men wearing all black came walking up the sidewalk to our left. "Why did Bowman send us here, anyway? Obviously Dr. Mayers didn't know much about *Caducuspetra* at the turn of the century."

Drew picked up a pebble from the sidewalk and threw it into the street. "Sometimes I feel like Bowman sends us on meaningless tasks just to keep us busy. You know, so we aren't sticking our noses into other concerns and being obstruent."

There might be some truth to that.

The two men stopped right in behind us, and before I could blink one of the guys threw a black bag over my head and wrestled my arms behind my back.

"Hey! What the hell?" I yelled.

"Who are you? What do you want?" Drew was obviously under attack as well.

"Shut up!" one of the men said forcefully, smacking me on the side of the head while pulling me to my feet.

I didn't have my gun with me. Why didn't I have my gun with me? I tried to muscle the man's grip from my arms, but he was incredibly strong. He held my arms back with one hand and with the other, he dug his fingers into my jeans pockets until he found my cell phone and pulled it out, throwing it to the ground.

I heard a car screech to a stop in front of us. The doors flew open and then I was blindly forced into the backseat of the car. Inside, Drew breathed quickly next to me. What the hell was happening?

It's Myers's men, my head explained.

Drew tried again to get some info from our captors. "What do you want from us?"

"Shut up," one of the men snapped.

A cell phone rang. "We've got them. ETA five minutes."

I had no idea if the men were watching me carefully, but I decided to take a risk. I began carefully working on the rope tied behind my back and by the time the car stopped it had loosened considerably. I hoped Drew was smart enough to be working on his ropes as well.

The doors opened and the men dragged us out of the car. We walked into a building and stumbled down some stairs. The poignant stench of moldy basement disturbed by nostrils as the vociferous sound of oversized machines whirred in my ears. We walked a few more steps, and then they forced us onto two chairs back to back. Our captor's heels walked toward a heavy door and slammed it. One man dialed a number on his cell. "We're here…. Yes…"

I took the opportunity to turn my head so my mouth was by Drew's ear and spoke softly, giving him directions.

"One, two, three!" I called, and busted out of my ropes. I whipped the black bag off of my head to see Drew already punching one of the guards in the face. The other guard came at me, but I was able to kick him in the knees before he could throw a punch. He toppled over to the ground in pain just as the other guard jabbed Drew in the stomach. I jumped up and hung from a pipe running through the exposed ceiling. I swung my legs back, smacked the man in the face with my feet and he went tumbling backwards, crashing into a stack of metal containers. Drew yelled for me to duck as he jumped up on the chair and then leapfrogged over my back, using his whole body to plow into a guard behind me.

Then the door opened. "STOP!"

I couldn't believe it. Agent Harper, my old boss from the CBB, stood in the doorway aiming his Glock at my head.

"I knew we'd meet again, Agent Hill." He walked closer, the guards still lying on the ground. "Now, be a good little agent and hand over the Schematics."

"What are you talking about?"

"Don't play ignorant!" He stopped a few feet closer to me but I only stared at him, showing no fear. He raised his voice a little and spoke through clenched teeth. "Give me the damn Schematics."

Drew didn't know who Harper was. "Listen buddy, we have no idea wha—" BANG! Drew fell to the ground with a grunt and lay at my feet holding his shoulder. My heart rate sped up to the same speed as a hummingbird's.

Harper spanned the room quickly and landed within inches of my face. "Give me the papers." His intense eyes bored a hole through mine.

Nerves flew rampantly through me, but I didn't allow them to surface. I knew he'd shoot me, and I didn't have a clue what papers he was talking about. "Listen Harper, I'd love to cooperate," I said, trying to steady my voice, "but I do not know what you are looking for."

He studied my eyes for another twenty seconds while Drew groaned on the floor. I wanted to bend down and help him stop the bleeding, but I knew I'd be shot if I moved.

A tiny hint of a smile made an appearance at the left corner of Harper's mouth. "You really don't know, do you?"

I remained silent.

Harper cracked an evil laugh. "Ethan's got you figured all wrong. You're oblivious to the truth." The smirk turned into a rather large and ugly smile. "Well, I guess we're back at square one, guys." Then with surprising speed, he took my arm and twisted it behind my back until I felt my shoulder crack and heard a painful pop from my forearm.

*   *   *   *

Sunday, October 26th

I woke up in a very dark room. Sleep was still on my mind as a horrible and moldy smell accompanied the dampness in the air. I was lying on some kind of dreadfully hard mattress, and as soon as I rolled over I felt intense pain in my left arm. I couldn't move it. There was no control. Panicking, I used my other hand to check if my left arm was actually there. Of course it was. One limp arm with incredible pain. It had to be broken in several places.

Where was I? Was I alone? My mind felt fuzzy as I tried to remember the last thing that happened to me.

Harper...

"He's nothing but a worthless piece of trash," a voice said in my memory. "Make him feel the pain."

I cautiously called out for Drew, but my voice came out scratchy and barely audible. I waited a few seconds, but there was no answer.

You're utterly alone, my heart called.

"Ava," I spoke out loud. "Ava, I need you..." and then my eyes closed, and I passed out.

222

Hunger pains forced my eyes open. My mouth was extremely dry, and I was disoriented. The room was spinning, even though I couldn't see anything through the darkness. The pain in my arm was difficult to endure, and now it felt like my brain was knocking itself into my skull. I leaned over the side of the bed and heaved onto the floor below.

A stranger's voice echoed through the halls of my mind. "Leave him there to rot."

Ava. My heart called desperately for Ava.

I wished I were dead.

* * * *

The creaking sound of a heavy metal door opening woke me up.

An urgent, whispered voice called my name. "Nolan. Get up. We've gotta get out of here quickly."

A small shaft of light shone through the door and into the dark room. I had been in a tiny concrete cell with a moldy cot and a moist floor. A dead rat sat in the corner of the room. I looked up at the blurry person standing in the doorway. She was wearing some kind of black leather bodysuit.

"Darcy?"

"Come on, Nolan! If we don't leave now you'll never get out of here." She reached out and grabbed the hand of my good arm, pulling me off the cot and onto my clumsy feet.

"Drink this," she ordered and shoved a small bottle towards me. I slowly drank in the sweet contents.

I stumbled out of the room into the hallway, almost falling to the ground several times, the muscles in my legs protesting from lack of use. The dim lights in the hallway were too bright and burned my eyes. Opening them only into slits, I saw a dead guard lying on the floor at the base of my door. Drew was waiting down the hall for us by an exit, sucking on a bottle similar to the one I had. As we approached, I noticed his eyes were black and blue, and his face was very swollen. His shirt was soaked with blood at the shoulder and upper chest.

"You look like hell, kid," he said to me.

"Same to you, buddy."

"Quit the chit-chat you two, and get up those stairs." Darcy had opened the heavy metal door to the fire exit and was waiting for us to ascend. We both stumbled and dragged ourselves up the stairs as Darcy followed behind us.

"Take the first-story exit," she called quietly, stifling back bursts of laughter at the sight of us.

My legs felt like they were made of jelly, and my left arm was throbbing with extreme pain. Even though I had only gone up about eight steps, I was out of breath as if I had just run a 5K race.

Darcy tried to keep her laughing under control, and even though I knew we must look ridiculous, I told her to shut up. "How long was I in there?"

"Same as me—almost four days." Drew used the handrail to pull himself up a few more stairs.

I could see the second-floor exit at the top of the next flight. "How did you find us, Darcy?"

"They took our cell phones," Drew answered, "but they didn't check my pants pocket for the emergency GPS button I had in there! Darcy gave me one before we left Dublin and I launched it when Harper's men bagged us. I knew things were not going well at that point."

Darcy climbed a few steps at a time and charged ahead of both Drew and me. "I got the signal, the IIA flew me to St. Ives, and I found you guys here in the basement of this old factory." Those little GPS buttons come in handy. My mind raced back to the night I left one on Ava's shoulder after I was forced to stab her.

"I took out the guards at the entrance door, and the rest of the place was abandoned." She pulled out her Glock and slowly opened the door at the landing of the stairs. "Stay here," Darcy whispered to us. Then she stuck her head out of the door and looked up and down the dark, empty space in front of us. "Still looks clear, but we've got to run our asses out of here quickly before Harper realizes you're gone. You think you boys can do that? I've got a car waiting out back."

"We'll do our best, babe, but my mind is still a little hazy, and I don't think it's sending the right messages to my legs."

Darcy laughed and said, "Let's go!" She shooed us out the door and then ran past us, leading the way through a large, dark warehouse. I willed my legs to move quickly but they were sluggish and weak, barely keeping up with Darcy as she jogged in her heeled boots toward an exit on the far end. We passed rows and rows of metal shelving units, but I couldn't see what was on them as we rushed by in the dark.

Suddenly, gunshots fired from behind us, ricocheting off metal and exploding a series of lights in the ceiling high above us. Glass rained down as Darcy turned her torso and expertly shot into the darkness behind us. I had to admit, she looked incredibly hot.

With a lot of effort, Drew pushed open the door as shots bounced off the walls around us, sounding out metallic tings. The door led right into the alley behind the building where a black SUV was waiting. Drew and I opened the door and dragged our tired bodies in while Darcy continued shooting behind us back into the building. She dove into the car just as the driver pulled away from the building.

Darcy pulled her legs into the moving car and shut the door as a few gunshots ricocheted off the hubcaps and bumper. Her strawberry-blond hair was loosely falling out of her high ponytail, and she was out of breath.

"Well boys, my job here is done. You'll be on a plane back to the US within the hour."

Drew reached over and grabbed her face in his hands. He stared sincerely into her eyes and said between breaths, "Thank you for rescuing us. You saved our lives. "

"Not a problem. I told you I'd be there for you when you needed me." And then as if I wasn't even in the car, they shared a passionate kiss.

Although my heart swarmed with sorrow wishing I could share such a wonderful moment with Ava, my heart was filled with joy and anticipation—we were actually headed home!

Chapter Nine

Wednesday, October 29th

Drew and I looked like war heroes returning from battle when we arrived back in Chicago late Wednesday afternoon. The IIA chartered a flight for us furnished with a medical staff to treat the injuries Drew and I suffered from. My arm had been broken in two places and my shoulder had been dislocated again. Drew had a fracture under his right eye socket and his nose was broken. He had a gunshot wound in his shoulder and needed surgery to repair the muscle.

We were driven back to the Midwest FBI headquarters in Milwaukee, where Drew received more treatment and the FBI doctors performed the same state-of-the-art laser surgery on me that they had done for Ava a few weeks before. Drew and I rested in the hospital wing until late that night.

It was almost 11:30 p.m. when Agent Bowman came into the hospital room Drew and I shared. "Agents, good work. I am proud of your efforts in Ireland and Cornwall. You were able to recover some important information."

Bowman sat down on the edge of Drew's bed. *"Caducuspetra Morbus."* He tapped his fingers together and stared out the window. "I've known for a while about *Caducuspetra*. I just didn't know that I did."

He's known about it?

There was a long silence as Agent Bowman stared out the window, thinking. Neither Drew nor I dared to say a word.

Then suddenly he stood up from the bed and cleared his throat, turning toward us.

"You boys know about genes, right?" We both nodded. "Of course you do."Bowman sat down on the visitor's chair in the

227

corner of the room, crossed his legs, and interlocked his fingers over his top knee. It was like he was settling in for a long lecture. "DNA is the building blocks of our body's trillion cells. Long, twisted ladders of tiny pieces of code contain the maps of genetic information that make our eyes blue or hair curly." He uncrossed his legs and continued the lesson, leaning forward so his elbows were on his knees, fingers interlaced. "What if your genes were missing parts of the DNA molecule in each cell? What if certain pieces of that ladder slowly disintegrated over a period of say, twenty years? Gradually the DNA chains would become weak, and eventually the whole ladder would collapse, leading to…death." He seemed to be thinking out loud.

I sat up in my bed a little. Could this have anything to do with Ava?

"We know these blue meteor rocks exhibit radiation capable of weakening DNA this way, depending on the size of the rock and the length of the exposure, of course." He got up from the chair, walked toward the door, and shut it. "Up until now, this problem has not been widely advertised, and a cure has not been necessary."

"Up until now, sir?" Drew asked.

"We have a double agent who is providing the agency with insider information from Myers's outfit. Our mole has indicated that Myers has been collecting the names of infected Americans for quite some time. For many decades there were isolated communities of people infected, but now the number is more widely spread. Myers believes there are almost twenty-thousand victims in the continental US alone." He paced the room silently for a few seconds while Drew and I waited patiently. "Recently he's been searching oversees and our double estimates Myers has learned the names of hundreds of others around the world that may be infected with *Caducuspetra*."

Drew spoke up. "What does he want with a list of infected people?"

"And that's the part of the story we are missing." The heels on Agent Bowman's shoes clicked as he walked to the window again. "Myers must know something we don't." Bowman stared out the window for a moment, thinking. "Intel believes he may try to engineer some type of antidote or cure. A million dollar enterprise sits before the creation of this cure, but I am hesitant to accept this as Myers's only motivation." He turned from the window. "You two have discovered that Myers believes the cure lies within the infected, but it is much more complicated than that." Bowman let out a loud sigh. "Agents, I think Myers needs something from these people to create his cure."

I suddenly wanted to jump up out of the bed and drive up to Stevens Point to be with Ava. There was no way in hell that I was going to sit here while she was on Myers's hit list.

Agent Bowman turned from the window and saw me pulling back the blankets. "I appreciate your enthusiasm, Agent Hill, but you can't run off to Miss Gardner just yet. I need to send you and Agent Smith down to Lena, Illinois, Myers's childhood hometown, to find out exactly what his father was researching when he died."

"And what about Ava?" My stomach turned butterflies.

"I just got off the phone with Agent Greene before I came up here." He thought about what to say next. "I won't insult your intelligence and try to tell you Miss Gardner is in no danger. Just last night Agent Greene and Miss Gardner narrowly missed a car bombing. I've sent extra protection to Stevens Point to follow Miss Gardner around the clock, just in case."

"Shouldn't we pull her out of there to be safe, sir?" A few extra guys weren't going to stop Myers, I was sure.

"We have no other indication that Myers or his men were in Stevens Point last night, and we'd like Miss Gardner to be able to live the most normal life plausible for as long as possible." Then he paused for a moment. "Believe me, she is well looked after."

"It had to be him. Why else would there be a random car bombing in a little central Wisconsin college town?" The tips of my ears growing hot with agitation.

Agent Bowman smiled and ignored my comment. "I'll have a car ready for you to take to Lena tomorrow morning." He walked around to the edge of my bed and patted my feet, but looked at Drew. "That is, unless either of you object to another mission so soon."

Something inside me said that in my condition, I probably shouldn't take the mission, but honestly there was no one else I trusted for the job.

Since neither of us replied, Agent Bowman said, "Good. Now you two get some rest," and he walked out the door.

Easier said than done. My heart was racing with worry over Ava's safety.

* * * *

Thursday, October 30th

Drew and I woke amazed at the marvels of modern medicine. Although we did not look our best, our injuries only felt like minor nuisances.

The trip to Lena was only supposed to take two and a half hours, but we ran into rush hour traffic around Chicago early in the morning. I spent the ride through the flatlands of Illinois on my tablet searching for anything I could about Myers or obscure genetics.

Drew kept yawning and exhaling loudly. He really looked miserable.

"Hey, are you sure you're up for this? You want me to drive for a while and you can take a nap?"

"Nope. Just crack me that energy drink in the console. I couldn't leave my buddy when he needs me most."

"Thanks, Drew. You know I'd do the same for you." It was true. There was no one else I'd rather be on this mission with. "I think we should start our search at the Lena Community Library," I suggested. I read from my tablet when Drew didn't comment. "Bowman knows Myers spent his childhood at the Stephenson County Children's Home because his parents died in a car accident when he was six."

Drew looked in the rearview mirror and then changed lanes. "We should go there. I bet they'd have some info for us."

"Maybe after we hit the library."

I wondered how Ava was doing and when this mission would be complete. Would it be soon that we'd have enough information to truly take down Myers and get Ava back in the operating room to restore her memory?

Lena, Illinois, was a small Midwestern community of three-thousand people. The Lena Library was a small, red brick building only a few blocks from the out-of-use railroad tracks that ran through town.

A very overweight woman, probably in her forties, was chugging a bottle of Mountain Dew behind the front checkout counter when we walked in the door. There was an empty bag of Cheetos on her desk and a suspect ring of orange cheese powder around her mouth. Drew shot me an eyes-wide-open look and I returned the sentiment. We awkwardly stood in front of her for a good twenty seconds before she opened her eyes, stopped chugging from the bottle, and noticed us. She jumped, startled, and choked a little on the soda.

"Oh good Lord almighty! You two startled me!" She laughed and wiped the Cheeto dust from her mouth with the back of her hand. "Can I help you gentlemen?"

I detected a slight southern accent hiding behind her words.

"Yes, we're looking for the public records, specifically archives of the census, old newspapers, and family records." The place was small and dated, and I hoped this wasn't a waste of time.

"We have a collection of newspapers on the microfiche machines in the basement, and there are several town hall record books down there as well." The large librarian got up from the chair and waddled around the circulation desk. "You two veterans? You look like you've been through a war!"

I was about to reply no, but Drew cut me off. "Yes. Just returned home." I had forgotten we don't normally offer our FBI status unless there is good reason to.

"Thanks for your service, boys. The country is in your debt." Her oversized backside bounced and jiggled as she led us through the library. I could barely turn my eyes from the spectacle before me, but finally looked away when I noticed Drew making obnoxious sexual gestures behind her back. I tried not to laugh, but a little snicker snuck out, so I faked a cough to cover it up.

We walked toward the back of the building; there wasn't another soul in the library. The librarian turned, "You two new to Lena? I know most everyone who lives in this little town and I don't think I've ever seen you fine young men around here before."

"We're just passing through, ma'am." Drew had a talent for quick thinking.

"Just passing through? Huh.....Well, welcome to Lena." We walked past the children's section and around a corner to a staircase. "We were in the process of taking all those old

232

newspaper scans and turning them into digital copies, but lately our volunteer staff have been busy preparing for the big town holiday festival in November. The whole scanning process is pretty much at a standstill at this point." She laughed a big chuckle and her butt bounced up and down as she did so. "You boys know how to use a microfiche machine, right?"

I had no idea what she was talking about, but Drew nodded his head.

At the bottom of the stairs the librarian showed us an area with two large microfiche machines on top of a long table pushed against a wall. Nearby were bookshelves of old leather-bound, oversized books.

"Good luck, dears. I'll be upstairs if you need anything." Then she turned and shuffled her way back down the hallway, humming an unfamiliar tune.

"Why don't you check out those books while I fire up the microfiche?" Drew suggested. He sat down in front of an oversized computer screen sitting on top of a computer box with a large dial attached. There was no keyboard, only a few buttons built into the front of the box. Under the monitor was a light shining up to a place where the user could put a piece of film to be read on the monitor.

While Drew got to work, I found the census record book from 1960–1970 and located Dr. Clennan and Mrs. Myrna Myers and their son Ethan Myers, residents of 519 Locust Street. I wrote down the information and put the book back on the shelf. Then I found county court records, town council meeting minutes, and many books recording marriages and divorces. But nothing seemed to be of help. I let out a sigh and turned to Drew. "Are you finding anything over there?"

"Nah. Not yet." He kept his eyes on the screen and turned the large dial on the machine until his phone vibrated and interrupted his work. He looked at the screen and then smiled a guilty grin and laughed quietly, trying to hide it from me.

"Nice try. What does she want?" I knew it was Darcy.

"Oh...you think it's..." Then he gave up his act. "Yeah, it's Darcy. She wants to know what we are up to."

"Doesn't she have anything better to do than text you all day?"

"I sure hope not," he said while texting.

I recognized that smile. "You really like her, don't you?"

He took a few seconds to muster up some courage, and then he said, "Yeah. I really, really do." He put down his phone and looked up at me, his face filled with complete sincerity. "It's so cliché but...but I've never felt about anyone else the way I feel about her. She stole my heart in the five days I spent with her." Then he let out a deep breath. "It sucks that she lives halfway around the world." His smile faded instantly.

"You'll find your way back to her." I smiled, wondering if I was talking to his heart or mine. "But for now, we have work to do."

"Yes, boss!" He saluted me, and then texted another message. I swiveled in my chair, and got back to reading books. I could tell Drew was still texting Darcy, however, since I heard him typing and snickering. "Oh wait, here's an article about Dr. Myers's research. Apparently he won a county science award for his advances in genetic medicine."

"Does it say anything specifically about the research?"

"Listen to this:

Dr. Myers was honored today for his unique discovery related to details concerning a rare DNA disorder. Certain strands of the DNA molecule in his patients were deteriorating and this led Dr. Myers to infer that the cure for this disease lies within the infected."

He turned to face me. "That part Myers ganked from his father, as we know. Then it goes on to describe the details of the ceremony and the address of the doctor's practice."

I let out a loud sigh. "Well, that wasn't very helpful." I went back to work scanning the books.

Drew continued scanning films for several minutes. "Wait, here's something else in the *Lena Review*."

March 29th, 1966

> *Longtime community board member, upstanding citizen, and respected town physician Clennan Myers and his wife, Myra, were tragically killed Thursday night in their home. The doctor and his wife were in bed when an intruder broke the window on the back door, unlocked the handle, and entered the house. The intruder was apparently seeking a specific antidote Dr. Myers was cultivating in his office, and when Dr. and Mrs. Myers confronted the intruder, a gun was pulled and they were shot. When emergency personnel arrived on the scene, both citizens were dead already. The couple's six-year-old son, Ethan, was asleep upstairs during the incident. The boy has been taken to the Stephenson County Children's Home as no relatives are in the area. The identity of the intruder is not being released at this time by local authorities as they are continuing their investigation."*

Drew turned from the screen and faced me. "I thought Myers's parents were killed in a car accident."

"I bet that's what the orphanage told Myers, not wanting a little kid to know his own parents were murdered. I wonder when he found out the truth." I thought about that for a moment. I would not be happy to find out my parents were murdered when I had thought all my life they died innocently in a car accident.

Drew scanned the article again. "So Dr. Myers actually created a cure, and Ethan Myers's parents were murdered for that cure. If I put two and two together, that means the intruder must have been suffering from *Caducuspetra*."

I tapped my pencil on the countertop, thinking. "If his father had already created the cure, why doesn't Ethan Myers have it now? Why has he been trying to re-create it?"

"Maybe the intruder stole the only sample Dr. Myers had made...*and*...maybe he stole the formula as well!" Drew took out his tablet and made a note.

"That could be entirely possible, I guess." I thought for a moment. "We need to find out who the intruder was. Maybe they still have the plans and we could, uh, borrow them."

"Sure, boss." Drew snickered and went back to surfing through the scanned newspapers. "Wait, wait, here's another article a couple days later." He read through it in his head and then summarized. "It looks like a few days after the doctor was killed they arrested a suspect. Let's see, blah blah—" he scanned a bit more, "—a woman named, let's see here...June Gardner."

"What? Let me see that! June Gardner?" I pushed Drew's rolling chair out of the way, and he crashed into the wall to his left, laughing. I slid mine over.

It said June Gardner.

"Ava's last name is Gardner. Do you think this person was related to Ava?" My jaw was slack in awe.

"Nah, it's just a coincidence, right?" But I could tell in Drew's voice that he thought there might be a chance June Gardner was related to Ava. Drew and I stared with disbelief at the article on the screen, deep in thought. My heart rate began to rise, and I felt beads of sweat gathering on my hairline.

"It can't be.... It can't be." My head was clouding over and my stomach was quickly turning sour.

"Hold on, here's another article from the following week."
Drew scrolled over to catch the article. "It says June Gardner,
from Platteville, Wisconsin, was tried for unintentional double
homicide and breaking and entering."

"Ava's grandparents lived in Platteville. It's Ava's
grandmother. It's gotta be." I said it slowly, letting it sink in.
"Ava's grandmother murdered Ethan Myers's parents." I looked
down at the floor when my heart realized what my mind didn't
want to admit. "He wants revenge."

"Wait, there's more, and this is odd. It says Mrs. Gardner
was sentenced to twenty years in the Galena County State Prison,
but was released after two days for reasons unknown."

" 'Reasons unknown' ? That makes no sense. Why would a
state prison release a sentenced murderer after two days?" I
suddenly wanted more than ever to call Ava, but there was a
possibility she had no idea about any of this—before or after the
memory wipe.

"What is the date on the article?"

"1966," Drew said as he searched the machine for more
information.

Suddenly our phones buzzed in tandem. Bowman had sent
us urgent texts—*Intel suggests you'll soon have company at the library.
Evacuate ASAP.*

Drew and I exchanged surprised looks, and then he quickly
pulled the film out of the machine while I shoved the books back
on the shelf. Upstairs we heard the librarian scream, and then a
rather large thud. Several footsteps scattered around the top
floor.

"There's more than one," Drew whispered.

"The only exits are upstairs. What are we going to do?" I
pulled the Glock from my belt. We only had seconds before
Myers's men figured out we were downstairs.

Drew looked around the room. A small rectangular window near the top of the wall had a pane of glass that opened outward. Drew pushed a table up against the wall, climbed on top of it, and pulled out the screen as I poked my head out the door. No one was coming down the stairs yet. When I looked back I could only see Drew's feet sneaking through the open window.

With my heart beating quickly, I hopped up onto the table and hoisted myself through the window with little effort. How did he get through there with his shoulder injured? Mine was miserable with pain.

Once out of the tiny window, Drew closed it quickly and then we ran our way around the side of the building toward the parking lot. When we got to the corner, Drew looked around the brick wall for sign of the intruders.

He turned back toward me and whispered, "I don't see anyone, but there's probably someone staking out the front door. Do you want to run for it?"

"I don't see what else we can do. The other guy'll be coming through the window any minute."

We ran through the back lawn toward the side parking lot where ours was still the only car present. About three feet out from the door I heard that familiar spitting sound and a bullet ricocheted off the hubcap. I lunged for the car and dove in just as another bullet hit the open door.

Drew started the car and threw it in reverse as a few more bullets rang out around us. Gravel spewed from the tires as Drew's car sped away from the library and out of town. I pulled my cell from my pocket and called Agent Bowman immediately to tell him we made it out safely.

"Great. Sorry my team didn't pick up any movement before they did. Were you able to find anything before Myers's men arrived?"

I told him what we had discovered and he sounded pleased. "Perfect. Just as I suspected. Good work, Agent Hill. Now you and Drew get up here quickly. My scientists have made a breakthrough in the case of the cure. I'll call Agent Greene and fill him in while you're heading back to Milwaukee."

Chapter Ten

Drew and I arrived back at headquarters late in the evening and were immediately rushed to the conference room on the second floor near Agent Bowman's office. There were several suited people sitting around a dark-grey oval table, waiting our arrival. Many agents had tablets in front of them, and a few were engaging in quiet conversation.

We took a seat in the only two empty office chairs pushed up to the table. Agent Bowman shut the door and then stood next to us, clearing his throat to gather everyone's attention. "Agents Hill and Smith, I applaud your dedication to this mission. Your discoveries have been instrumental in our advances toward the arrest of Ethan Myers. Before we can pull the trigger on this operation, we need to compile our information to create a plan of attack. Agent Gibson, please report first."

A small man with an alarmingly bushy and unkempt beard spoke up rather excitedly. He had a ponytail and oversized front teeth that reminded me of those on a small rodent. "The genetics department has discovered the key to the cure for *Caducuspetra Morbus*. We are certain Ethan Myers is ravenously searching for the Desirable Eight—a term he's coined for eight citizens who fit a very explicit set of genetic requirements. Up until now we haven't been cognizant of the precise formula, but recently we have concocted a plausible hypothesis based on the latest and most respected genetic research around the world."

He paused for a big breath and Agent Bowman cut in. "Wonderful work, Agent Gibson. What are these specific requirements?"

"We are certain on three counts: the victim must be female, brown haired, and must be of Great British descent." Some of the agents took notes on their tablets. "We know the other qualities are harmonious with exposure to meteoric radiation as well as an unknown certain level of disintegration within gene pairs.

"But?" Agent Bowman sensed Gibson had something else to say.

Agent Gibson smiled. "But, without a manifestation Myers calls 'The Schematics,' we are somewhat bewildered as to what the rest of the recipe could entail."

"And does Mr. Myers have the Schematics in his possession at this time?"

"We believe he does not." Agent Gibson cleared his throat and pushed his glasses up his nose a bit. "These young ladies we are finding dead…well, sir, we believe Myers is killing them somewhat unintentionally. Autopsies suggest Myers is looking for something within their brains and, of course, he is not a brain surgeon."

"Hmmm…" Bowman walked the perimeter of the room. "Any other pertinent information to report at this time?"

"Yes, it should also be noted that although evidence suggests Ava Gardner fits what we know of the profile for one of the Desirable Eight, we are certain she will be useless in contributing to the cure."

A small murmur came over the group.

"Why so?"

"Because Miss Gardner underwent gene therapy last August. Agent Greene strengthened her already weakened genes. The suspected formula requires genes that have been weakened to a certain degree and Miss Gardner no longer possesses such genes."

241

"I see. Thank you for the update, Agent Gibson." Then he turned to another man sitting to his right. "Agent Richardson, please report."

"Recent discoveries from Agent Hill and Agent Smith have indicated that although Miss Gardner might not precisely fit the profile for one of the Desirable Eight, Ethan Myers will most likely pursue her as revenge for her grandmother murdering his parents. Through our source of informants, we can roughly track Mr. Myers's activity, but we do not know his exact location at this point in time. Although we believe Miss Gardner's well-being is possibly in danger, we are unsure if Myers is currently focused on locating the Desirable Eight, or more interested in pursuing Miss Gardner."

"Thank you. Recommendations?" Agent Bowman clicked the pen in his hand.

"We recommend securing the identity of the Desirable Eight before extracting Miss Gardner. Agent Greene will ostensibly be able to protect Miss Gardner, and we'll most likely know when Mr. Myers migrates north to Stevens Point."

Most likely? I did not like the sound of that. I felt a strong need to head up to Ava and help Adam keep guard.

"Very well, then. This meeting is adjourned. Back to work, agents. Let's uncover the identity of these people before Myers does."

Drew and I slowly stood up from the table, not exactly knowing what to do next when Agent Bowman said, "Not you two. Stay here for a moment." Agent Bowman continued once the room cleared. "I'm not sure I agree with my advisors completely. I think it's best if you two travel to Stevens Point in the morning and stay on the lookout for Myers or his men. Our mole is stellar, but then again, can you ever completely trust a mole?" He stared at us as if he expected us to answer, but we knew the question was rhetorical.

With fluttery excitement in my heart, I left the conference room. I knew Ava still didn't know who I was, but it was entirely possible I could see her beautiful face from afar every day until we could capture Myers and take Ava back to the operating room.

Things were looking up.

*   *   *   *   *

Friday, October 31st

I actually got a better night's rest than I had in quite some time. The prospect of being in the same town as Ava calmed my heart. Even so, the morning came quickly and Drew and I were ready to leave around nine.

I hadn't remembered it was Halloween until we pulled into a gas station in Plover and a slutty pirate was pumping gas into the Buick next to us.

"What'd ya say we hit a costume party tonight?" Drew's eyes got wide. "College girls!" he mouthed to me with his back to the pirate. "I bet we could muster up some costumes lickety-split."

"Oh really, grandpa from 1950?" I smiled at his vocabulary choices. "Let's just get to Stevens Point and settle in before we make plans for the evening. I told Adam we'd meet him at the coffee shop around two."

"Oh golly gee mister, that sure is swell!"

I had no idea what had gotten into Drew, but it was entertaining. He hopped in the car and drove us the last few miles north to Stevens Point, all the way spewing out his favorite catchphrases from half a century ago.

Agent Greene was waiting at a small table in the back when we arrived at the cozy little coffee shop near the riverfront. He had ordered three small coffees and was sipping on one of them. There were several patrons, mostly college-aged, listening to their iPods and reading out of textbooks. A couple played checkers pulled from the shelf of games nearby.

Adam appeared suspiciously nervous, but greeted us with smiles and handshakes. "Welcome back to American soil, boys." It sounded a bit odd coming from a man with a British accent.

"So how's my girl?" Adam winced slightly when I asked. "Is she alright?"

"Well…yes…I assume."

"What the hell do you mean, 'I assume'? Haven't you been following her around all day every day for the last few weeks?"

Adam picked at the napkin under his coffee mug. "Sort of. Something happened and Ava is a tad grumpy towards me at the moment. She hasn't spoken to me in a few days."

Drew laughed out loud, but I was not amused. He better not have tried to hurt her.

"What'd ya do? Try to put the moves on her?" Drew tipped backward onto two legs of his chair and laughed loudly.

I didn't see what was so funny.

"No, no….There was just some rubbish prank the frat kids played. It was mean and…well, anyway…it's no matter, she's fine. I've been keeping tabs on her without her knowing. But I need to get her back on my side, or I may not be able to continue to monitor her as closely as I would like to. You know, from a medical standpoint."

"Just tell her the truth. She's a smart woman." I couldn't believe some frat prank would have angered her too much.

"I would, mate, but she won't listen to me right now." His eyebrows lowered in frustration.

Drew leaned forward and poked a finger in the air in Adam's direction. "Here's a genius idea—just figure out where she's going tonight, corner her with your debonair charm and wit, and she's putty in your hands. I've done it a million times."

I believed that about Drew.

"Going tonight?" Adam asked, perplexed.

"Yeah!" Drew said obnoxiously. "It's Halloween! All college girls go out to party on Halloween night." Drew's phone buzzed and he swiped the screen. Smiling, he sent a text message.

"Right...right. Halloween night. Brilliant...I can do that." Adam looked out the window in deep thought.

"Anyway, what else can you tell us about Ava? Is she still blacking out?"

"Yes, but the episodes are becoming shorter and occurring less often. I am able to pull her out of them quickly, and minimize the danger to her brain."

"That's good at least."

Drew's phone vibrated a continuous buzz. "It's Bowman," he said before answering. He had a quick conversation and then put down the phone and took a long drink from his coffee, holding our curiosity over our heads before filling us in. "Intel indicates Myers is on the move again. They're pretty sure he's headed for Stevens Point. Myers is planning his revenge on Ava tonight."

I jumped up, heart pumping, ready to swing into action.

Drew grabbed my arm and pulled me back down into the wooden chair. "Hold on there, buckaroo. Intel has confirmed Myers halfway across the country right now. Even with the fastest jet, he won't arrive until the Halloween moon is high in the sky. Sit down and enjoy your brew." And then he closed his eyes and took a deep drink from his cup.

I, however, would not be able to enjoy myself at all. I turned to Adam, "Where is she right now? We need to be with her."

Adam took out his phone. "The GPS indicates she's at home. I'll go park my car a few blocks down from her house and watch her door for the rest of the afternoon."

"I'll come with you." I put my phone in my pocket in preparation of leaving.

"No, no. I'll have a go at it alone. I have more research documents to read anyway." Adam drained the last sip from his mug, and then stood up from the table. "Keep me posted on the plan for tonight. I'll see you two later."

"See ya, British Buddy! Have fun on lookout duty!" Drew smiled as Adam left the shop, but once he left Drew leaned over toward me with a completely serious expression, "There's something fishy about that dude."

"I told you that a month ago!" I stared at Drew for a few seconds. "I can't wait to get this night over with and get Ava back in my arms."

"Don't jump the gun, my friend. You have a long road ahead of you when it comes to getting back with your woman."

"I know, but one day closer is one day closer."

"Ooh! That's a good one." Then he sang to me with a smile, "One day closer is one day closer."

I laughed. "I'll take a twenty-percent cut if that one hits the charts!"

"Deal, dude!"

*　　*　　*　　*

That evening Drew and I were eating take-out pizza in my hotel room when I got a call from Agent Bowman informing us that Myers should be arriving in Point around eleven that night. Bowman gave explicit instructions to find Ava and get her out of town sooner than later. If we were still around when Myers arrived, we should take out his men but bring Myers into custody.

I called Adam right away to relay the news.

"No problem, Nolan. I know exactly where the girls are going. I'll have her trusting me again and back to you straight away."

"Fine, but hurry. I don't want any surprises from Myers." *This needs to be pulled off without any complications,* my heart warned.

"Remember, Nolan, if you end up on campus for some reason, it's imperative to Ava's health for you to stay out of her sight until we get back to headquarters where we can put her under anesthesia. Ava's brain still isn't ready to see you yet."

"Look Adam, it's been twenty-one long and excruciating days without her. I don't think I can—"

But he cut me off, raising his voice above mine. "Trust me, Agent Hill. You could do irremediable damage to her brain by allowing her to interact with you. If you truly want what's best for her, you'll stay away."

I begrudgingly replied, "Fine, I'll try."But I yearned for Ava so badly at that point I couldn't in good conscience whole-heartedly agree to such terms.

I hung up the phone just as Drew's buzzed on the table. He picked it up, swiping the screen. "Bowman says he's sending a tactical team up here by jet. They'll land near the Plover rendezvous point in about an hour. We're supposed to go out there and meet with them at the safe house."

"Let's get this show on the road 'cause I'm taking that punk down if it's the last thing I do."

"Oh, look at you! Two horrible clichés in one sentence."

"Shut up, Drew!" I grabbed a pillow from the bed and threw it hard at Drew's head. The force knocked him off the edge of the bed, taking the box of half eaten pizza to the floor with him. Drew laughed as he sat up and chucked a few pieces at me. I ducked and they smacked the wall behind me, squirting pizza sauce over the paint.

"Dude! It looks like a murder scene in here!" I said, peeling pizza off the wall.

Drew picked the rest of the pizza off the carpet and threw it back into the box, laughing. "Yeah, maybe an insect murder scene. I'm going to go clean the pizza out of my ears and change. I'll be back here in twenty." Drew left my room and shut the door.

I got off the bed, finding myself in an incredible mood. Tonight was going to be the first step in the long journey of Ava and me getting our lives back to normal. A smile contentedly rested on my lips as I showered and shaved and then changed into my black cargo pants and FBI raid shirt.

Drew knocked on the door just as I was ready to leave. "It's showtime, baby!"

"Let's do this."

We hopped in the Tahoe and headed south down I-39 toward the Plover exit. My heart was flying high as I pictured Adam taking Ava into his car and driving her to the rendezvous point. I could see her gorgeous face again in a matter of hours.

We pulled into the parking lot near a memorial dedicated to veterans from the area. Behind the statues and benches was a tiny serene lake, and off to the west stood a small cabin labeled Visitor's Center. The agency designated a safe house in the back of the center where agents in the immediate area could find refuge should they need it. There were two black Tahoes parked in the lot with a ring of men standing around talking. They greeted us upon arrival, and I recognized a few guys from training.

A stocky and muscular man much older than the others approached us. He wore a clean goatee and his face was sharp and chiseled, radiating intimidation. He spoke in a low voice. "Agent Hill, Agent Smith, I'm Agent Mathy, captain of this mission. Agent Bowman wanted me to inform you that our mole has discovered that Myers has rounded up a team of his best men from the Midwest CBB chapters to secure Miss Gardner this evening. We expect he will not show his face here in Stevens Point, but has sent his men to do his dirty work. Our goal tonight is to keep Miss Gardner safe from any counter attacks Myers's team employs and extract her without the public even knowing we're here."

Someone from behind Agent Mathy handed him a small box. "Thank you," he said. "Here are your earpieces. It is imperative you follow any commands given by me." He handed the box to Drew, and we each took out a tiny black earpiece.

"Agent Greene has been instructed to transport Miss Gardner to this point no later than twenty-one hundred hours. Myers's team isn't expected to arrive here for another two and a half hours, so half of this tactical team will wait at this location for Agent Green to arrive and the other half will head to campus to stake out the area."

"I'll head with the team to campus," I informed Agent Mathy.

He continued, ignoring my request. "Agent Hill and Agent Smith, you stay with the other four here. I will contact you if there is a need."

Disappointment drilled deep within me. How could I just sit here and wait?

"Please familiarize yourself with the team members and maps of campus, specifically the Student Center, should you be requested to join us." He pointed toward the other agents behind him looking at maps on their tablets. His phone rang, "Excuse me, agents." He answered as he walked away from us.

Although the other guys were supposed to be studying maps, when I walked over to them they were checking the score of the Packers' game and talking sports statistics. One of the guys pulled up the campus map and then handed me his tablet.

Drew was digging through a box of high-tech gadgets when his phone rang. "It's Darcy," he said with a smile. He answered the phone just as he walked away, "Hey, baby!"

Why would she be calling now? It's the middle of the night in Ireland.

My watch read 8:30 and the butterflies danced wildly in my stomach. I let out a deep breath and wondered what Ava and Adam were doing at this very moment. The guys talked sports for a while as I tried to study the maps, and then Drew rejoined the group a few minutes later.

"How's Darcy?" I asked.

"Fine, I think. Well, actually she sounded weird, like something was bothering her but didn't offer an explanation. Apparently she couldn't sleep and wanted to know what I was up to. She's happy to know we've almost got Myers."

Suddenly Agent Mathy returned to the group, hanging up his phone. "Boys, Intel just intercepted an unidentified phone call to Ava's cell. Myers may be trying to confirm her location. They might be closer than we thought." Then he turned to an agent behind me. "Get Agent Greene over to the Center immediately."

"Yes, sir." The agent turned on his phone, apparently dialing Adam's number.

Agent Mathy yelled to the team, "Move out, everyone! We need to get on campus, now!" All the men jumped into their cars and peeled out of the parking lot and onto the highway. With my heart beating overtime, we zoomed north for several miles and exited quickly onto Division Street.

Drew looked over at my apprehensive state as he sped through the empty streets. "Hey, kiddo, don't barf on my freshly detailed leather seats."

"I can't promise you that." I blew out an anxious lungful of air. "I just want to get this all over with."

Why had all my first FBI missions become so personal?

Drew drove down Portage Street and into Parking Lot R. The tactical team had pulled in right in front of us and all the men got out. Agent Mathy barked out directions as I felt my head dizzying with fear and anticipation. What was going to happen in the next hour? What if I came face to face with Myers again? I couldn't afford to botch it up like last time.

I heard nothing Agent Mathy said. The group broke up and dispersed towards the Student Center. Drew grabbed my arm and pulled me towards the others.

"Adam and Ava are inside." He knew I hadn't heard a word Mathy had said. "Intel believes Myers's men will be here within minutes. We need to rush inside and fight them off while Adam pulls Ava out the back service door."

I stalked silently alongside Drew, looking carefully behind us every twenty feet or so. It was dark on campus, and the October night air was bitterly cold. As we approached the building I could hear the low booming of dance music coming from inside. Ava must be at a Halloween dance.

We approached the side basement door, and Drew tried the handle. It was locked, so he pulled a lock-pick from his belt and expertly opened the door within seconds. We found ourselves immersed in a vestibule soaked in almost complete darkness. Loud beeping announced our presence. With confidence, I rushed to a box on the wall, pried the faceplate off and pulled a red wired from the back, snipping it quickly with a tool from my pocket. The beeping stopped immediately.

"Sexy," Drew teased and then touched his earpiece. "Outlier and Raven are in the east service entrance."

"Copy that. Proceed to underground entrance," I heard in my ear.

Drew pulled from his pocket a small black gadget a little bigger than a deck of cards and turned it on. It glowed bright green and displayed a map of the area we were standing in.

Suddenly bright red arrows lit up, indicating which way to proceed. Drew hit the flashlight app on his cell phone and illuminated the empty hallway before us. The GPS device showed a few little yellow stars scattered throughout the map, warning us where enemy agents were hiding.

"They're here. Be ready, Agent Hill."

My heartbeat quickened wondering if Ava had been taken to the safe house yet or not. We sped through the hallways using the GPS device to take twists and turns through the basement service areas. We eventually approached a closed door labeled *tunnel.*

Our earpieces spoke up, "All agents are in place. Prepare to attack on my count."

My heart rate was through the roof and my armpits soaked through my undershirt. I held my Glock pointing to the ground, eyes wide with anticipation for what was coming.

Drew consulted the device. "There are two guys stationed just down the hall from this door on the left. The other FBI agents will advance from the opposite end and we'll meet in the middle." Then he stuck the device back in his pocket and stared me in the eyes. "This is it, Nolan. Remember all those physical tests you aced at Quantico? You can do this!"

Agent Bowman buzzed in our ear to advance, and Drew kicked the door open. We ran, hugging the right wall. As we approached the spot where Drew's device had indicated men hiding, we slowed down and crouched near the floor. It was dark in the underground pathway, which was lit only by warm yellow service lights every fifty feet.

Then I noticed it as Drew did—a slight movement in the doorframe down the hall.

Drew took the shot and got the man in the neck. Although that was one down, it gave away our position and suddenly the hallway was showered with bullets. Drew went to the other side of the hall to split up the targets, and we advanced on the enemy, shooting with confidence. Adrenaline flowed swiftly through my veins as Drew and I took down several men.

Suddenly the shooting stopped and Drew gave me the sign to hold fire. He dug the GPS device out of his pocket and checked for stars.

"We've cleared them out of this area, but there are several down past the open space ahead. Let's go!" He ran forward, and I followed. We cautiously approached a large open area, scanning the scene from the cover of the door. This part of the underground tunnel was apparently a storage area. There were racks after racks of boxes, crates, and barrels. The sheer amount of hiding places would make this more than challenging.

Drew was still holding the gadget, and we spotted eight men stationed around the room. Drew pressed his earpiece. "Outlier and Raven, stationed at the warehouse east entrance."

Our earpieces rang out, "Copy that. The rest of the team is holding at the west entrance. Go on my signal."

The next twelve minutes moved quickly through my mind, but slowly through my heart.

When Agent Mathy gave the go-ahead, the team charged the warehouse. Our opponents were dressed like us—all black— except they had nylon ski masks on. They were using the element of surprise— popping out of corners and jumping from hideouts between crates and boxes. I narrowly missed being hit several times. Not having much field experience, I surprised myself, injuring a few of Myers's men, and distracting others while Drew took them out. We worked well as a team, reading each other's minds and anticipating the next move of our partner.

We worked the perimeter of the room, disarming many and shooting others. Even though I felt well prepared for combat during training, this authentic raid was nothing like I had imagined. My shoulder and forearm were still healing from

Harper's torture, and this fight was more physically demanding than anything I had done since training. My survival instincts kicked in, guiding me to throw punches and to be in heightened awareness of everything around me.

In the heat of the fight, I witnessed a bullet hit a box close to Drew's ear. As he turned to shoot at his attacker, a tiny man jumped out from the corner, bounded off a wooden barrel, and kicked Drew in the side of the head. He fell to the ground and the attacker stood over him for several seconds with his gun pointed at Drew's fallen chest, clearly deciding whether or not to shoot.

I witnessed it all from behind a large shelf, and before the attacker could take out Drew, I kicked out the man's knees from behind. He fell to the ground, his body crashing into a stack of empty wooden crates. Drew stood up, head bleeding, and obviously pissed off. He yanked his assailant's legs out from under the pile of boxes, pulling off his ski mask in the process.

What we saw forced me to gasp and Drew to drop the legs instantly in shock. There, lying in front of us, was not a man but a woman.

Darcy McCombe.

She frantically found her mask and stood up, running along the back wall of the warehouse and out the west entrance, Drew still frozen from shock and devastating heartbreak.

Suddenly the earpieces spoke in our ears, "Myers's men have retreated. Still no sign of Agent Greene or Miss Gardner at the rendezvous point. All team members search the Center."

Drew turned to me, pointing behind him. "I gonna confront her. You head up these stairs. They'll lead you right out the back door. Find Adam!" And before I could even agree, he ran off down the dark hallway and toward the outside door.

I scaled the stairs two at a time and busted through the heavy metal doors at the top. How could Darcy be here in Wisconsin?

Why was she fighting for Myers's team? I suddenly felt very sick. Had she been playing us the entire time?

I emerged into a dark alleyway at the back of the Student Center. The cold air took my breath away, but I was so sweaty my skin didn't seem to notice the temperature change. I jogged down the perimeter of the building, keeping my eyes open for movement. It seemed like we took out most of Myers's men, but I had no idea where the survivors retreated to. I half expected to bump into Darcy again around the corner.

Down at the end of the brick wall I saw Adam. I tapped my earpiece and reported that Agent Greene was in my sight. I approached, holding my Glock down at the ground, anger filling my heart.

"God, Adam! What the hell were you thinking? You were supposed to get her out of here hours ago!"

Chapter Eleven

It was only a handful of minutes later when I excruciatingly left my sweet Ava in the possibly incompetent hands of Agent Greene and ran through the courtyards of the Student Center, Glock at the ready in case Myers's men were waiting for stragglers like me. I found Drew waiting by his Tahoe, pacing and looking angrier than I had ever seen him before.

"She used me." He kicked the tire and then raised his voice to a yell. "Even her accent was freakin' fake, Nolan! She's on Myers's team and I've unknowingly been feeding her information this whole time!" He punched the side of his Tahoe, leaving a slight dent and grunting loudly.

My heart sank in frustration and defeat, but I knew my friend needed some comfort. "Come on, Drew. It's not your fault. We had no idea."

"Dammit! I thought I knew her! I was falling for her!"

"Where is she now?" I scanned the parking lot around me. "Did she get away?"

He paused a few seconds before answering. "No, I tied her up. She's in the backseat."

"What?" I moved over to look in the back window. There in the dark backseat of Drew's Tahoe sat Darcy with her wrists and ankles bound together. "How did you do that?"

"I knocked her out with the butt of my gun first. She came to just a few minutes ago." He actually looked a little embarrassed.

"And what are you going to do with her?"

"I hadn't thought that far ahead." Drew's face exhibited a rare state of disgust and perplexity all at the same time.

Agent Mathy buzzed in my earpiece. "Outlier, Raven, report."

I stared at Drew, silently asking which one of us would respond. When Drew didn't move I pushed the button on my earpiece. "Raven and Outlier are leaving the Center. ETA ten minutes."

Drew walked around to the Tahoe as I opened the door to get in the passenger's side.

A voice with an American accent sounded from the darkness of the backseat. "Nice to see you again, Agent Hill."

Without turning around I replied to Darcy. "You sound much sexier with your phony accent."

Drew started the ignition and left the parking lot, still looking mad as hell.

"Let me explain," Darcy started.

"Shut up!" Drew yelled passionately from the front seat.

BOOM!

A loud explosion half a block behind the Student Center rocked the car. Drew slammed on the breaks and Darcy bounced off the back of Drew's seat. Startled, I looked outside my window and saw the roof of a house covered in wild fire and billowing smoke. Bits of roof rained down from the sky. My mouth dropped in shock.

It's Ava's house, my heart knew.

"Turn around, Drew! Ava's there." Suddenly Agent Mathy's voice rang out in my earpiece. "Outlier, Raven, have you cleared campus?"

"Yes, we're heading north on Division," Drew answered.

"Are you aware of an explosion near Miss Gardner's residence?"

"Affirmative. Intel observed an immense jump on their satellite thermal sensors and suspected bomb activity. They're looking into it now."

Darcy spoke, unconcerned from the backseat. "It's Ethan's fail-safe. He probably decided he wants her dead…tonight."

My stomach turned uncomfortably. "Do we have a 10-20 on Ava?" I frantically asked Agent Mathy.

"Negative, her location is unknown. We are waiting for a report from Agent Greene."

I was downright nauseous and my head was pounding. We had to go back to her house and see if we could find her.

Drew asked Mathy for further instructions. "Should we report back to the rendezvous point or stay here?"

There was a pause that took up several seconds. "Sir?" Drew asked again.

"Agent Greene just called into Base Ops requesting an emergency transport order for two. He's with Miss Gardner, and they're alive."

I let out a loud sigh of relief, but the nausea didn't completely pass.

"Head to the safe house and wait for further instructions. My team will arrive in ten minutes."

"Copy that." Drew merged onto Highway 59 and headed south toward Plover. We all sat silently thinking our own thoughts.

Darcy's fake-sounding voice cut through the silence. "Honey, I can help you if you let me explain."

"Don't you dare call me that!" Drew yelled, slamming his fist on the steering wheel. There was resentment in his voice, and heartbreak in his eyes.

"Drew," she pleaded. But before she could continue, Drew turned around in his seat and jabbed her with a syringe right in her thigh. Her eyes rolled and then closed, and she slumped over in the seat. The Tahoe swerved off the road slightly, but Drew caught control and pulled us straight.

Somewhat horrified, I retreated back against the window. "What the hell was that?!"

"Dammit! I can't listen to her crap anymore. That'll put her out for an hour or so until we can pass her off to Mathy."

"Fine," I accepted. Then I added, "Don't you ever think about doing that to me." I saw Drew smile out of the corner of his mouth. Mission accomplished—Drew's mood had shifted ever so slightly.

I stared through the dark window as Darcy's words rang out in my ears over and over again. He wants her dead tonight *Find her right now,* my brain instructed.

I took out my phone and texted Adam—*Where are you?*

I stared at the screen. Nothing. Several minutes passed and still no reply. I looked up and out the windshield at the passing road signs. We were almost there. I texted Adam again, but he still hadn't answered by the time we arrived at the parking lot of the safe house.

There were two Tahoes in the lot, but no other cars. As soon as Drew threw the car in park, I had my door open and I approached Agent Mathy, who stood away from the group of agents, talking on his phone.

"Have you heard from her?" I asked. "Is she okay?"

Mathy held up one finger while he finished his call. I paced back and forth, waiting impatiently.

Finally, he hung up his call. "Agent Hill, calm yourself."

"Where is she?" My voice grew uncontrollably loud. "Greene's not following protocol!"

Mathy said nothing, but collectedly stared into my eyes, trying to find one shred of sense inside me. "Agent Hill, although your behavior is unwarranted, you are correct on one account. Agent Greene never reported to the Portage County airport for extraction. He's not answering his cell, and he's disabled the GPS within his cell and his car."

"Why would Agent Greene knowingly disable his GPS?" Drew questioned.

"He wouldn't! He and Ava must have been captured!" I was freaking out, expecting the worse.

"I doubt he's been captured, although that's a scenario we can't discount at this point in time. Let's give Intel a chance to locate him. The agency has the most sophisticated satellite equipment in the world."

I can't just sit here and wait.

I paced back and forth, breathing heavily while Drew timidly approached Agent Mathy. "Sir, on another note, we've captured a hostage."

I had almost forgotten about Darcy.

"Excuse me?" Agent Mathy responded with annoyance.

"A hostage. In my Tahoe, sir." He pointed behind him. "She's tied up in the backseat."

Agent Mathy walked a few steps toward the vehicle. "Who is it?"

"Darcy McCombe. She plays for Myers's team," I confessed.

Agent Mathy looked in the window and then pulled out his cell and texted someone. I looked at mine. Still nothing from Adam.

"Agents! Intel has tracked Agent Greene's car heading south on 59 toward Madison. Agent Bowman infers he's heading toward Myers's new secret headquarters."

"What? He's taking her straight to Myers?" I was beyond furious.

Drew chimed in behind me. "How does Greene know where Myers's secret headquarters are?"

"Haven't you figured it out?" Agent Math asked condescendingly. "Agent Greene is a double agent."

My insides instantly caught fire. "No! He can't take her to Myers!"

The other agents had circled in around Agent Mathy. "I'm not sure what motivation he has to take Ava to Myers, but the FBI trusts Agent Greene. He must have a real and legit reason." "That's bullshit!" The other men murmured their disapproval of my outburst. I inched closer to Mathy. "We barely know anything about that idiot!"

"Agent Hill, stand down or you will not be allowed to continue as part of this mission. Hell, I don't think you should even be here now. You're in too deep already." Then he looked me dead in the eyes. "Maybe you don't know much about Agent Greene, but the agency has full confidence in his loyalties."

I took another step forward and opened my mouth to dispute, but Drew swung his arm in front of my chest, physically jolting me back and knocking some sense into me. "Get a hold of yourself."

I grabbed a hold of my emotions and took a deep breath. Drew addressed Agent Mathy, "What do we do now?"

"We get in the vehicles and follow Agent Greene's trajectory. Intel will continue to track Agent Greene remotely and give us our directions." The men immediately left the circle and headed back to the Tahoes.

Drew called after Agent Mathy, "And the hostage, sir?" but Mathy kept walking and then jumped in one of the Tahoes as it pulled away.

Chapter Twelve

We were an hour down the road when Darcy's phone rang out from the dash where Adam had stashed it. I picked it up and read the screen out loud. *Adam's on his way with Ava. Report your location immediately.*

Darcy was still passed out in the backseat. "It's Myers. Should I respond?" I asked.

Drew stayed focused on the road. "I could pretend to be her."

"Give me the phone." Darcy commanded. I hadn't even seen her wake up. Perhaps she had been faking for a while.

"Dream on. We're not letting you converse with your evil master."

"Give me the phone so he doesn't suspect I've been captured." She stuck her palm up to the front seat. "Come on!" she screamed. "You'll blow my cover!"

"What are you talking about?" I asked.

The phone buzzed again and I read the screen out loud again: *Alliance protocol. Reply within 180 seconds or you're out.*

"Reply, reply! Come on!" Darcy yelled urgently.

I looked over at Drew for confirmation, but he kept driving, looking angrily out the windshield. "You have sixty seconds to explain yourself and if I am not convinced, I'm throwing this phone out the window."

"Just give me the—" Darcy started, but I lowered my window and held the phone out the crack.

"Fine! Fine!" Darcy's spoke quickly but with an underlying petition in her words. "First of all, you have to know I'm on the same team as you—"

Drew interrupted, shouting at her. "Then tell me why you were with Myers's men tonight! Why did you try to kill me?"

"I'm a double, Drew. I work for Myers and the IIA."

"Then we are decidedly not on the same team. I want nothing to do with that rat bastard."

Ignoring Drew's ranting, she went on, quickly. "I've known Myers for several years. He needed someone with an Irish background to do his research related to *Caducuspetra Morbus*. He doesn't know I've been sending his secrets back to the IIA."

"Then you're Irish? What's with the American accent?" I inquired.

Still talking rapidly, she continued. "I was born in Ireland and moved to the US when I was four. My father was IIA, placed in the US for a special assignment. My mother decided to move us to Illinois to be with my dad, and also because she had family in the midwest. We ended up staying for the remainder of my school years. I picked up the American accent as a child in grammar school and it feels most comfortable for me still. I moved back to Ireland when I was eighteen and joined the IIA. I've been working for them for the past ten years."

"That's all very interesting, but I still don't appreciate being used...or shot at." I could tell Drew was relaxing a bit but still holding a grudge, with good reason. "Nolan, drop the phone out the window," he instructed.

"Wait!" she pleaded. "If I hadn't attacked you, I would have proved to my teammates where my alliance falls. I couldn't risk that. Not now that we're so close to blowing Myers's operation wide open."

I was starting to believe Darcy, but I needed a little more information before I was ready to trust her. "How did you get in with Myers?"

"I went undercover for the IIA and spent years working my way into Myers's inner circle. That's where I met Agent Greene and we discovered we were both doubles. We've been working together for the last nine months to gather enough information for the agency to take down Myers. We're almost there. If Adam doesn't blow it tonight and if you let me reply to Myers, I can lead you right to his front door."

I looked at Drew and he returned a glance. "Give it to her."

"Actually, you'll have to text for me, my hands are still tied up," she replied, nodding behind her.

"Fine, what should I say to him?"

"Text, *Got separated from team at Center. On route now. Hurry.*"

I thought for a few seconds about giving Myers a piece of my mind instead, but decided I better play it safe for the time being, and texted only what Darcy said.

Drew spoke next. "So, the whole time we were in Ireland...?"

"Yes, I was feeding Myers the info you boys found, but only because we believe Myers will be the only one to put all the pieces together. We need him to discover the cure for us before we could take him down. There is a legitimate need for a cure of this kind throughout the US and parts of Europe, and that's part of my mission as a double agent."

"And what about in St. Ives?" Drew questioned.

"Myers had you captured and roughed up without me knowing anything about it. Once I realized what had happened, I discovered where you were taken, and broke you out when I thought no one would be around." She squirmed a bit in the backseat. "God, Drew, did you have to clock me so hard? My head is pounding!"

"Sorry, Darce." Drew was starting to thaw out a little.

Darcy's phone rang out in my hands. I swiped the screen. *Hurry back. I'll need you at dawn.*

"Looks like he bought it," I said.

"Nolan, untie her hands."

"Are you sure?" I whispered. This was all a beautiful story, but could we really trust Darcy just yet?

"Just do it," Drew replied.

I untied the ropes restraining her hands behind her back and she instantly rubbed her wrists and then her right temple. "Thanks, Nolan."

"No problem." I checked my phone. Still no new messages from Adam or anyone else.

Darcy asked me to call Agent Mathy so she could give him exact directions to Myers's headquarters, and then she laid down in the backseat and went to sleep.

*　　*　　*　　*

It was 3:30 in the morning when we approached downtown Chicago. I was incredibly tired, but had offered to stay awake with Drew while he drove, so on our way out of Wisconsin we stopped quickly just north of Milwaukee in Delafield for coffee.

Drew woke Darcy as we approached the Windy City. "Darcy, wake up. You've got to get us to Myers's front door."

She sat up and looked out the window, trying to get her bearings. She turned on her phone's GPS and then instructed Drew to get off the Kennedy Expressway and take the Dan Ryan to Garfield Boulevard.

Seeing the city reminded me of the years I spent attending college and when I was recruited to train for the CBB. I thought of the undying excitement that coursed through my soul during that period of my life, and how it paled to the passion of the one summer in Wisconsin Dells with Ava.

"Guns at the ready, agents." Drew said half jokingly as he pulled into a sketchy south-side neighborhood. Abandoned storefronts lined the streets, fires roared out of barrels in the alleyways, and groups of young men shouted obscenities at us as we drove by. Most of the cars on the street looked like they belonged in a junkyard, but a Mercedes was scattered every few blocks or so. I had no doubt where that Mercedes owner earned his money.

"Darcy, are you sure this is it? Why would Myers choose one of the most dangerous areas of Chicago for his hideout?"

"Not sure. Perhaps he wants to make sure no one stumbles into his research." She was looking out the window, rubbing her eyes. "Turn here on South Prairie and park in the public lot two blocks down."

"Public lot? At four in the morning? You in with the South Side, Darcy?"

"Go to the second floor ramp," Darcy replied. "Just trust me."

Drew snorted loudly. "Oh, right. Trust you. Good one."

Darcy's phone rang on the dash, so I picked it up and checked the screen. It was a text from Adam—*We're here. Where are you?*

I handed it back to Darcy, excited at the prospect of seeing Ava soon. I wondered if she was sleeping, or awake and scared to death. A huge ball of sympathetic panic fired up inside me.

"Nolan, call Agent Mathy," Darcy instructed as we pulled into the parking garage. "Ask him to have mission tech hack into Myers's security system and put the parking garage video on a loop. I'll give them the location."

I did as Darcy said, and within minutes we received word we could proceed.

"Okay Nolan, let's go get your girl!" Darcy exclaimed.

Flying high with excitement and somewhat paralyzed with terror, I exited the car and Drew hit the locks. The parking garage was completely empty at this time of night, and it radiated an eerie feeling of impending danger. Darcy's heeled boots clicked too loudly on the concrete as she led us over to the elevator.

When the doors opened, Darcy looked in and then turned toward us. "There's a camera pointed at the northeast wall. Stand over there and you'll miss it." We followed Darcy's instructions and stood where she pointed. "I'll stand over here. I need Myers to see I've arrived."

As the doors closed, Darcy pulled a tiny silver disk from her pocket and stuck it to the wall of the elevator. "Bug killer," she explained. "You can talk freely." Then she pressed the button labeled B2 at the same time as the tenth floor button. The panel above the buttons suddenly came to life as it turned into a small computer screen. *Enter passcode,* it read. Darcy peeled down the plastic advertisement above the screen to reveal a hidden keyboard on a hinge. She typed in a long password and shut the keyboard again.

The elevator gently glided down what felt like two floors, and then it violently shifted directions and somehow began to move backward horizontally. The sudden change surprised Drew and me, and we were flung to the floor. We scrambled back to our posts by the wall so the camera wouldn't see us. Darcy, who expected the switch, had held tight to the handrail and was still standing, laughing at us.

Drew looked at Darcy. "A little heads up next time, please!"

"Ah, but that was too funny!" She smiled widely.

I clung to the railing as we continued to travel parallel to the ground for several minutes. I wondered if we could possibly be under Lake Michigan.

Darcy read my mind. "Myers built his lab under Washington Park. It's virtually undetectable by FBI satellites, and it has been impenetrable until now." She smirked. "When the elevator stops, you'll have to stay in the vestibule right outside it for a few moments while I check in with Myers. I've got to confirm his progress on the cure before we bust up his operation."

"We've got to get Ava out of there no matter what," I protested.

Darcy stayed calm and tried to spread the feeling to me. "Trust me, Nolan, she's safe under the watch of Adam and me."

"I apologize, Darcy, but it's a bit challenging trusting anyone these days. Ava needs to be out of Myers's reach as quickly as possible."

The elevator began to slow down, preparing to stop. Then Darcy took off her wristwatch and turned toward Drew. "I'll communicate with you when it's time to advance." She stared intently into his eyes as she fastened the slightly masculine black watch around his left wrist. Drew's perplexed gaze was stuck on hers, unsure if he should listen to his heart or his brain. And then without waiting for any sign that he wanted one, she laid a tender kiss on his lips.

My eyes and heart sank down to the ground. When would I be able to kiss Ava again?

Finally, the elevator came to a stop and the door opened, breaking up their kiss. Darcy pulled away abruptly and, without giving Drew another glance, walked confidently through a dark and empty waiting area before us. She punched another code into the keypad on the wall, and a steel door slid open with a hiss of pressure being released. Darcy walked through the door, and it slid shut the second her heels cleared the threshold, leaving us in the dim room all by ourselves.

Drew stood stunned, still shocked from the kiss. "God," he said, wiping his lips with the back of his hand, "women really know how to mess with us guys, don't they? One second I want to smash her face in and now I want to—" He scrunched up his nose and made some movement with his hips, but I quickly cut him off.

"Hold it right there, hound dog. Let's see if we can get out of this place alive before you start planning your next overnighter with Darcy."

Our instructions were to stay, so we sat on the floor to the right of the elevator doors and contemplated what we might be facing when we were allowed through the door.

It wasn't long before I began feeling jittery. "I can't just sit here and wait." I stood up and paced the perimeter of the room.

"Dude. Relax. We've gotta let her set us up before we storm the castle."

He was right. I sat back down, but had trouble calming myself.

It was more than thirty excruciating minutes before we heard Mathy's voice in our ears. "Raven, Outlier. We're...par...arage. Can't...we...code..."

Drew pressed the button on his earpiece. "Sir, you're breaking up."

"...hold post...ission tech...cryption."

"We're deep under the park." I looked up at the ceiling, thinking about what was above our heads, and then took out my phone. "I've got no reception."

"Guess we're on our own down here," Drew said, pocketing his phone. "Wonder how long she's going to take back there," he said, pointing at the door Darcy had walked through.

With his arm extended it was easy to notice. "The watch," I said, pointing. "It's counting down."

Drew studied the face for a moment. "It's at twenty-nine minutes and twenty-seven seconds." He put the watch up to his ear and then jumped up from the ground quickly like he had just sat on a bee's nest. "That bitch! It's a bomb!" Drew frantically attempted to get the watch off, but there was no traditional watch fastener, only a tiny box with an up and down arrow button.

"Stop! If it is a bomb, we need to be careful. Come here." I waved for Drew to move his arm near my hands. I carefully studied the watch, and when I put it to my ear it sounded just like a watch and nothing more. "I don't think it's a bomb. But I do think she wants us to do something in the next twenty-eight and a half minutes."

Drew screamed at his wrist, "Why are so you cryptic, Darcy?"

And as if she had heard him, the watch spoke to us. "Adam's coming back to let you through the door. Follow his instructions carefully. Oh, and check the cabinet."

Drew yelled at the watch, "Darcy! Darcy, can you hear me?" He lifted the watch to his ear but heard nothing.

"Check the cabinet?" I repeated, perplexed. I turned around, looking for any kind of storage unit, but found nothing.

Almost immediately the heavy, metal door began to slowly slide open. Drew and I approached the entrance and as soon as Adam's face appeared in my sight I punched him hard in the jaw.

Man, that felt good.

He fell to the floor and I stood over him, looking down on the punk. "That's for trying to steal my girl." He groaned and rolled over from his side to his back. Although I knew this would be the perfect vantage point from which to kick him squarely in the nuts, I knew I needed Adam to help me get Ava out of Myers's grip. I offered a hand to help him up.

He reluctantly accepted and stood, rubbing his jaw. "I don't think I deserved that, mate."

"Are you really a double?" I asked quietly.

"This is not the place," Adam replied grumpily. Then he turned and led us through a clean, grey metal hallway with curved walls like a tunnel. A strip of blue lights glowed at the point where the wall met the floor.

At the end of the hall Adam stopped in front of a door cracked open to give us more instructions. "We're going to have to take out the guards on the other side so they don't alarm Myers to your presence."

"Hey, you know anything about this watch?" Drew held out his wrist for Adam to see. "It's Darcy's."

"No," he said barely looking. "After we take out the guards, we'll advance through and enter the viewing room outside the operating room where Myers is holding Ava. Darcy's in there with her right now."

I felt that familiar nervous feeling zooming around in my belly, mixed with adrenaline, sleepiness, and anger. I was a complete emotional mess and wasn't sure if I could handle what was in store for me.

"Why is he holding her?" Drew asked. "If he wanted her dead, why hasn't he done it already?"

"He's preparing to take a sample of her DNA. He's not sure, but believes she might be one of the Desirable Eight. All of us here," he pointed to Drew and me, then back to himself, "know she can't be."

"So go in there and tell Myers Ava's not one of the Eight!" I challenged.

"Darcy believes we should allow Myers to realize on his own that Ava's genes are not weakened to the point he needs them to be."

"Can't you just take a DNA sample with a cotton swab and a lab kit?" Drew questioned. "What's with the operating room?"

"Not this kind of sample. Myers needs a specific gene part that has disintegrated just the right amount from a cell deep within her brain. He knows my training in neuro-genetics and has asked me to perform the operation."

"Absolutely not! What's the problem with just busting in and whisking her out of there right now?" There was no way I would

271

allow Adam slice her head open again—last time that didn't go so well.

Drew came to the conclusion before I did. "Myers isn't much closer to the cure than we are, is he?"

"No. The agencies don't want Darcy and me to risk revealing our true selves yet. We believe Myers has more to discover and he is the only one with access to the correct resources.

"It's in his father's research," I spoke quietly.

Adam continued, ignoring my discovery. "We need him to create the cure for us before we take him down. If we can get him to decide he doesn't need Ava's DNA for the cure, then we can get her out of here without him suspecting anything."

"But he wants revenge for Ava's grandmother killing his parents!" I frantically whispered. "If he realizes he doesn't need her for the cure, then he'll undoubtedly kill her right there on the spot!"

"Excuse me? Ava's grandmother killed Myers's parents?" Adam looked genuinely surprised. "Blimey," he said in a whisper.

"It's a long story," Drew replied. The watch on his wrist spoke to us again, "Get in here! What's taking so long?"

"Twenty-four minutes," Drew whispered to me.

"Let's go!" Adam pushed the door open and silently snuck forward.

Three guards sat attentively around a half moon grey desk occupied with computer screens and keyboards. The men drank from coffee mugs and were dressed in khaki uniforms, completely oblivious to the intruders standing behind them.

"Agent Raddemann, you're back quickly," one of the guards stated.

Agent Raddemann?

Adam didn't reply, but threw a crippling uppercut, knocking the guard off his chair. Drew and I rushed in and took out the other two men as they sprang to their feet, grabbing for their guns. Within seconds we had knocked out and disarmed all three. Adam snatched the key ring off one of their belts as we stepped over their bodies and quickly entered a hallway beyond the desk.

As Adam led the way I was overcome with the oddest feeling, as if cold pressure from the park above us was pushing down on our heads. I closed my eyes tight and shook my head, trying to chase away the impending gloom surrounding my very being.

We entered a small dark room lined with a tilted wall of windows revealing an operating room beyond it. There were chairs for observers and even a screen for displaying close-ups from the surgery. The lights were off in this room, the darkness shielding us from view.

Inside the white operating room, Ava was strapped to a medical table and draped in a hospital gown, her eyes closed. A gag was positioned across her mouth. My heart leapt when I saw her so near me, looking so helpless. Had she been knocked unconscious? Darcy and two other men stood nearby.

"Why can't we hear what they're saying?" Drew asked.

"The intercom system is not on. Stay here while I go in. No one will be tempted to look in here if you don't bring attention to yourself. I'll clear my throat two times loudly if I want you to come in and back me up." Then he left the viewing area and entered the operating room, locking the door behind him.

Curious, I tried the door we entered through. "He locked us in," I said, when the door wouldn't move.

"I'm not sure this is going the way we'd like it to," Drew said somewhat nervously, trying again to get the watch off.

"I couldn't have said it better." I walked over to Drew and crouched down. "Give me one good reason why I shouldn't bust open that door right now and steal Ava away."

"Might I remind you we are in Myers's funhouse, and if the rest of it is anything like that whacked-out elevator, we're in trouble. We are basically at the mercy of two"—he used air quotes for emphasis—"double agents, one of whom may want to bomb my arm off, and the other is about to slice your lover's brain wide open."

He was right. We needed a real plan in order to end this thing in our favor.

The people through the window busied themselves around the room, preparing. They washed instruments, brought in sterile linens and solutions, and laid out surgical tools. Adam checked Ava's vitals and Darcy attended to some computers in the corner. Ava's eyes were still closed when Adam bent down near her face and whispered something into her ear. I was so intent on watching Ava that I hadn't noticed Drew crouched down on the floor.

"What are you doing?" I asked.

"I've got the overwhelming feeling that we're walking right into a trap. Presently I don't trust Adam or Darcy, and I can't fathom a way out of here for us."

Scattered around Drew on the floor were several small tech objects. I noticed the GPS device he used to identify hiding enemy agents in the Student Center, a few tablets of different sizes, and a long, skinny device somewhat like a keyboard but turned vertically. Positioned at the top of this machine was a small square monitor and a probe that extended off the end about four inches. Drew was waving this one over Darcy's watch.

"Hot damn, it isn't explosive! It's just counting down." He smiled and then looked up through the window at Darcy as if he was asking her a question. "What's supposed to happen in nineteen minutes?"

"Dude! Where do you keep all those gadgets?"

274

"Never underestimate the real estate in your cargo pantaloons, friend!"

I laughed. It felt good to laugh.

Drew picked up the long, skinny device. "This little guy can scan a radius of fifty feet for environmental abnormalities, explosive devices, weird biometric readings—you know, anything we should be aware of before we bust in there and thrown down!"

Drew was always prepared. The machine beeped rapidly, and I tried to read the monitor, but the data was unfamiliar and I had no idea what was displayed.

When I looked up again Adam was dressed in a surgical gown, holding Ava's hand with both of his and staring into her open eyes. Adam placed the anesthesia mask over Ava's mouth. It was difficult to be sure, but I thought I saw a tear flow from her eye and land on the table.

"Everything looks normal. No sign of explosives or harmful toxins—wait....Wait, what is...?" Drew typed on the strange keyboard and looked quizzically at the screen. He rubbed his eyes and muttered under his breath.

"What?"

"Wait, let me scan again. This must be a mistake." He typed in a command and then waited while the machine beeped for a few moments. He looked down while he waited. "Sixteen minutes on the watch."

Suddenly we could hear Adam's voice over the intercom. Through the window, I could see Myers, dressed in a medical gown, standing against the back wall of the room.

"Sir?" Adam said to Myers, "The Desflurane is not entering the mask. Something is wrong with your anesthetic machine."

"Fix it!" Myers barked. Darcy rushed over and they played with the hoses and tubes for a few seconds.

What were they up to?

Drew spoke up at my side. "No, it's reading the same.... Huh...."

"What!" I was getting impatient.

"I'm getting an abnormal reading from...well, from Ava." He continued typing on the machine.

"Then give her Methohexital intravenously!" Myers snapped.

Darcy spoke up. "Sir, your supply has been depleted."

Myers gave a loud grunt of disapproval and frustration.

"Drew, what do you mean, a strange reading?" I asked impatiently.

"It's her body. There is some type of foreign substance in her body." Adam wrinkled his nose and played around with the machine.

"Is it dangerous? Did Myers pump her veins with something? Drugs? Did he drug her?"

An angry fire burned within me again, but my attention was pulled back through the window when Myers's voice became much louder.

"This is unacceptable!" Myers paced the operating room while Darcy and Adam quickly prepared instruments. "I suppose we are forced to proceed without placing Miss Gardner under anesthesia."

Ava whined loudly and squirmed on the table, tears pouring from her eyes.

"Drew! What's the deal? We've gotta get in there!" My body was shaking, revving up and ready to break loose.

Just like my heart.

Myers's demeanor changed rapidly as he realized for the first time that Ava was awake.

"Ah, Miss Ava Gardner, I finally get to meet you." He walked over to where she was lying, but stayed behind her head so she couldn't see him. "Can't say it's a pleasure, though. Your very name makes me want to vomit right here on the floor." His laugh was disgusting. "Though not because of lack of beauty. You've got that one covered, my dear." He took one oversized plump hand and stroked her brown hair.

"Get your hands off her," I whispered through gritted teeth. Myers continued to stroke her hair. "Mr. Hill is a lucky man. Very lucky indeed."

So Myers had no idea her memory had been wiped.

Then he dropped her hair and looked up quickly as if another thought popped into his brain. "Or perhaps there is someone else who's been enjoying your beauty lately. Someone who I thought was one of mine, but recently has proven differently."

Adam shifted his weight slightly but otherwise showed no change in demeanor.

Drew interrupted, "No drugs…well, I can't be one hundred percent sure. It looks like there is some type of synthetic agent in her body, but it's not matching with any of the molecular compositions of the chemicals programmed in this machine." Drew looked confused. "I guess we'll only know if we can take a sample of her blood and run it through the lab back at headquarters." He looked up. "Nine minutes. What are we going to do in nine minutes?"

Still standing behind Ava, Myers continued his speech. "Miss Gardner, you possess something that I want. Something that I need to complete my very reason for existence. Forty-nine years ago my parents were murdered for a small vial of medicine—a prototype my father had been experimenting with." He addressed Ava as if she were the only person in the room. "I have some of the best chemists in the world trying to re-create the formula, yet they all tell me something is missing." He stroked her hair again, and Ava tried to pull loose from the straps holding her wrists down. She began to sob when she realized it was no use. Then Ethan laughed under his breath. "Funny how the very person I want desperately to destroy is the very person I need desperately to keep alive. If only I had known before." He shook the thought out of his mind.

Then he lowered his head down to her ear and spoke quietly. "A slice of your DNA from a single cell deep within your brain. This won't hurt a bit." She closed her eyes tightly, squeezing tears out of her eyes as his loud, repulsive laugh filled the room.

I clenched my teeth together, trying to hold back my urge to bust through the windows. "Drew," I said, my leg shaking. "I can't wait much longer."

"Cabinets," Drew muttered. Out of the corner of my eye I saw him get up and start walking the perimeter of the room, but I couldn't peel my eyes from looking through the glass in front of me. Myers was careful to stay where Ava couldn't get a good look at him. "I have to say, Miss Gardner, my track record hasn't been too successful thus far. Those young ladies weren't meant to die. You, on the other hand..." Myers showed his teeth, but he was not smiling. "I guess you're lucky I've assigned Agent Raddemann to do the honors."

He turned to face Adam, "Now's the time. Let's begin."

But Adam stood, not moving.

"That's it, I'm going in." I stood up from my crouching position on the floor when Drew startled me.

"I know what the countdown means!" He rushed over to my side, speaking quickly, only inches from my face. "One night in Dublin, Darcy told me about a mission where she followed a lead on a Belgian freelance bomb maker the IIA had been searching for. She was hoping to lure him into custody by posing as a client interested in his work."

Drew left my side again and quickly returned to the cabinets stuck on the opposite wall. He frantically searched through them while he spoke. "She met up with him deep in the underground club scene of Brussels. Unfortunately, she wasn't able to catch him that night because the guy had created a special watch that emitted high-frequency ultraviolet rays he'd engineered in a lab."

Myers's voice came over the intercom again, sounding a much like a disgruntled parent. "Agent Raddemann, do as I say. Begin the surgery."

My attention turned back into the operating room—Adam was still holding his ground. Myers was going to blow soon.

"Yes!" Drew had found some type of spray can and pulled it off the shelf. "Everyone in a two mile radius was suddenly hit with an intense dose of UV rays and—"

"They all got sunburned?" I snapped, perhaps due to my current state of stress.

"No, smart ass. UV radiation has so much energy it is able to actually knock electrons away from their atoms, causing molecules to split." He walked over to me and looked at his watch. "In three minutes this watch is going to send out a micro-blast of UV radiation and cause everyone in a half a mile radius to fall unconscious and possibly will suffer some serious cell damage."

"Not much better than a bomb on your wrist," I said, concerned. "What do we do about it?"

He stared me in the eye, and held up the can. "She left us an aerosol can of ozone in the cabinet!"

"Ozone? Like the layer of gases up in our atmosphere?"

"Exactly. Seconds before the freelance bomb maker set off his watch, he sprayed a dome of synthetic ozone around his body, intending to scatter and absorb the UV and protect himself."

"So in a few minutes that watch will knock out everyone in Myers's headquarters, except for us?"

"Only for several minutes, and only those who aren't protected by the ozone spray."

"What about Ava?" I turned to look through the observation window, but heard a loud click behind me. A gun cocked right behind my head. "How useful. I'll take that, Agent Smith."

Dammit! Harper. Of course—he was still Myers's right-hand man.

He yanked the can out of Drew's hands. "Put your hands up and slowly turn around, both of you."

Myer's voice boomed from the intercom. "Fine then. Darcy, hand me the scalpel. It's time for me to finally take my revenge, with or without you, Agent Raddemann."

"No!" Adam and I yelled at the same time. I turned from Harper to look through the window.

Harper kicked Drew in the stomach, and then grabbed my right hand and twisted it behind my back, holding me captive. I struggled while we heard Myers over the intercom.

"Just as I suspected, Agent Raddemann. I concluded a short time ago that you haven't exactly been loyal to me." He looked calm, yet irritated. "Perhaps your loyalties lie with someone very near us."

Drew popped up from the ground, kicking Harper's gun from his hand and catching it in midair. The trick startled Harper enough to loosen his grip, and I twisted around until I had him in the same position he had just held me in. I slammed his face up against the glass hard and stared through the window, over Harper's shoulder, holding him hostage while he struggled to get loose.

Myers stood only a few inches from Adam's face. "Do you love her, Adam? Have you fallen for the very stink of this earth?"

He didn't have to say a word—his eyes told the truth of his heart.

With my heart in my throat I went right to Ava's face. Did she love him, too?

No!

There it was, right in her eyes. The end to us. The end to my existence. I involuntarily released my hold on Harper and fell to my knees, hunched over with excruciating pain in my chest.

Drew kicked Harper in the jaw but he bounced up quickly and threw a punch back at Drew. I couldn't move. My world had started spinning.

Ava!

That British demon stole my sweet Ava! My stomach turned sour, my head pounded, and my heart was on fire. I suddenly felt like I couldn't breathe, like all the air had been sucked out of the room.

"Two minutes, Nolan!" Drew yelled, but it sounded like he was at the end of a long tunnel. Harper growled and I barely heard items breaking around the room as Drew battled Harper.

This was all Myers's fault. Not caring about everything around me, I stood and wandered toward the door, planning on busting through and ending Myers right then and there. But I only made it about three steps when I fell to the floor, dizzy and disoriented. My body had given up.

"Nolan, get up! I need you!" Drew's ragged voice called for help behind me. "My Glock!" Harper and Drew still in combat, faces bloody and looking exhausted.

My mind went back to the old bartender in Dublin— *'The man who is worthwhile is the one who can smile when everything is dead wrong.'*

Was I really ready to give up on Ava? In Ireland I swore I would fight for her, even if I died trying.

"Thirty seconds, Nolan!"

I lifted my head off the ground and looked through the window at the most captivating woman I had ever met, lying helpless on the table. A woman who had shown me the true beauty of life. She had offered me comfort and ecstasy, and given my life real meaning. She held every inch of my heart.

As if she could hear, I pressed my hands up against the window and spoke to her. "I'll be the one who loves you the most."

And then as if I had just downed a can of adrenaline, I took the Glock from my waistband and pulled the trigger. Harper fell to the ground instantly. Drew ran over to me.

"Ten seconds!" We huddled together and watched Drew's watch counting down. "I'm going to spray the ozone," Drew said." Hold your breath and close your eyes!"

Drew sprayed a cloud of gas around us, and then held his wrist with the watch as far from his body as he could. I counted down in my head, hoping Drew was right about all this.

A series of high-pitched beeps rang out just as a massive burst of invisible energy sent three successive waves through the room, blowing papers, blasting pictures off the wall, and shattering the glass windows of the observation room.

My ears felt like I was deep underwater and my head experienced an uncomfortable squeeze of pressure, but I otherwise felt alright.

A few seconds later Drew told me to open my eyes. "It worked! Let's go!"

I looked through the window inside the operating room. Two of Myer's men and Adam lay on the floor unconscious, but no one else was in the room. Cabinets, furniture and medical supplies had toppled over and a large metal cabinet has shifted in front of the exit to the operating room.

"Where's Ava?" I screamed. "Was she affected by the UV?"

Drew used his pistol to shoot out the door and then entered the room, yelling for Darcy. I crouched down and felt Adam's pulse. He was alive.

"Adam! Where did they go?" I slapped his cheeks, hoping he would come to quickly.

"Darcy's gone, too." Drew tried to move the cabinet unsuccessfully and began carefully tracing the perimeter of the room with another one of his tech gadgets.

"When will they wake up?"

"Probably a few minutes." Drew stopped at a black box that looked like a thermostat stuck to the wall. He lifted a false front to display a touch-sensitive screen. "I bet this opens a secret outlet." He tried to guess the code with no success.

The more time we wasted, the farther Myers would get with Ava. I filled a metal container partway with cold water from the sink, and then splashed it on Adam's face. He opened his eyes and sat up, gasping for air.

"What the bloody hell?" He looked around still breathing heavily. "Owe! My head! What happened?"

"It's a long story that we don't have time for right now."

Adam rubbed his eyes and looked around the room quizzically. A line of blood dripped down from his nose as he sat up.

I moved in closer. "Adam, focus! Where did they go?"

"I can't hear well." He pulled on his ear lobes and moved his jaw back and forth. "Who?"

"Ava! Where did Myers take her?"

I pulled Adam to his feet as he stumbled over his words, looking stunned. "I...I don't know. I have no ruddy idea."

Drew turned from the box and said calmly, "Adam, you don't happen to know the code to this thing, do ya?"

"No," Adam replied as he continued groaning and rubbing his head. He grabbed a stack of paper towels and pressed it to his nose. "Oh hell, I'm bleeding from the ears, too!"

With a hiss, a section of the tiled wall cracked open and swung out to reveal a dark tunnel behind it. Drew smiled and said, "*Caducuspetra Morbus.*"

"Come on, Adam," I said. "You know your way around here better than us. You've got to get us to that girl."

Adam made his way down the tunnel, Drew and I desperately following.

Epilogue

The hospital gown flew back behind me as I ran insanely through the parking garage, following the directions the pretty strawberry-blond lady had whispered to me. "Adam!" I yelled through tears, wondering if whatever that strange blast was had killed him. I knew Myers and his men must be only steps behind me, but I had no idea where I was or where I was going.

My muscles were weak and I felt nauseous from the drugs Adam had given me. Only a few cars were scattered throughout the lot so I could see out over the railings. The sun was just barely rising between the skyscrapers.

Skyscrapers? There are no skyscrapers in Stevens Point. Where am I?

"Ava! Stop!" someone yelled behind me. I turned to look and tripped over my clumsy feet. I fell hard, scraping my knee, wrist, and palm on the pavement. A wicked sting proved I had peeled a few layers of skin back in all three places. I screamed in pain and then in terror as I looked behind me, spotting a man dressed all in black running after me.

I forced my legs to stand and run up the ramp, blood dripping down my shins and toward my bare feet. I had nowhere to go. I was freezing.

This was definitely the last day of my life.

A bullet flew by my legs. "Adam!" I desperately cried out, hoping he'd magically jump out from behind the nearest car and whisk me away to safety. I was crying so intensely that mucus was pouring out of my nose and tears were blocking my view.

Suddenly a long, black car came roaring down the ramp ahead of me. It swung around, screeching its tires and coming to rest within ten feet of my body. The passenger side window rolled down and the person in the driver's seat pointed a gun right out the window.

"Get down!" he yelled.

I collapsed to the ground and covered my head just as three shots— louder than anything I had ever heard in my life—rang out through the parking garage.

When the noise stopped echoing, I heard my name. "Ava, sweetheart. Get in!"

My attacker lay still on the cement floor. I stood from my crouched position and looked at my rescuer in the car.

My jaw fell open with shock. "Dad?"

I couldn't believe it. My father was here, shooting a gun and swinging his car around like a regular old James Bond.

"Get in the car! Now!" He leaned over and opened the passenger's side door.

I quickly slid in as Dad peeled out and zoomed down the parking ramp and onto the street, breaking through a wooden barricade across the exit.

My mouth hung open, eyes wide, as I tried to take in the truth of the last few minutes of my life. I stared at my father, not knowing what to say.

Dad pointed to a bag on the floor at my feet. "I brought you a change of clothes. There's also a blanket."

I couldn't speak.

He kept his eyes on the road. "Are you okay, sweetie? Did Myers hurt you in any way?"

"Dad...I'm fine...I just..." Why the hell was my dad here? And how did he know about Myers?

"Honey, I've got a lot to tell you. But—"

"—I'd say," I interrupted, sharply.

"Fine. You have the right to be upset with me." He let out a deep breath. "But please, just listen to the whole story before you...react."

"First, just tell me the truth: You are actually my father, right?"

I was completely serious but my dad laughed.

"Yes, dear. I am your father." He took a deep breath and let it out loudly. "I'm just not entirely the person you always thought I was."

"What do you mean?" I was somewhat terrified to hear his answer.

My father looked nervous. "I knew this day would eventually come. I just didn't expect the truth to arrive quite in this manner." He turned onto the Dan Ryan Expressway heading north toward Wisconsin and sat silently for a few moments.

"Dad?" Tears began to well up in my eyes and my voice cracked.

"I don't work for a bank. I never have."

"Okay…" I said with worry in my voice and tears sliding down my cheeks.

"I am a special consultant for the FBI." He looked over at me but I didn't react, so he continued. "I spend most of my days working in an office, conducting research and advising missions. When I was younger I was out in the field like Nolan."

"Nolan?" How did my dad know about Nolan? I barely knew about Nolan.

"That's right, you don't have….Oh, Ava, I'm so sorry I haven't protected you."

His concerned stare was unsettling, and I was still frozen with shock.

My dad was FBI?

"Darling, at least put the blanket on. You'll catch pneumonia."

I pulled the blanket onto my lap just to humor him. Right now I could feel nothing—no pain, no discomfort.

"As you know, your mother and I have been overseas visiting Laura, but I was also working on a case for the agency." He reached over to grab my hand. "We thought Myers got everything he wanted from us last August and that you'd be safe now. I learned just yesterday that Myers was ready to launch his assault on you and so I spent most of the night flying back to the US, sick with worry that you weren't safe." Then he stared out the windshield and muttered to himself, "Bowman assured me you'd be safe."

I didn't know much of what he was talking about. "So Mom knows all about this…life of yours?"

"Yes. Your mother has always been very supportive of my career choices."

I closed my eyes and hoped that when I woke up, this entire day would just be a dream. I'd be in Stevens Point blissfully falling for Adam and enjoying the feeling of new love.

"Speaking of, I have strict orders to bring you straight home to your mother. She's been crazy worried about you, just as I have been." He looked over to me for some form of acceptance, but I kept my eyes closed, begging for sleep to come. "It's a long way home, and I can imagine you're exhausted, honey. But before you rest you have to hear one more thing."

I didn't know if I could take any more news, but I opened my eyes anyway. "Are you sure it can't wait, Dad?"

"I can't foresee the future, and I would hate for me to never have the chance to tell you this again, so I think you better hear this now."

I couldn't find any words.

"That scar you have over your heart…"

I instinctively felt my chest with my hand.

"It's not from when you fell off your bike when you were four."

"Dad…"

He lowered his voice, even though we were the only two in the car. "Nineteen years ago your grandmother and I desperately needed a hiding place." He stopped for a moment, apparently looking for the right words. "There's a secret inside of you, Ava. A secret you need to spend great efforts to defend, or very soon millions of Americans could find themselves at death's door."

Acknowledgements

Thanks again are due to my awesome husband, Wes, for supporting my choice to write. I'm sure you're sick of me staring at my computer. I love you endlessly.

He edits, he compliments, and he does it all generously! Without you, Carl Stratman, Ava and Nolan wouldn't pop off the page. Thank you, thank you, thank you!

To my amazing graphic designer, Hannah Christian Hess, for once again blowing me out of the water with your amazing cover design. Thank you so much!
http://www.hannahchristian.com/

To Lena, the voice of reason and advice in my ear. I thank you for continuing to feed the fire of my dream.

To the Carrier Series fans, for taking this journey with me! I hope you've enjoyed the second installment of the adventures of Ava and Nolan! Keep reading—there's a lot more to Ava and Nolan's journey!

Diana Ryan lives in the great state of Wisconsin with her husband and two young children. Although writing was not her first career, publishing novels has always been on her bucket list. In her free time, she enjoys watching live theater, playing piano, hanging out with her family, and of course, writing sequels to Ava and Nolan's adventures. *The Defender* is the second novel Ryan has written in *The Carrier Series.*

62268292R00165